THE HAUNTING
OF
MUDDY CREEK

TARYN'S CAMERA BOOK 7

Rebecca Patrick-Howard

For Clarence.

This book is a work of fiction. Any similarities to any person or place are purely coincidental.

Want access to FREE books (audio, print, and digital), prizes, and new releases before anyone else? Then sign up for Rebecca's VIP mailing list. She promises she won't spam you! *And she'll never sell your information or use it for anything other than sending you her newsletter.) You may easily opt out at any time.*

http://eepurl.com/Srwkn

TABLE OF CONTENTS

The Haunting of Muddy Creek   1
Bloody Moor, Book 8 Excerpt   167
A Broom with a View Excerpt 183
About the Author   208
Let's Connect   209
Rebecca's Books   211

ONE

A re you sure you want to go up there and get in the middle of all that?"

Matt's voice was non-accusatory, but Taryn knew he was worried about her. They'd been friends for most of her life. She often knew what he felt, and what he was going to say before he did.

Taryn grinned, unable to hide the fact that his worry and care comforted her, and continued packing her pink duffle bag. She would be gone for three weeks, four tops. It wouldn't be a long job. The drive to West Virginia and back would be the worst part, and she had plenty of music stocked up for the trip. The CDs she'd burned the night before all read West Virginia: The Long Drive to Nowhere.

Still, short job or not, it didn't mean she had to skimp on necessities. Pausing, she surveyed the two suitcases already parked in the doorway. Should she be embarrassed that one of them contained nothing but shoes?

Nah.

"I'll be fine," she promised Matt, turning her attention back to her longtime friend/sometimes boyfriend. "I've been warned about the media but they said that, for the most part, the attention will be on the court house and downtown. I'll be miles from that."

She felt Matt frown through the phone. "Have you been watching that lady on that news channel? Frieda Bowen, her name is. She's there already, covering the case. I've tried tuning in a few times to get an idea of what the climate is up there, but I can only handle a few minutes of her at a time."

Taryn grimaced. "Tell me about it. I usually agree with her, but she seems to get very angry very quickly. She's done a lot for children's rights, though. I can't fault her that. She's just so..."

"Mean?" Matt offered. Taryn laughed. "I wish I could go up there with you, or that you would just bite the bullet and fly."

She knew he was worried about the long car ride from Nashville, about the possibility of her doing damage to her muscles and joints now that her medical condition had progressed. Sitting for long periods of time was becoming increasingly harder. But she'd put her foot down about it. She was not going to be limited by the amount of luggage she could take just because a long car ride was going to be a little uncomfortable. "Nope. Not with all those restrictions they're putting on luggage

1

these days. I can spend in gas driving up there for what they want to charge for my extra bags."

"Well, I'll still meet you in a few days. I'm flying into Huntington and renting a car," Matt reminded her.

Matt lived two states away, in Florida. So far they'd been making their relationship work by traveling back and forth to see one another. Taryn, a freelance artist, set her own schedules and hours, so she was about as flexible as they came. Matt, however, worked for NASA and couldn't pop in and out when he pleased. They tended to frown upon that. The distance hadn't been detrimental so far, though both were prone to occasional bouts of loneliness.

Taryn wasn't sure how much longer it could continue. Eventually, one of them would have to make a move. She knew it would need to be her. Matt wasn't going to budge. He loved his job too much. And who wouldn't? He'd wanted to work for NASA since he was eight years old.

"I guess the timing is a little off," Taryn sighed at last. She threw the last extra battery for her camera into the duffle bag then flung herself down on the bed. It bounced beneath her, giving her a little thrill as she was momentarily tossed into the air.

Taryn was by herself a lot. She had to make her own entertainment.

"What do you mean?"

"The, er, incident was over a year ago, but they're just now going to trial," she explained. "If they'd hired me to come up and paint that school a little sooner, or a little later, then I wouldn't be right in the middle of the three-ring circus."

"Wonder why they hired you now?"

"I have no earthly idea. You'd think they'd have enough going on, right? Maybe they're hoping for extra attention since they've got the country's eye. It's not often the big networks are interested in anything that happens there. I know West Virginia, have been there for three different job assignments, and even I couldn't find this place on the map," Taryn said.

Matt snorted and she could imagine him shuddering at the thought. They'd both grown up in suburban Nashville. Although he didn't mind the occasional weekend in the cabin, and loved his solitude and to be alone with his thoughts, he was about as far away from being a country boy as he could get. He enjoyed his high-priced coffee and artisan bread as much as he did a walk on a (well-manicured and landscaped) nature trail.

"They're wanting to rebuild the old school and turn it into an Appalachian Heritage Center, with a museum and concert hall and stuff. That costs money, and you know the county doesn't have it. Maybe they're hoping to catch the eye of a philanthropist or something with all the news people hounding the area. I say why not," Taryn laughed. "Why not use Frieda Bowen while you can?"

2

Matt was quiet for a moment and, together, they shared the companionable silence. Taryn let her mind play around on the events that had led to her hiring, about the lofty (yet somehow desperate) email appeal the PTA had sent.

Would she, due to the "tragedy and sensitivity of the situation", consider lowering her rates? Could she come as soon as possible? Would she mind signing a media waiver so that her name and likeness could be used...?

Matt was the one to finally mention the elephant in the room.

"Do you have any feelings about what happened?" he asked. "I mean, have you...?"

"No, nothing." Taryn glanced over at her beloved Nikon, Miss Dixie, who observed the proceedings from her perch atop Taryn's dresser. "I looked at the pictures of the school. You know, before it looked...the way it does now. I felt fine. Nothing strange."

"But sometimes you don't get anything until the camera does," Matt pointed out.

"Right." Taryn bit her lip and closed her eyes. "I mean, I feel bad about what happened. People died, of course. Murdered, if you believe the news stories. The fact that I am going to be in the same town as CNN's trending story is kind of weird. I do feel strange about that. I've never really been in the middle of things before; I always seem to be at the end before I realize anything is even going on. But I'll just be there, doing my job, on the other side of the county with the old school. Whatever circus is going on downtown won't concern me."

"I hope it won't...," Matt replied, his voice trailing off.

From her vantage point on her bed, Taryn could see her living room. The television flickered in the evening light. The sound was on "mute" but throngs of journalists and cameramen engulfed the courthouse steps of Haven Hollow, county seat of Venters County. A middle-aged, red-faced attorney, sweat pouring from her head, looked like a deer in headlights.

"Day two of the Muddy Creek Six Jury Selection..." flashed across the bottom of her screen. Frieda Bowen, with her thick, black eyeliner and frosted hair, was on a split screen, gesturing with animation.

Taryn closed her eyes and exhaled softly. What had she gotten herself into?

TWO

*B*efore she'd left Nashville, Taryn had gone through her bookshelf and pulled out the copy of the one book by Lucy Dawson that she still owned. It had somehow survived the multiple moves and was still in good condition, even though it was more than fifteen years old.

Lucy Dawson was Haven Hollow's most famous resident—a children's book author who had won multiple awards and was one of the bestselling novelists in the country. As someone rarely seen in public, and who shared few details of her personal life, a certain amount of mystique was built up around her that was almost as legendary as her writings.

Taryn felt it only fitting to share the journey with her beautifully illustrated copy, even if the circumstances were not ideal.

"The Boy in the Tree." Taryn looked at the book now and carried it outside to the table by her motel room door. She'd meant to read it before she left but hadn't had time. She did now, though.

A great deal of activity shuffled around Taryn as she opened the first page. As an artist that worked in a variety of settings, she'd learned to tune out the world around her and concentrate on the goal at hand. So now, with feet stomping back and forth, coal trucks barreling down the main street just a few feet behind her, and calls of maintenance workers shouting across the parking lot, she began to read.

It was a story that had stuck with her through the years.

Lenny Laker was a poor boy who lived in a little town in a little world. He had a little bed in a little room in a little house.

But Lenny Laker was not little. He was big.

His big feet hung off the end of his little bed and scraped the wall at night.

When he tried to sit at the little kitchen table his head touched the ceiling of his little house.

He was bigger than all the other kids in his little school. "One day I am going to find a bigger world," he'd tell everyone he knew every day. They would laugh at him, though, and poke fun. Then they grew angry.

"There is no bigger world, Lenny," they would tell him. "You're just making that up."

Soon, Lenny no longer had any friends. Nobody would talk to him. They didn't want to hear about the bigger world; they were happy in their little beds in their little houses in their little town. They didn't like Lenny anymore and he grew very lonely.

One day as he was taking a walk in the little woods behind his little house, he saw a big tree. It was the biggest tree he'd ever seen. Lenny had tried climbing other trees, but they were all so small that he'd reached the top in a matter of seconds. This one, however, towered above him so high that he couldn't even see the top branches.

"I'm going to climb that tree," he said to himself. And so, he began to climb. He climbed and climbed and climbed and when he reached the top, hours later, he looked around at the world before him. His little town was at the very bottom, no bigger than a pinprick. The rest of the world, however, spread out for miles. Off in the distance he saw big houses, houses where his head would not touch the ceiling, where his feet would not hang off the end of his bed.

Excited, Lenny climbed down and returned to school. He tried telling the others about what he'd seen but they did not believe him. Each day, though, he returned to the tree and climbed to the top. And each day he saw more and more.

His friends and teacher, however, did not want to hear about that other world. It made them angry.

Then, one day when he was telling them about the big waterfall he'd seen miles away, the one that was so big that it would take days to slide down, his little friends decided they'd had enough. They all took off through the woods and ran until they found the tree. Once there, instead of climbing to the top, they began chopping it down. They chopped and chopped until it was gone.

When it finally fell to the forest ground with a mighty "thud" they cheered and laughed with glee.

Lenny did not cry or grow angry, though. Instead, he smiled and walked away.

They did not know it, but he'd found lots of trees on his adventures. There would always be more to climb.

                                 * * *

TARYN HAD A MEETING with the superintendent and other members of the school
board the following morning. In the meantime, however, since she'd arrived much
earlier than she'd anticipated and had already unpacked, she decided take advantage
of what daylight hours she had left. She would visit Muddy Creek Elementary, her
new job site.

Taryn preferred her first impressions to be undiluted, pure, without any outside
influence of a well-meaning person towering over her and filling the air with
aimless chatter. Although all her employers wanted to give her the "grand tour",
when she was able to, she preferred walking around by herself, getting a feel for the
job site without any preconceived ideas.

It was another reason why she'd avoided the news as much as possible.

Eden Inn was the one motel in the entire county and it was neither biblical,
beautiful, or an inn. It was also full of reporters.

From the outside, its weedy parking lot and sidewalks stained with air-
conditioning condensation weren't exactly going to win it any high reviews on Yelp
(she knew; she'd looked). Still, while it might not have been the Ritz, Taryn was
okay with it and bid it a fond little farewell as she drove away. Though independent
and used to being alone, since every member of her family was now gone, Taryn was
prone to loneliness and would go for days without seeing a soul if she didn't make
an effort. Sometimes forced human interaction was good for her. Besides, she'd
stayed in so many questionable places over the years, from torrid hostels to flea-
infested campsites, that she thought she'd built up a pretty good tolerance to most
anything that could kill her. It was her own body turning on itself that was doing
that at the moment.

As she drove down Haven Hollow's Main Street, Taryn had the opportunity to
survey most of what the town had to offer. There were only four main roads
downtown and they all seemed to drift off into the mountains, winding through the
trees like snakes until they vanished. She followed one of those roads now, listening
intently as the Australian voice on her GPS system guided her.

Along the way she'd passed empty storefront after empty storefront. A lone gas
station that promised "bait, fried chicken, and hunting licenses" was located next to
a condemned clapboard building across from the courthouse. She could barely see
any of these for the masses of people camped out on the steps of the modest, two-
story stone building. Clutching microphones and notebooks, they spilled over into

the gas station's lot, swirling around the pumps like ants. Court wasn't even in session but that didn't stop them from coming out, afraid they'd miss something.

She'd had to slow down as she drove past them and many had paused and peered at her through her tinted windows, trying to ascertain whether or not she was anyone of importance.

She wasn't, not to them anyway. They'd learn that soon enough. She was just there to paint.

Taryn passed a KFC, two pizza places with homemade signs, and a country diner. All were full.

"Trial's good for business, at least," she murmured as she leaned on the gas and sped on out of town. There wasn't much else to see. Although the tiny town was picturesque, with the mountains towering over the nineteenth century buildings, it was as dead as most small towns she'd visited.

She hated that. Taryn was a big fan of the past.

The twisting county road was a burrow of trees. As she zigzagged along the small county road she took time to appreciate the foliage pressing in around her. It was early November, so most of the leaves remained, but their density spread over her like a thick blanket. There were times she was unable to see the sky; the canopy formed a ceiling above her, allowing in only spots of blue here and there. What sunlight the trees didn't block out, the mountains did. It was only 3:00 pm and it felt like dusk. Despite the splendor of it all for a moment Taryn, someone who had never had a problem with tight places, felt suffocated.

"Geeze, I'm getting weak," she muttered. She was also the only car on the road, a fact she was thankful for since she was taking most of the curves in the opposite lane.

There were patches of houses here and there, mostly grouped together like little communes. For the most part, however, the dirt and gravel roads that snaked off the main line were the only indications that anyone lived there at all. She was struck by the seclusion of it all. And by the tiny wooden houses that stood next to mailboxes along the way. They lacked doors, but were too open to be outhouses. They contained no windows, no insulation of any kind. Some were painted but most were not.

Taryn would need to ask someone about those.

For company, she fiddled around in the passenger seat until she found her Best of Motown CD and tuned it to Otis. It wasn't a drive that called for happy, peppy music.

Indeed, it wasn't a *job* that called for much lightheartedness at all.

Taryn saw the school a quarter of a mile before she reached it. Despite the fact that it set back off the road over an embankment in a small valley, and was partially hidden by the vegetation growing wildly around it, there was no mistaking that Pepto Bismal color.

The Muddy Creek PTA had come up with the provocative idea of painting the elementary school deep red, a tribute to the Muddy Creek Cardinals who had won the county-wide basketball championship from 1987-1990.

Nobody had counted on the elements; over the years, the school had faded to a bright, unmistakable, blushing pink.

"*My colors are blush and bashful*," Taryn giggled when she'd first seen the picture. She could quote "Steel Magnolias" all day long.

At least, the part of the school that could still be *seen* was pink.

"All the king's horses, and all the king's men," Taryn whispered as the building came into full view.

The school had been blown to pieces, parts of it strewn as far back as the field and creek behind it.

That was, of course, why Taryn had been called in for the job in the first place: to put Muddy Creek Elementary back together again.

* * *

TARYN EXPECTED TO FEEL a sense of sadness, a tug of melancholia, as she walked around the remains of the once vibrant (and still vibrant in its tacky way) school. She was surprised at what she felt instead: repulsion.

Confused, she stood knee-deep in weeds and observed the building before her. She was overcome with the urge to scratch at her legs, swipe at her arms and nape of her neck. It had nothing to do with the swarms of bugs in the air.

The school had been closed for many years, since she was a little girl. The fire had happened only last year, however, long after Muddy Creek consolidated with two other nearby country schools to make the much bigger (and more modern) Pleasant Grove Elementary.

It had been many years since those hallways had heard the happy, cheerful voices of children as the soles of their new shoes squeaked on the newly-waxed tiles. A long time since the rotten swings with their rusty chains had been moved back and forth by anything other than the wind. The newest generation of the county's children wouldn't even be able to remember a time when the school had been open.

"Huh," Taryn spoke with puzzlement as she stood before the front entrance with her hands on her hips. She was surprised by her antipathy.

Normally, Taryn was head over heels for anything old, abandoned, and neglected. She felt the same way over old houses that some people felt about abandoned animals. But this one...

"I don't like it," she whispered as she crossed her arms over her chest and shivered slightly.

It was isolated, pushed back away from the rest of civilization like it had been forgotten long before anyone stopped remembering it. With its location over the embankment and the heavy foliage, one could almost drive right past it and not know it was there. If not for the color, they probably would.

The side that remained intact with its offensive pink paint was in poor condition—a condition that was just as poor as the side that had been burnt. Cracks formed in windows; big holes gaped in others. From deep inside, blackness oozed out and seemed to consider Taryn carefully. She was reminded of a big, toothless mouth of a giant, waiting to gobble up the children that moved too close.

In its abandonment, weeds had grown through the drive that encircled the school. Spindly vines grew up the sides and poked their way through the doors and windows. Plaster crumbled and littered the ground, ground overgrown with stringy wildflowers and thorny shrubs.

The other side of the school, the damaged side, was better in its own way. It was in complete ruin, but at least it was an excusable ruin. The fact that it had burned almost pardoned its appearance. Still...

Although it had been more than a year since the fire, Taryn could still smell the acrid scent of the smoke. It had left behind a rottenness that permeated the air, and she gagged, unable to help herself. Could nobody else smell it? It was like a sewer, a terrible stench that made her eyes water. She didn't know how they'd be able to fix that. If they were going to get the school back together and renovate it, they'd have to do something about it.

"Oh man, this is going to be a problem," Taryn said as she paced around the building, moving at a much faster pace than she would usually.

Taryn always took along her camera, Miss Dixie, with her, especially at the first meeting when she was introducing herself to the building she'd be working with. Miss Dixie was her second set of eyes; she liked for her camera to gain her first impressions early on and both preferred to dive into the work immediately.

But, this time, neither had any interest in pausing long enough to capture any moment they were having.

"What do you think?" Taryn asked, glancing down at her chest where Miss Dixie bounced along with each step. "Call it a day and do this tomorrow?"

Miss Dixie did not appear to have any objections to this plan.

The sun had set over the mountains, and the darkness that had started settling over her in the car was growing increasingly thicker as she made the loop. A long shadow loomed overhead and stretched its gangly fingers over the building and towards Taryn, as though reaching for her. The blackness was cold, eating through the mild warmth of the day. The bits that touched her were chilling. Damp.

She was reminded of a wet, cold grave.

Although she felt silly, and a little ashamed of herself, Taryn quickened her pace. It was ridiculous; she'd been in much more harrowing situations. But you can't control what you feel. Logic can fly right out the door when you're scared.

And Taryn had learned to trust her instincts.

"I'll get pictures tomorrow," she whispered to the wind that had started picking up.

When she reached her car she paused, her hand on her door. A one-lane road ran off the parking lot and she studied it now. A glossy blue gate had been newly installed, keeping trespassers out. A security camera looked down at the entrance. It was almost comical, such newness and technology in contrast to the broken-down building that shared its space.

But it made sense.

Lucy Dawson, celebrated children's author, lived a mile up the road.

Taryn felt a slight, uncontrollable thrill as she looked at the mailbox with the "Dawson" name. She was a fan. Her books had been a little young for Taryn, she was in high school when the middle school books were released, but she'd secretly enjoyed them anyway. The characters, whimsical misfits that lived in their own little worlds, had appealed to her. She'd even written an in-depth thesis about "The Girl in the Well" in high school.

Lucy inhabited the log cabin her great grandfather had built, or so Taryn had read. She'd lived there most of her adult life. Before that, she'd grown up in a nearby hollow. She'd worked as a waitress at the local drive-in as a teenager. Three roads in the county were named after her family. She was a local, one of them.

So everyone in town was shocked when, on a September evening thirteen months earlier, she'd set off a homemade pipe bomb, destroying the very school she'd attended, killing seven people she'd known as a child.

THREE

So, how's the motel?"

Taryn picked up her traveling blanket, a fleece she'd picked up at the Wal-Mart after the Christmas sales, and spread it out on the couch before answering Matt. When she was satisfied that it covered enough of the cushions, she gingerly lowered herself onto it. The couch bowed in the middle, and the fabric reeked of cigarette smoke, but it wasn't the worst thing she'd ever sat on.

"We–lllll...." She faltered, feeling slightly defensive of the Eden Inn. "It's not too bad."

"Tell me about it," Matt prompted cheerfully.

Feeling fairly confident that the couch wasn't going to fall apart under her now, Taryn pulled up her legs and stretched them out before her. She leaned back on one of the bed pillows she'd placed behind her back and surveyed what would be her home for the next few weeks.

"It's different," she replied at last. "I guess it's mostly used for long-term guests. Like maybe people staying here for the mines or something."

"Yeah?"

"Yeah," she nodded, even though he couldn't see her. "First of all, there's, like, four beds in here. Five if you count the fact that the couch folds out."

"Geeze."

"Yep. Two doubles," Taryn counted, "one king, and one single. It's a big room. Looks like they knocked out a wall, maybe, and made one out of two. I could have a party. Or at least a sleepover."

"So is it nice?"

Taryn snickered. "I wouldn't go that far. I mean, you can tell that it's mostly used by men who are here for work. It's got that kind of indoor/outdoor carpet, and I can't tell if it's meant to be brown, or that's just what color it is now."

"Ew." Taryn could feel Matt crinkling his nose across the distance. As a Virgo, he was fastidious and organized. He didn't do dirt or clutter.

"The bedspreads are those old floral slick ones, kind of quilted. The ones they never wash?" Now she was teasing him a little, hoping to make him cringe.

"Uh huh..."

"I went ahead and took them off of the bed I'm sleeping on. The sheets and blankets underneath looked okay. I'm glad I have my own pillows, though."

There was a dampness present that she hoped wasn't going to be an issue for her joints or allergies; she'd turned the heat on high for awhile in an attempt to burn some of it off. The room, which lacked a window in the cinder block walls, was dingy and dusty. It carried traces of perspiration, smoke, and homesickness.

"And there's nowhere else to stay?"

"Nope," Taryn exhaled noisily. "But it's okay. It's a room. I'm all right."

True, the bathroom had mold and mildew and the shower was barely big enough for her slight frame to turn around in, but the toilet was clean, the mattresses were soft enough, and she had cable and Wi-Fi. Someone had thoughtfully left a bouquet of silk flowers on the small, wobbly table, too. She didn't know if it was the school board or the motel, but she decided to be touched either way.

"It's not the worst place I've stayed."

And that much was true.

Taryn had an unusual job, and it sometimes called for unique travel arrangements. An artist by trade, Taryn was not only skilled with the paintbrush, but she ran her own small freelancing business and had for years. As someone who had always had a penchant for the past, and believed that there was no such thing as an old building without a personality, her clients hired her to recreate yesterday for them. Old houses, old businesses, even old barns—she was called in to paint them and recreate them in such a way that they appeared new and full of life on her canvas.

Sometimes the paintings were used for sentimental reasons. Perhaps a historical society wanted a complete reconstruction of a county landmark to hang in their museum. Sometimes it was used as a blueprint. Indeed, she worked with a fair number of architects, and her paintings were often the only complete rendering of how the building had once looked.

With degrees both in art and historical preservation, Taryn used her knowledge of historical architecture and her imagination to render the past to life.

Her imagination and knowledge, in fact, had been enough in the past to get the job done. She'd been able to "see" the past because she wanted her to because she was terrific at visualizing.

Then things changed.

Taryn no longer had to use her imagination to envision the past...now she really did see it.

An empty room devoid of furnishings, with peeling wallpaper and rodent droppings on the floor, was suddenly transformed into a glittering parlor with a marble-topped table set for tea.

The fallen beams of a dilapidated barn rose and straightened; a fresh coat of paint gleamed in the sunlight as a colt playfully bucked in what was once the overgrown and forgotten field behind it.

She could see those things.

Well, her camera had something to do with that. In the beginning, it was only through Miss Dixie that the past had come to life. And it had been sporadic at best. Her camera was the conduit through which she grasped the impossible.

That had also changed.

Miss Dixie still provided her with a window but, more and more, she was able to see without its assistance.

Whatever veil that had once separated time and death was no longer as dense and opaque as it had once been.

*　　　*　　　*

"WE WANT TO THANK YOU for taking the time out of your busy schedule to come up and do this for us." The portly, middle-aged man with the half-moons under his arms bustled around his office, barely casting a glance at Taryn.

"Oh, it's no problem," Taryn assured him. "It's my job."

And, of course, she was getting paid to be there. That seemed relevant. She had a big heart, but a girl had to eat.

"As you can imagine, it's been a madhouse around here," the superintendent grumbled. Taryn nodded sympathetically as he wiped the sweat gathering on his shiny forehead with a damp tissue. It was at least fifteen degrees hotter inside his cramped, airless office than it was outside.

Venters County's Board of Education was located in a compound made up of double-wide trailers. Wooden planks acted as sidewalks and connected the half dozen or so buildings that served as temporary offices until the county's new, state-of-the-art residence was finished. So far, they'd been at their "temporary" site for more than a year.

"It's not so bad," Mr. Hamilton had explained when he'd first welcomed Taryn inside. "Our old building was falling apart at the seams. A WPA building, if you know what that is. Cold in the winter, hotter than hell in the summer. Well, you can see it as you drive out of town. It was the old high school until they built that new one ten years ago. We keep getting shuffled around."

A knock on the door now had him pausing, the stack of papers in his hands trembling slightly. From the two empty bottles of Tums on his desk, Taryn imagined that his stress level was at an all-time high.

"It's me, Roy," the deep, male voice on the other side called.

The look of relief on the pale man's face had Taryn feeling sorry for him. "Come in," he called.

The man who strolled through the door had olive skin and a head full of pitch black hair. He was in his late thirties or early forties, so close to her age, and she could tell from his stocky frame and the way he carried himself that he'd once played sports, probably football. He smiled politely at Taryn but kept his face impassive. She was sure he'd met a lot of people that didn't have the best intentions; most of Haven Hollow was keeping its guard up these days.

"Jamey, this is Taryn Magill," the superintendent intoned, gesturing towards her. "She's here to put our school back together again."

The other man's shoulders relaxed a little, and his smile warmed. "I know who you are then," he said, his eyes twinkling. "It's nice to meet you. I'm Jamey Winters, high school principal extraordinaire."

He was, without a doubt, the best-looking principal she'd ever seen. She wouldn't have minded being called into his office.

"I don't know about putting it back together again, but I am going to try," she told him modestly.

It was, in fact, the high school's PTO that had raised the funds to hire her. She was taking only a fraction of her usual fees, considering the circumstances. She wasn't sure how they'd heard of her, or what they knew. Taryn had earned some notoriety with her second talent, the supernatural one, and was occasionally recognized for it—though she never brought it up or openly advertised it herself.

"I can't wait to see what you do," Jamey said. His face softened then. "I went to Muddy Creek myself. I have a soft spot for it."

"Yeah?" she asked, interested. "I might hit you up with some questions then. I like to get a feel for a place's history while I'm working. I like to put as much of its soul into my work as possible. They're not just inanimate objects to me, these places I work with."

A flicker of something passed over his face, a shadow, but then it was gone. It was probably just stress. She was, after all, asking one more thing from a person who undoubtedly had a lot on his plate already.

"Do you believe places have memories, Miss Magill? That they have souls?"

"Very much," she nodded.

"Hmmm," he replied. She was unable to read his expression now but her sense of smell, which had always been unnaturally strong, picked up something not unlike nervousness. But when he shrugged and grinned she thought she might be imagining it. "Then my wife and I will have you over for dinner one night. Tell you all the gory details."

The room quieted as his words fell like lead. The three of them exchanged looks and Taryn's face reddened at Jamey's embarrassment.

"You know, I don't mean...," his voice trailed off as he looked at the floor.

14

"Oh well, we know you didn't, boy," Mr. Hamilton boomed at last. He turned to Taryn. "Fact is, I'll be glad when all this nonsense is over and done with. Life can get back to normal. And nobody will ever have to talk about it again."

*   *   *

MAIN STREET WAS DESERTED as Taryn drove back to her motel. With only a handful of restaurants in town, and most of them pizza parlors, she wasn't going to have a healthy or varied diet while she was there. She'd only been there two nights and had already eaten at three of them. Still, the Stromboli she'd had for supper was good, and the mom 'n pop place was charming with the old jukebox that seemed to stop at 1990 and the cracked leather chairs.

It truly was a town that appeared to roll up the streets when the sun went down. The one stoplight on Main turned to a caution light at night, and it blinked orange now, casting an eerie glow in front of the court house. Nobody stood on the steps milling around; it was a ghost town. She'd seen a group of the reporters standing around by their cars in the motel's parking lot earlier. A few had given her cursory glances, but mostly she didn't seem to register on their radars. They had bigger fish to fry. To them, she was probably just another journalist, someone else coming on late to the scene to make a name for herself with her editor.

With no other streetlamps on the road, the boarded-up storefronts hid in the shadows, ghosts of small towns past. Ancient meters glowed in her headlights and garbage cans overflowed onto the cracked sidewalks.

"Probably hard to keep up with all the people," Taryn remarked, recognizing the irony of the now-empty streets.

Around her, the mountains rose straight up into the sky, murky silhouettes that colorless clouds embraced. When she got out of her car, she caught a whiff of cigarette smoke and rain. Her joints were aching; she would need to take medicine when she got inside. The dampness always made it worse.

"I am getting old," Taryn frowned as she searched in her backpack for the motel key. "When I can predict rain from my aching knees, I've crossed the threshold."

Somewhere, several miles away, another woman studied the mountains rising around her and also felt the rain coming on in her bones. Rain, and something else...

FOUR

*T*aryn stood with her back to the gym. She could feel its vastness behind her, slowly opening like a mouth ready to swallow her whole.

Before her, the long, gloomy hallway carried on for eternity, the miles of open doors between her and the end little comfort with their feeble attempts at light.

The soft music that spilled towards her swelled within the shadows and built around her, seeping inside her skin. She caught the words "blue eyes" and something else and then the line began repeating itself over and over again until she thought she might scream. The endless loop was as unnerving as the darkness that seemed to be alive.

When she felt the icy tendrils gently lace themselves over her neck, she began to run. On and on she ran, her tennis shoes softly thumping on the tile below. Their plodding rose above the ghastly music.

She ran as hard as she ever had, her chest heaved and fell from the effort, but as she looked in horror, the end was suddenly much further away. She hastened her speed, making her legs pump faster and faster, but it was of no use. Then, behind her, a slam.

Taryn screeched but did not pause or look over her shoulder, not even after another door slammed, and then another.

They were catching up with her now. There was only one more between her and whatever chased her. Her legs ached; she began to slow down when the heart in her chest felt as though it might jump right on out.

When the last door behind her bolted shut, Taryn screamed.

FIVE

*T*aryn walked around the chilly motel room, pale rays of morning filtering through the space between the dirty floor and heavy door. She'd wanted to make it out to the school by sunrise but hadn't quite gotten up in time. After her nightmare, she'd gotten sucked into a "House Hunters: International" marathon and didn't fall back asleep until the wee hours of the morning. As it was, she was running on three hours of sleep and a gallon of caffeine.

From the television hovering precariously atop the ancient bureau, the morning news chattered, and the glare flashed random colors around the room.

Taryn was not a morning person, but mornings and sunsets offered the best light.

Hair damp from a shower intended to wake her, Taryn started a braid to tame the unruly waves that fell to her shoulders. Her hands felt heavy with fatigue. The water pressure in the tiny bathroom had been all but nonexistent. She'd run out of shampoo (never, in her life, had she used up the shampoo and conditioner at the same time). And she was stuck drinking the same warm, flat two liters of Coke she'd been nursing all night since she forgot to hit the gas station to restock and didn't have any change for the vending machine.

The morning was not going as planned.

To make it worse, Miss Dixie appeared to be judging her from across the room.

"Yeah, yeah, yeah," Taryn grumbled, stalking over to her camera. "I see you looking at me."

Feeling foolish, Taryn turned the camera around so that it was facing the wall, her face now reflected on the LCD screen. And yet, she somehow felt oddly better. She might joke that Miss Dixie was often her eyes, but, in fact, sometimes she felt like Miss Dixie had her own eyes. And maybe even a soul.

Taryn wouldn't start painting today or even sketching. She generally spent the first few days walking around the property, snapping pictures of the features that called to her. She'd then return to her room and upload the images to her laptop. From there, Taryn would go through them one by one, studying the building and what Miss Dixie had captured. She found that this helped her get a better feel for what she was working with. When she was offsite and didn't have the building right in front of her, she could use the images for help with late-night painting sessions.

Taryn knew she'd never make a real living as a photographer; her work lay with her paintings. The photos were just for her. Still, a month back she'd had a small showing of her photography at a Nashville art gallery, and it had gone very well. A former client had set it up for her, and she knew she wouldn't have gotten the gig without her benefactor's string pulling, but Taryn had managed to sell several of the shots and the owner was setting up another one in the spring.

That was something.

Sighing, Taryn stretched her leg out in front of her and winced. The pain was worse. It seemed to be getting a little worse every day. A few short years ago, she'd never heard of Ehlers-Danlos Syndrome, the connective tissue disorder that was wreaking havoc on her joints and organs. Now she dealt with the repercussions of having it almost every day.

Suddenly, Taryn's attention was drawn away from her aching leg and to the television screen. "...Muddy Creek..." she heard an announcer say so she walked back to the bed and lowered herself to the fleece blanket she'd spread over it.

The screen was instantly filled with a live view of the court house. Although it was barely daylight, the steps were covered with swarms of people. Some held homemade signs with the words "Murderer" and "Killer" scrawled on them. Media hounds staked out spots on the grass and sidewalk, looking for spectators willing to talk. (None had to look very hard.) There must have been three dozen people already gathered on the steps, and from the sounds of the cars racing down the street outside her room, more were on their way.

Taryn groaned. She'd have to get in the middle of that to reach the school.

As though on cue, the shot of the court house disappeared, and one of the school loomed before her. Taryn turned up the volume as she studied the once impeccable and somewhat charming country school appear on the screen.

"For almost forty-five years the Muddy Creek Elementary School was a thriving, welcoming, center of community for the residents of this small West Virginia town," the heavily made-up face of Frieda Bowen intoned. "Most years, the small school only saw one-hundred fifty students at a single time. It was a place where everyone knew everyone, and everybody felt safe."

The camera zoomed in on an athletic, thirtysomething brunette with two toddlers at her side. "I went to school here, yeah," she declared, smacking her lips as she spoke. "Went there all the way through elementary school. I loved Muddy Creek! I was hoping these would get to go there, too. But then it closed. It was just awful what happened. I hope she hangs!"

Taryn winced. She understood why people were angry, but open hostility was not something she was comfortable with. Taryn still feared lynch mobs. No wonder Lucy Dawson had installed the gate and security camera. She wondered if they were enough.

18

Another shot, this one of an elderly woman in a swing. The words "rsing Home" could be seen on the brick wall behind her.

"My sister, Marilu Evans, was a schoolteacher there for forty years," she stated in a soft, but firm, voice. "She loved it more than anything. We grew up down the road from it. Attended the original school even before they built that one. Our daddy worked the mines until he passed. I'm the only one left now. She never thought that school would be her death..." A single tear escaped from her eye and slid down her wrinkled cheek. Taryn shook her head with sadness.

Another picture flashed on the screen, an image of a tall, unsmiling woman with thick, short-cropped hair standing in front of a library shelf, surrounded by somber eight-year-olds.

Taryn trembled again. Of course. She was one of the people killed that night. She hadn't remembered her name but knew she'd been one of the teachers.

They'd all been teachers.

"This small, isolated county that nobody had ever heard of before will never forget what happened that fateful night," Frieda charged. Her crazy looking eyes were almost wild as she stared down the camera before her. She was all but shaking with excitement. "What was meant to be a joyous occasion, a reunion, a time for reconnecting, would end in senseless tragedy..."

Taryn shook her head and rolled her eyes. That "nobody had ever heard of"? She imagined that went over well with the local people. It was a second away from pissing her off. Still, the new footage of the little school, a blazing inferno, was a sight to see. Taryn had seen the material before, but it continued to amaze her. One entire side of the building was a wall of flames, the black smoke dense.

"Today, opening statements for the trial of Lucy Dawson..."

Taryn considered the face of the woman they now showed, but she tuned out Frieda.

Lucy Dawson was not a large woman. Barely five feet tall and hunched over slightly, she looked like a child next to the officers that flanked her as they marched her up the court house stairs. The video was taken months ago, at an arraignment. Back then she'd been fifteen pounds heavier, but she'd looked younger. The peasant skirt and loose-fitting blouse billowed around her as she moved, both trailing behind her like a cape. She was not an attractive woman by any means, but she was impressive looking. Her long tangled hair fell nearly to her waist. Her ruddy cheeks were plump, her forehead high and shiny. The thick bifocals took up half her face and slipped down her nose as she walked, but nobody offered to push them up for her.

For some reason, that bothered Taryn. Couldn't someone have helped her?

When a bystander shoved against Lucy and caught her off balance, she nearly tumbled to the ground. The older officer grabbed her under the arms and straightened her, his mouth set in a hard line. The other one seemed to give her a push. Even in the short piece of footage, their roughness was evident. The jeering, taunting, and spitting were all obvious as well.

Even though the woman was accused of a cold, calculated murder Taryn found herself growing a little sick to her stomach. She didn't like seeing anyone picked on or mistreated—no matter what they'd done.

When the news program began displaying pictures of the deceased, seven who had died the night Lucy Dawson had decided to play "Independence Day", Taryn turned it off. Now, with the sound gone, she could hear the excited chatter of the journalists outside, the ones who hadn't yet left. They sounded like a group of athletes, getting ready to head off for the Big Game. Their laughing, jostling, and animated calls to one another were almost festive. Soon, she'd be all alone in the motel, everyone else in the thick of the action down the street.

"Eh, what the hell," Taryn mumbled, allowing herself to fall backward onto the bed. "I've got plenty of time."

She wasn't yet ready to face that school, not after what she'd just seen. Miss Dixie would have to get over it.

* * *

THE GIRL THAT lounged behind the dusty counter had her feet propped up on an empty toilet paper box and a Cosmo magazine balanced on her lap. She sipped on a root beer. (Maybe. It might have been a real one. Taryn couldn't see real well.)

Taryn would put her around nineteen, although she had one of those older, kind of worn-looking faces that was deceptive.

"Hey, I hate to be a bother," Taryn began, a hint of apology in her tone, "but I was wondering if you all have any hair dryers up here. Mine doesn't seem to be working."

Taryn rarely dried her hair with a blow dryer, preferring to let it air dry so it didn't frizz, but the weather report was calling for a cold front. She didn't want to get sick. Sicker than she already was, anyway.

The girl barely acknowledged her. She was currently engrossed in a quiz, circling her answers with blue Maybelline eyeliner. Beside her on a small television screen, Dr. Oz excitedly gestured to something in a bottle while his audience leaned forward with rapturous attention.

Taryn coughed politely.

"Um...," the girl heaved a sigh at last, rolling her eyes in the process. "We don't, like, keep any here."

"Oh, okay then," Taryn replied, feeling foolish. Used to working alone the majority of the time, Taryn didn't always do well with people. She was known to be socially awkward at times, especially if the other person was even less communicative and outgoing than her. It was one of the reasons she got along so well with Matt—both were rather shy introverts who enjoyed quietness and alone time. They were perfectly happy sitting together on the couch, reading separate books, all afternoon long.

The girl, however, suddenly seemed to have a change of heart. Or maybe she was just bored.

"I can, like, look around though," she shrugged. "Somebody might have left one here."

Taryn got a flash of someone going off and leaving a nice straightener or hair dryer and that going right into the housekeeper's purse instead of the Lost and Found. Not that she could blame them; those suckers were expensive.

"That would be nice, thanks," Taryn replied. "I'm in Room 16."

"No problem," the girl said with another shrug. "You one of them reporters here?"

"No, I'm actually here to paint the school," Taryn explained. "Well, not paint the building, but to paint a picture of it."

With her explanation, Taryn now held more interest to the girl before her.

The girl's eyes lit up with interest. "Yeah? Really? That's cool, that's cool. I took art in high school. It was my favorite class."

Seeking an opportunity to learn more information about her surroundings, Taryn leaned forward on the counter and brushed a stray strand of hair from her face. "So you from here?"

"Everyone's from here," the girl snorted. "Nobody actually moves here or anything." Her stringy hair was held back in a plastic butterfly clip—something Taryn hadn't seen in ages. The thick eyeliner and lipstick were applied heavily, but carefully. She'd apparently taken her time getting herself ready that morning. Her skin was far too brown for it to have been a natural tan, considering the season. Still, it didn't have an orange tint to it. Tanning bed, Taryn guessed. There was one on every corner there.

Looking at her, Taryn was again struck by the changes the small town was experiencing from the influx of visitors and attention. She tried to imagine being a local and waking up one morning to the hordes of people, the continuous line of traffic, the cameras...She figured people felt a mixture of overwhelming excitement and immense irritation and distrust. After all, it wasn't the first time outsiders had come into their mountains with their cameras and tape recorders and shown the world only a partial story of what was really going on. They couldn't trust what was being relayed to the masses.

"It's a pretty place," Taryn offered truthfully.

The girl rolled her eyes again and sniffed. "It's okay. There's literally nothing to do here. Used to have a skating rink when I was a kid. Now, even that's closed."

That was a picture Taryn saw painted all too often. Small towns everywhere were drying up and closing down, giving way to urban sprawl and big box stores. It wounded her.

"Did you go to the school?"

Now, technically, the county had four elementary schools, including one within the city limits. But they both knew which "school" she was talking about.

"I didn't, no," the girl answered. "I went here in town. But my cousins did. We always laughed about it, about how far out in the country it was."

Taryn started then laughed aloud herself. There was one two-lane highway running into the county. The coal company had built it a few years before. The county itself had fewer than five-thousand people. There was no Wal-Mart, no Kroger, no clothing stores (besides a few church-sponsored charity shops), and only a handful of restaurants. There wasn't a single subdivision in the entire county. Road names actually included the word "Hollow" on them—she had passed a few on the drive to the school. How far out did a place have to be to qualify as "country" there?

"You having trouble with the reporters or anything?"

She was nosy, but she couldn't help it.

"Naw," the girl replied. "I mean, they ask a lot of questions and stuff, but they're okay. Police have only been here twice in the past week. That probably woulda happened anyway, you know?"

Taryn nodded. She'd heard one of them making fun of the town earlier, calling the residents "all rednecks" and later referring to them as being "so inbred they were turning blue." But they hadn't realized she was in her room and could hear them. Or else they figured she wouldn't care; after all, she was just a guest there herself.

"But, yeah, that woman," the girl interjected into Taryn's racing thoughts, "she was always weird. Always."

At first, Taryn thought she might be referring to Frieda Bowen. Taryn had heard Frieda was also staying at the motel, though she had a hard time believing it. But then, on instinct, she realized the girl was talking about Lucy. Sensing an opportunity, she ran with it. "She was kind of your town celebrity before she was your, er, *celebrity*, wasn't she? Because of her books?"

"Yeah, yeah. I never read 'em though," she said. "And nobody never saw her. She didn't, like, leave the house much. My mom said she used to get out and do stuff, used to go all over the country for book signings and to be on TV. But none of that went on in my life. She's always been right there at that house by the school as long as I can remember."

"That's what I'd heard, too," Taryn confided. "So was she kind of a recluse?"

"Dunno. I guess. She went to school with my mom back in the day. Mom said she was weird even then."

Taryn made a mental note of that. She never knew when she might need some of the random information she collected and carried around.

"Well, I'd better get on to work," Taryn said at last. She might want to talk more, and she didn't want to wear out her welcome while it was still early. She pointed to the vacant parking lot. "Gonna hit the road and avoid the traffic while they're all eating or whatever they're doing. It's quiet out there."

The sun was starting to drop down behind the mountains. If she timed it just right she'd hit the school at twilight and still get in some good shots. She had time to make the magic hour.

"Okay, no problem," the girl sang as Taryn turned to leave. "Oh, and by the way, my name's Sandy."

Taryn had a feeling she'd be seeing a lot of Sandy.

* * *

SOMEWHERE, A PACK OF DOGS BARKED. They could have been on the other side of the school or the other side of the mountain. The location and valley floor's acoustics made it hard to tell.

These were not friendly, sociable "yips" but low, angry bays and growls. The hostile symphony added a sinister quality to the already isolated and eerie setting. Taryn had already been around the building once, snapping pictures as her feet quietly disturbed the fallen leaves strewn on the spongy ground. And now the sun had almost entirely faded away. The oblong school was becoming a black outline against the purple sky, a shadowy ghost with the dark line of ridgetops closing in behind it.

Taryn shuddered a little and self-consciously pulled her cardigan tighter around her shoulders. She'd taken around two dozen photos but wasn't satisfied. She'd need to return for more, preferably when she had more daylight to work with.

Taryn had always possessed the talent of seeing the past, even before she could literally see it. She'd always been able to look at a building, or park or empty field, and visualize what it had once looked like; she'd seen everything as it had once been when it thrived. It was why she'd gone into Historic Preservation. Taryn's love of history had her living with the past secured firmly around her, just the way she liked it. She saw into the past the way fortune tellers were meant to see into the future. Where others saw a dilapidated farmhouse with broken windows and collapsed roof she saw a couple pushing off on the wooden porch swing, caught the aroma of fried chicken wafting through an open window, and heard children giggling as they darted across the wooden floors.

Try as she might, however, Taryn was having trouble seeing anything with Muddy Creek Elementary.

"Don't let the incident that's going on now cloud your judgment or imagination with what went on then," she scolded herself, looking away from the burned-out section and, instead, focusing on the side that was "only" damaged from neglect. "Just pretend that the other thing didn't happen..."

Of course, she couldn't logically act like the school hadn't been blown up with a homemade bomb–that seven people weren't dead because of one woman's alleged madness. There was no way she could avoid thinking about that; Taryn's compassion alone wouldn't let her forget it, much less the gaping black holes in the cinderblocks

With the last flickers of light now dissipating, Taryn studied the back of the school as she walked towards her car. She really put her mind to work, attempting to evoke imagery that was having difficulty coming. She focused on the classroom windows and pretended she could hear happy children inside. Singing. Teachers reading aloud from primers. Little voices reciting the Pledge of Allegiance in unison.

Instead of broken glass, she tried seeing colorful construction paper taped to the windows, artwork by stubby little hands. Rather than the putrid scent of standing water, she made herself pick up on the scents of a cafeteria kitchen–those rectangle pizzas and soft chocolate chip cookies.

And, for a moment anyway, it worked. She could almost see and feel it the way it had once been. She was there, standing outside the school on a gray, fall day. Children laughed and sang. Music drifted through the open windows. Pumpkin spice and apple cider filled the air. School buses began dipping over the side of the hill, ready to take eager students back home to their parents.

Suddenly, however, the intense itching on her arm had her breaking the mood and slapping at herself in annoyance. Then came the itching on her neck, on her ankles, in her other hand...

When Taryn looked down, she was startled to see every inch of skin covered in hundreds of tiny mosquitos. Her ankles were black.

"Ew, ew!" Taryn yelped as she continued to swat at the air and slap at her skin. "Get off!"

That standing water, suspected but not yet seen, had created a new set of problems.

Taryn danced around in a circle, waving at the air like a crazy person. As she dashed the rest of the way to her car, mumbling and griping with each new bite, Miss Dixie vaulted back and forth on her chest keeping rhythm.

Inside, she locked the door in defiance, a satisfactory if not a logical decision. Welts were already cropping up on her pale skin.

"Well, damn," Taryn muttered as she cranked the engine.

A light flashed then, a light that shouldn't have been there at all. A light from inside of the school. At first, she'd thought it was a flashlight, that someone was exploring the old place. Maybe a kid, or perhaps even an optimistic journalist hoping for a new angle on the story. Perhaps someone had followed her, deciding she was someone of importance after all.

But it wasn't a small, probing flashlight beam. As it flickered again, she saw the room nearest her fill with light–the desks piled upon one another, the blackboard against the wall, chairs pushed against the door. It only remained lit for a second or two, but it was obvious that the light was an overhead one, fluorescent.

Troubled, Taryn still tried to shrug it off as she pulled away. She didn't think the electricity could still be on, but stranger things had happened. Maybe there was a short.

Still, she refused to look back.

SIX

*S*he'd collapsed on the bed, sleepy and achy, not long after she returned to her motel room. However, she'd tossed and turned until she'd finally given it up got up at 2:00 am, frustrated and still tired yet unable to sleep.

"May as well work," Taryn lamented, remembering how her grandmother had done the same. She'd lived with her grandmother off and on throughout her childhood and then until she'd passed away. Taryn still missed her and felt a pang when she ran her fingers over the antique ring that hugged her left ring finger. A present from her grandfather to her grandmother on one of their anniversaries.

Stella had been a significant figure in Taryn's life, and the most stable one after Matt. Her parents were good people with good intentions, but they'd been neglectful of Taryn in more ways than one. They'd been wrapped up in their jobs, in each other, and had little love or attention leftover for the daughter they didn't really understand. When she'd asked to move in with her grandmother, she knew her mother had been secretly relieved.

With the television on for background noise, Taryn flipped open her laptop and popped in Miss Dixie's SD card. "Might as well see what I've got so far..."

She'd taken fifty-six photos of the school that evening. "Dang," she said, impressed with herself. "I was busier than I thought!"

It wasn't uncommon for Taryn to get lost in her work. She could take hundreds of photos without registering it, or totally lose track of time and not realize that she'd been painting for five hours straight until her hand started cramping.

The photos popped out of her through the glare of the computer screen, all lined up in neat little rows. She studied the thumbnails, trying to figure out where she wanted to start.

"Miss Dixie sees things that I don't always notice," she'd explained to Matt once. "There's something different about every place that is unique to it. Miss Dixie usually finds those features a lot faster than me."

There were the windows in the antebellum home in Georgia, the extraordinary wood carvings in the row house in New York, the twisted wrought iron on the porches and balconies on the place in Memphis...

It wasn't just buildings that Taryn and her camera were drawn to. On a backpacking trip to Croatia when she was in college she'd been drawn to the colorful laundry that hung from the ancient buildings. Blue jeans and red miniskirts had flapped in the wind, draped between crumbling stone edifices. On a job in Montana she'd planned on being mesmerized by the glorious mountains, but Miss Dixie had picked up on the mind-boggling sky: sunrise, sunset, thunderstorms, even midnight...there was a subtle magnificence about the wide open space above them there. And, on Jekyll Island in Georgia, it was the Spanish moss. Whether it hung from live oaks or lampposts, Miss Dixie had discovered something magical in it and featured it in most of her photos.

She didn't yet know what Muddy Creek Elementary would have in store for her.

It certainly was bright, though.

Taryn giggled. Then, remembering Beaches, "It looks like a flamingo threw up in here!"

It was times like these she wished she had a close girlfriend, someone she could quote "Steel Magnolias" with or discuss Barbara Hershey's Hilary.

Taryn was suddenly hit with a pang for Matt then, a slight yearning that made her want to hear his voice. It was too late, even for them. He'd be dead to the world and, with his early mornings, getting up in a couple of hours. She wouldn't disturb him.

"I need some friends," Taryn muttered.

She had acquaintances, people she could exchange emails and messages with. She'd met lots of other women on assignment. Melissa, for instance, back in Kentucky was someone she still spoke to regularly and even saw on occasion. But there wasn't anyone in her life she could just go out for a drink with, drag along with her to listen to live music, hit the Macy's Black Friday sales with...

"Huh." Taryn had gazed at the thumbnails for a good five minutes. Her attention not been piqued by any one shot in particular, but now it settled on one towards the end. The picture had been taken about ten minutes before the Great Mosquito Attack.

Curious at what she was looking at, Taryn clicked on the image and enlarged it.

The light she'd seen in the classroom window was on again. It flickered through the broken window, casting a warm glow into the blackening night. She didn't know how she'd missed it when she'd been there. "It must have happened so fast I just didn't see it," Taryn murmured.

At first, she thought her flash might have come on and she was simply looking at a reflection of Miss Dixie through the glass. When she zoomed in on the picture, though, she knew it wasn't her camera. Sure enough, the light was on inside the classroom. It became apparent, then, why she'd missed it in person.

It hadn't been on then.

Taryn was no longer looking at a broken window and neglected classroom. The room in the picture was bright, organized, and full of life. Although she could only see a portion of the room through the two windows, and she'd been standing back pretty far when the shot was made, she could still see the rows of desks, the little orange plastic chairs pushed neatly under them. There was writing on the blackboard. A cluttered desk with stacks of folders and papers stood solidly in the front of the room. Multi-colored streamers dangled from the ceiling. Fluorescent overhead lights illuminated the lively scene.

"Oh no," Taryn groaned, the implication of what she saw sinking in.

Although her camera did, on occasion, pick up insignificant peeks of the past, the hollowness in the pit of her stomach assured Taryn that this was no random glimpse back in time. It was a preview of things to come.

"Welcome to Muddy Creek," she called over to Miss Dixie. "Looks like we're going to have our hands full."

SEVEN

So was it just the one picture then?"

Taryn nodded, despite the fact that Matt couldn't see her head bobbing through the phone. His voice sounded so good to her. They talked every day, and sometimes more than once, but she always welcomed hearing from him. The familiarly was reassuring.

"Just the one," she said in between crunches of crispy bacon, "so far."

"There might not be any others," Matt mused thoughtfully. "That's happened before."

"Not this time," Taryn said, a little surprised at the unintended force in her voice.

"But you've become more sensitive, we've discovered. So it's possible this doesn't mean anything at all."

"It means something, I am sure of it," she declared.

"Okay. I just don't want you getting worked up and upset if there's nothing to get excited about."

Taryn bristled, the cold burst of air hitting her stomach with a punch. Some people got hot and saw red when they were angry–Taryn grew cold and blue.

"I am not 'worked up,'" she said evenly, keeping her voice low and measured. It was her first morning eating breakfast in the small diner downtown. The "fried chicken place," she'd heard the reporters call it. The small room was crowded and she didn't want to cause a scene.

Not that most of them would've noticed her anyway. Everyone seemed to be barking on phones, mesmerized by their laptop screens, or conversing frantically with the people squeezed in next to them.

"Okay, okay," Matt said, attempting to soothe her. "It's just that we've seen the things that can happen and they're not always good. The road isn't always worth going down."

"The road hasn't always been easy, but the result has always been worth it," Taryn argued, remembering some of the things that she'd helped put to rest in the past. Sure, she'd almost been killed once or twice (okay, maybe more) but with each incident, she'd become a little more powerful, a little more focused.

"This is why I'm here, Matt," she stated firmly.

"Well, you're mainly there to paint that school. Keep that in mind, no matter what; it's still just a job."

"Not here as in Muddy Creek but here," Taryn tried again.

"Ah." Matt wouldn't argue that point with her. In fact, if there was one thing they agreed on it was the power of the universe and destiny. Matt was a big believer in purpose, in things that were meant to be.

It was the only way he could describe his relationship with Taryn.

"Do you need me to do anything?"

"Nah," Taryn shrugged. "Nothing's happened yet. I'll let you know, though."

"This time, just make sure you let me know before something crazy happens," Matt added drily. "I'm getting a little old for all this excitement."

"Me too, dude, me too."

* * *

IN THE FULL MORNING LIGHT, the school didn't look nearly as intimidating as it had at dusk. The sky had been slate gray over the past few days, colorless. Today, however, had seen a turn for the better with the weather. Taryn was surprised at how much the blue sky, fluffy clouds, and bright sunshine prettied up the valley. Even with the severe neglect, the school looked like something from a painting. Hopefully, her own painting would look just as good.

By the time she finished, it would look as though you could walk through the front doors. Viewers would swear they could hear the sounds of the morning bell, and the shuffling of little feet. All of the darkness associated with what the place had become would be gone.

"getting excited about this job now," Taryn sang to herself, trying to pump herself up.

The school only looked at her warily. It was still playing its cards too close to the vest.

Always wary of snakes, she'd tugged on a pair of scuffed cowboy boots. It was now cold enough to wear long sleeves, especially in the morning, although the sun warmed her through the flannel of her shirt. She might have to strip down to her tank later in the afternoon. Her unruly hair was pulled up in a ponytail and hidden beneath a John Denver baseball cap–Thank God I'm A Country Boy.

"Okay, then. Let's do this!"

As she made her way to the building, the tall weeds still glistened with dew. They left wet patches on her jeans and soon her tan boots were muddy brown. The Civil

Wars rang through her earbuds. She was still mourning their breakup and hoped that by sheer will alone they might eventually get back together.

Taryn enjoyed creating her own soundtrack to her life, shutting out the external world around her. She rarely went anywhere without her music. It had saved her on more than one occasion. When her fiancé, Andrew, had died several years before she'd gone through a deep depression. It was the unsettling Allison Moorer and the hopefulness of Kelly Willis that had finally dragged her back out into the sunshine.

Her songs were her friends, as corny (and a little pathetic) as that sounded.

Taryn stopped moving and stood back to study the windows that flanked the school's main entrance. They were mostly intact; only a few thin cracks splintered the glass around the edges. The other windows were either broken or covered with vegetation. These, however, sparkled in the muted sunlight. Reflected in the panes were the outlines of the lofty mountains that surrounded the school. The leaves already changing colors and Taryn could see orange, red, and yellow blurs reflected in the window panes.

She paced in front of the entrance at leisure, taking shots from every angle. When Taryn examined the images on her LCD screen, it was almost possible to forget that the school was in such poor shape. When she was only looking at the windows, it could just as well have been a regular Tuesday morning; the kids tucked away safely inside.

Taryn smiled to herself and squatted down. She aimed the camera at the vine-covered front door and carefully focused Mis Dixie on the scene before her. At about the time she pressed her finger down, however, a movement caught her eye from another window. Caught off guard, Taryn lost her balance and tumbled to the ground, landing on the damp grass.

"Well, damn," she muttered as she wiped the seat of her pants and straightened the camera strap.

The flash of white had been quick, but she hadn't imagined it. Another reflection maybe?

Taryn stepped closer to the building and peered at the window where she'd seen the movement. "Nope, not a reflection," Taryn said aloud. "There's no glass in that window."

A bird then. Had to have been a bird.

Only it had seemed much larger. And more fluid.

She'd have to shrug it off, though. She couldn't let herself get spooked so early in the game.

"Ghosts can't hurt people," Taryn reminded herself. "And nobody said this school was haunted."

Pulling herself together, Taryn turned Miss Dixie back on and aimed her at the entrance once again. "Okay, let's give this another shot," she declared with authority. "I've got this."

This time, the burst of movement was much more than a simple flash–it was a deliberate action. After the initial burst caught the corner of her eye again, Taryn watched in fascination as the silvery shadow dashed before the broken glass and paused briefly before vanishing into the ragged obscurity of the room behind it.

"Oh," Taryn yelped in surprise, involuntarily flinching from the sight.

When nothing more happened, Taryn let out a long sigh of breath she'd unconsciously been holding. More curious now than frightened, she took a single step towards the building, Miss Dixie held before her like a shield, her finger still hovering over the shutter button. The dead leaves crinkled under her feet. Otherwise, the late morning was quiet. Not a single gnat or bird lingered above her or sang its song through the trees. It was almost eerily still, in fact.

Cautiously, she made her way to the open window. Careful of the shards of glass that still clung to the rotten wood, she brushed aside the climbing plants and peered inside. There wasn't much to see. A mountain of desks, the kind shaped like little individual tables with openings under the top, took up the center of the floor. A graffiti-filled blackboard watched from the front of the room; someone had taken spray paint to it. A sad looking bulletin board still held the faded remnants of construction paper and cut-out balloon letters announcing spelling contest winners.

Those winners are now adults with children of their own, Taryn thought with irony.

The classroom door was open, but she couldn't see beyond; the hallway was pitch black. With the sun hidden behind the leaden clouds that once again formed out of nowhere, the room was murky and dim.

Outside, a granddaddy longlegs quietly worked its way up her arm. Taryn stepped back from the window, not wanting to press her luck, when something moved inside again. On instinct, she pressed the shutter button and the room was instantly illuminated, the artificial brightness momentarily blinding.

A little brown field mouse ran out from under a broken chair and scurried from the room, peeved at the disruption.

"Ha," Taryn grinned, shaking her head.

Maybe it had just been a mouse, she thought. Maybe she was overreacting. About all of it.

She was putting Miss Dixie's lens cap back on when the rumbling of tires on loose gravel had her recoiling in surprise. It was the first vehicle she'd seen since visiting the school. Taryn looked up just in time to see an old, red Jeep flying past the school, sending stones soaring through the air like tiny bullets. The driver moved like a bat out of hell, the Jeep sliding and skidding from one side of the narrow road to the other. Linda Ronstadt blasted through the scratchy speakers. Before the vehicle climbed the embankment to the main road and disappeared around the corner Taryn caught sight of long, grayish brown hair whipping through the open window.

"Lucy Dawson," Taryn murmured, bemused at the sighting. She'd just seen what dozens of reporters had been trying to see for weeks. It made her wonder why more weren't camped out at the school.

The cry that came from behind her was chilling. For a brief moment, in her confusion, Taryn thought she was the one calling out—the earsplitting sound was that close. She knew it couldn't be, however. Aside from the fact that her mouth was closed, such a high-pitched wail could have only belonged to a child. Only a child could cry so passionately, without regard to embarrassment or pride.

Eyes wide and the hairs on the back of her neck raised at attention, Taryn turned back to the building.

It was, of course, still empty.

EIGHT

I'd like to thank you for having me over," Taryn said politely.

The tall, willowy blond accepted the store-bought pie with a gracious smile. Taryn tried not to stare at Heather Winters with complete disgust. Jamey's wife was quite possibly the most beautiful creature she'd ever seen. "Jealousy" did not even begin to describe the emotion running through Taryn's veins.

"Well, I told Jamey we needed to have you over as soon as he told me about you," the woman replied warmly. She threaded her arm through Taryn's and gently led her into the living room.

Taryn looked down and noticed beautifully manicured fingernails at the end of a smooth, tan hand. Next to her, Taryn was pale, freckled, and sported jagged nails that had permanent paint and charcoal ground under them. She was mortified to be up against such a creature.

She wasn't sure how much money a school principal could earn, but whatever it was it must have gone far in Haven Hollow. The Winters had a striking home–a large, brand new, Tudor style house on several acres. The snowy white carpet she now walked over in her bare feet (Taryn's mother had been big on people taking their shoes off at the door and it was now habit), was so soft and clean it felt like walking on clouds. The décor was a mix of shabby chic and antiques. From the chipped-paint buffet with its display of farm kitchen cookware to the mahogany hall tree with the vintage hats artfully balanced on its "limbs," everything looked as though it had come straight out of *Country Living* magazine.

Taryn dug it.

"You've got a lovely home," she said, feeling both shy and awkward. Taryn had never been good with small talk. She didn't normally even use the word "lovely."

"Oh, thank you," Heather blushed prettily.

Damn, Taryn thought. *Perfect teeth and she's modest too. I hate this woman.*

She didn't really, of course. Taryn might not have been psychic but she was usually pretty good at reading people. (Of course, when she was wrong she was really wrong.) Her gut instinct told her that Heather Winters was a good egg.

Later, as she sat across from a tired-but-friendly Jamey and his sparkling wife she felt right at home with the two. Jamey filled the women in on the school antics of the day and when the conversation lulled Heather made sure she asked the appropriate questions of Taryn to ensure she continued to feel wanted and included.

"So how long have you been painting?" Heather asked.

"Off and on most of my life," Taryn answered, "but it wasn't until high school and college that I really started taking it seriously. I wanted to major in Art in college but I knew it wasn't the kind of degree that would lead to a lot of jobs. I'm not much of a teacher, no offense Jamey."

Jamey sent her a laugh. "At least you were smart enough to know that! I wish some of these other teachers would figure it out sooner. So what did you end up going into?"

"Historical Preservation and Art. I wanted to combine the two," Taryn explained. "I'm lucky to be able to have a job that I love. Although it has its drawbacks, of course, it's mostly a lot of fun."

What she didn't add was that some days the drawbacks were almost *too* tough. Her health was failing and that was not something she could continue to ignore. Ehlers-Danlos Syndrome, a connective tissue disorder, left her in an extreme amount of pain. Without a cure, she could only manage the pain with strong medications that left her tired and sick to her stomach. Of more immediate concern, though, was that she'd recently been diagnosed with an aortic aneurism. There were no real treatment options available for that, either. They were taking a watch-and-wait approach to it. The fatigue, pain, and gastrointestinal issues it caused seemed to get a little worse every day, though. She couldn't ignore it forever.

"We love to travel," Heather said. "Over the summer we took a cruise through the Bahamas with some friends."

"That sounds like fun. I've never been on a cruise," Taryn said.

"Heather here has to get out every once in awhile or she starts to get stir crazy," Jamey grinned.

"It's true," Heather said. "I love it here and it's my home but sometimes enough is *enough*."

"Have you all ever lived anywhere else?"

"We went to college at Marshall and lived there for five years," Jamey said.

"Is that where you all met?"

The couple looked at each other and shared a laugh. When Jamey reached over and took his wife's hand in his and squeezed her elegant fingers, for a moment Taryn felt a little pang of real jealousy. Their closeness was not a show; this was a couple that truly loved and enjoyed one another. Taryn shared a similar closeness with Matt, but the distance prohibited them from having that daily sharing-of-lives interaction that most couples enjoyed.

"We're both from right here," Heather replied with a soft smile. "We've actually been together since Middle School. Since I was twelve years old."

"Really?" Taryn was pleasantly surprised. You didn't see that happen very often. "That's really cool."

"Of course, there were a few break ups here and there," Jamey said playfully. "This one here dumped me twice so that she could sow her wild oats."

"Oh please." Heather rolled her eyes and swatted at her husband. "Don't let him fool you. Every girl in the school wanted him. I had to fight so many girls that I still have the bruises to show for it."

Taryn didn't doubt it. Jamey was still an attractive man and she could only imagine what he would've looked like in high school. She wanted to ask about children but it was obvious they didn't have any, their house was far too clean and organized, and it wasn't any of her business.

When dinner was over, and after Taryn helped clear the table (in spite of Heather's protests that she was a guest), they all gathered in a family room. Jamey busied himself with building a fire in the fireplace and Heather stretched out on a small loveseat, a soft blanket toss her over her feet. "It feels so good to just come home and relax at the end of the day. The store was packed today. I didn't get a break until after noon."

"Heather works at the pharmacy here in town," Jamey called over his shoulder. "As you can imagine, our town has more than its usual share of visitors these days."

"I've sold more candy bars and Cokes in the past three weeks than I've sold in two years. Those reporters are trying to stay awake I guess. And you wouldn't believe the number of prescriptions for Xanax and Valium we've filled."

"It's hard to drive through them sometimes to get to the school," Taryn said. Although she, too, was a visitor to the area and technically not any different, she wanted to commiserate with her hosts.

"They've mostly been okay," Heather said, "and I guess it's good for our business, but I'll be glad when things go back to normal. I can't take all this excitement."

Taryn was a little surprised by Heather's reaction. As she sat in their nice house, eating their nice meal, and looking at their nice things she couldn't help but wonder why they'd continue to stick around the town. They'd been out–had attended college, traveled around a little, etc. They didn't seem to have children so it didn't look like they were necessarily tied to the community in ways a lot of others were. If anything Taryn would've thought that the influx of visitors from around the country would've been exciting to them, allowed them to be the bridge between the community members they might feel disconnected to and the rest of the world they wanted to be a part of.

But perhaps she had misread the situation. After all, in front of their nice, new house they had matching four wheelers and coordinating trucks. Jamey's hunting trophies were hanging on the wall above the fireplace, along with a collection of antique firearms. Perhaps they were, what her friend Melissa sometimes called people, rednecks with money. Down home at heart, just with a little more extra cash that allowed them to buy nicer toys than most.

"I was wondering if you all could tell me about the school," Taryn said. "Since you're both from here."

"I can," Jamey replied, "because I went to Muddy Creek. Heather went to the city school, though. She was upper class."

"Ha," Heather snorted. "We just have the one middle school and one high school but there are four elementary schools. Or there were, anyway. Now there are two."

"I loved Muddy Creek," Jamey said. He settled onto the loveseat by his wife's feet. By habit, it seemed, he placed her legs in his lab and began rubbing her claves. Taryn thought it looked fabulous. "It was a great school."

"It's really cute," Taryn prompted. "I bet when it was still open it was a nice place."

"It was," he agreed. "It was small, you know? Not that many students. Everyone knew everyone, though, and we were all friends. I still remember being out there running around the playground, playing kick ball with my buddies, eating breakfast in the cafeteria every morning–and that was back when the cooks were really allowed to cook. Now everything is state mandated and frozen."

"School food used to be worth eating," Heather added. "It's horrible now."

Taryn could agree with that. Only, her cafeteria's food had *always* been bad. She must have missed the quality period. "Did you have any favorite teachers?"

Jamey paused and looked up at the ceiling, as though searching for the right answer. "Well..."

"Honey, you know it was Mrs. Evans," Heather said teasingly.

A dark cloud passed briefly over Jamey's face before he grimaced. "She was a mean, hateful woman," he explained. "I'm embarrassed to admit it now, considering my chosen career field, but the kids just hated her. Including me. I had her for fourth grade. First day of school they had to bring in extra trash cans and sit them around the room. Kids were throwing up because they were afraid to be in there. Her reputation preceded her."

Taryn laughed. "You're kidding!"

"I kid you not," Jamey said. "That woman could scare a bear. She'd scream and yell and...well, it wasn't pretty. I couldn't do a damn thing right in her class." He shook his head and grinned, but the smile didn't reach his eyes.

Heather chuckled. "Not sorry I missed that."

"In hindsight, she was probably just doing her best. Some of us were a bunch of hellions. And the experience certainly helped me get to where I am today. Of course, some of her, er, unorthodox teaching methods would not be tolerated in today's classrooms. The parents wouldn't allow it."

"The parents are a little overprotective of their precious snowflakes," Heather explained.

"Snowflakes?" Taryn asked, confused.

"*Snowflakes*," Heather lamented, rolling her eyes in exaggeration. "The parents believe little Jenny and little Michael are extra-special. There has never been another child like them and never will be. They are the most beautiful, the most charming, the most talented...well, you get the picture."

Taryn did.

"The other teachers were good, though," Jamey continued, sending his wife a look. "Miss Adair was my first grade teacher. She used to bring her dog to school with her. Nobody cared about those things back then, about allergies or pet anxieties or anything. Dog's name was Holly and used to roam up and down the hallways and visit the other classrooms. The kids loved it."

Taryn tried to picture a dog roaming around her old school and couldn't. A bird had gotten inside once, though, and there had been some excitement.

"And then there was Mr. Scott. Everyone loved him. He was my fifth grade teacher. He came from the other side of the state. I don't know what brought him here. He was young, probably early twenties. Of course, back then he felt like an old man to us, although not nearly as old as our fathers. Maybe our big brother. At a time when all the other teachers were mostly middle-aged women in long skirts and orthopedic shoes, in our minds anyway, he wore silk shirts, a gold chain, and visited the tanning bed. Our fathers were mostly miners, railroad workers, or farmers. We'd never seen a man who got manicures, not outside of television anyway."

Taryn smiled, immediately envisioning a young, good-looking man mesmerizing a group of youngsters as he stood before their desks, his thick gold chain catching the overhead light.

"He'd play rock music in class, talk about movies and plays he'd seen, and showed us vacation pictures of his trips to the Virgin Islands. It was the first time a lot of us ever thought about life outside the county. It's hard to believe now but there were kids back then who had literally never been outside of the county. He kind of made us think it was possible to do big things, go places."

Taryn could almost see the young, idealistic teacher in the small mountain school, playing the radio for his fresh-faced kids and passing around images of unnaturally blue water and white sand. "That's nice," she said, meaning it.

"Yeah," Jamey shrugged. "I remember once, after social studies, he passed around paper towels and plastic forks and stuff and taught us all how to set a table and use the right utensils. Like any of *us* were going to be five-star dining anytime soon. But that's just the way he was. He wanted to show us a bigger world. Oh, and then there was Mrs. Jennings. She had narcolepsy. She taught second grade and would doze off in the middle of teaching. We used to play pranks on her. Didn't learn much that year but man we had us some fun."

The three of them laughed now, all entertained by Jamey's descriptions of his childhood educators. "Yeah," he grumbled happily. "There were some great teachers there. I miss them."

The room fell silent. The smile on Heather's face froze and Jamey ducked his head, unable to meet Taryn's eyes. She, herself, looked away and found herself unnaturally interested in a magazine stand beside her, her face burning hot.

He'd had good teachers at Muddy Creek. "Had" being the operative word.

Thanks to Lucy Dawson, they were now all dead.

* * *

TARYN SLUMPED AGAINST the pressed-wood headboard and exhaled nosily. It had been a long day, an even longer evening. She'd spent all morning and afternoon at the school where she'd taken hundreds of pictures. Her plans of grabbing fried chicken and holing up in her motel room for the rest of the night had been thwarted by the call from Jamey, inviting her to dinner.

Had she known how attractive her hostess was going to be, she'd have taken more care with her appearance. She would've at least hopped in the shower before heading over. Even now, Taryn could feel the stench of the stagnant water from the valley and the school clinging to her. She wondered if Jamey and Heather had caught it as well.

Sniffing now, Taryn caught a whiff of the decay and neglect and wrinkled her nose. "Eh, crap," she muttered. She was dog tired and wanted to curl under the covers and flip on the television but she knew if she wallered around on the bed the odor would never disappear. It would cling to her for weeks. The thought of taking it back home to Nashville with her had Taryn jumping out of the bed and scampering to the tiny bathroom, shedding layers of clothing as she went.

Her phone rang twice as the hot water poured down. Both calls were from Matt. She'd call him back later. The water pressure wasn't great, but the heat felt wonderful on her clammy skin.

"Taryn's water isn't hot enough unless you can boil a chicken in it," Matt liked to tell people.

Remembering the mosquitos and gnats that had surrounded her, the slimy weeds that brushed at her thighs, and the stench of excrement from the animals that had made the general area their dumping ground had Taryn scrubbing at her skin with the motel's generic shower gel. Her sense of smell had always been unnaturally strong, but this was different. She was breathing it, *tasting* it.

Taryn scowled and scrubbed harder.

When her water started running cool she quickly rinsed her hair and turned off the faucet. Like everything else in the motel room, it didn't work like it should; it took all her strength and a few kicks to get it off. As she wrapped the towel around her shoulders, Taryn was surprised to look down and see her red, raw skin glaring up at her.

"Oops," she groaned. "Looks like I got a little overzealous there."

The cold blast of air that smacked her in the face when she opened the bathroom door had her fighting for breath. With the steamy heat of the bathroom behind her, Taryn braced herself against the chill. The temperature had dropped a good twenty degrees in the short amount of time she'd been bathing.

"What the–" Taryn muttered, stomping over to the thermostat.

It read seventy-nine degrees, normal.

"Great. Is this broken, too?"

A gasp behind her, a sharp intake of breath, had her spinning on her heel. Hackles up, she was prepared to come face-to-face with an intruder, someone who had let themselves in when she was at her most vulnerable.

The room was empty.

Taryn stood motionless, water trickling down her legs and pooling at her feet. She slowed her breathing, taking inaudible breaths. A block away she could hear the faint sounds of a car radio. Someone slammed a door a few rooms down. Intermittent drops of water fell from the shower faucet, their metallic echo amplified by the quietness.

Taryn was still, but the room was not. There was something with her.

The scent was earthy– dirt mixed with creek water and something else...an animal, perhaps? It wasn't unpleasant, nor was it unfamiliar. She'd smelled it before but couldn't put her finger on where.

The air stirred around her, the currents moving swiftly as bursts of air whipped across her stomach and back. Something was moving, and moving quickly.

"Hello?" Taryn ventured, her voice cracking with fear.

The freezing hand that landed on her elbow was gentle, tentative. The small fingers lightly brushed her forearm. She didn't need to be able to see the invader to know it was a child.

"Oh my God," Taryn whispered in a rush. She closed her eyes and stood as still as a stone, willing whatever was there to remain placid.

The pressure eased for a second and then, again, the frozen fingers fell on her, this time more confident as they dug into her skin–little things that groped and prodded.

Taryn couldn't breathe.

Her instinct was to scream—to shriek and run from the room. Towel and all. But she couldn't move.

Just when tears of terror threatened to spill, a soft noise came from the front door. The weight on her arm disappeared. In an instant, the air seemed to change. Something invisible shifted inside the room. Within seconds she could feel the warmth starting to seep back, though she remained frozen in place. Taryn knew whatever had been there was gone.

The sound came again, a rustling that sounded human. And alive. As Taryn watched, a folded-up piece of paper slowly crawled towards her from under the door, inching its way across the soiled carpet. When the movement stopped, hurried footsteps faded down the sidewalk and into the night.

Clutching her towel to her chest, Taryn walked the length of the floor and knelt to the auspicious intruder. Almost fearing what she would find, she unfolded the document as a foreboding unease settled in around her. One short paragraph was written in large, loopy handwriting in the middle of the page.

Her eyes began to scan the note but she stopped short when the signature at the bottom had her doing a double take. Taryn blinked, shook her head, and looked again.

Lucy Dawson.

Somehow, the most famous woman in town had braved the throngs of reporters camped out in that very motel to find her, Taryn. She exhaled noisily and bowed her head.

She'd just been officially invited to the party.

NINE

I don't know that you should do this." Matt's concern resounded through her head as Taryn's little car leisurely pushed past the decrepit pink schoolhouse and began climbing the mountain behind it.

"Me either," she'd agreed, not taking his words lightly. She was also concerned. "But I think I *have* to."

"Have you learned nothing?" Matt had asked. "After everything?"

It was true; he was right. She'd been through a lot in the past two years. Her life had gone from fairly ordinary, sometimes boring, to exhilarating and sometimes scary. In addition to the revelations she received through Miss Dixie, she was becoming more sensitive with the energy that cleaved to the places she'd visited and worked at. She no longer needed Miss Dixie for communication and visions–they were finding her on their own, now.

And then there was her illness. Ehlers-Danlos Syndrome. EDS. She was beginning to hate those letters. It was slowly causing her connective tissue to fall apart. And the pain wasn't even the worst part; sometimes the fatigue and neurological issues were overwhelming. She'd gone from a person who'd readily jumped into her car with her camera, ready to explore and wiggle through any abandoned building that caught her interest to someone who could barely climb out of bed some days.

Thankfully, a legal settlement she'd received in the past year meant that she no longer had to rely on her work to pay the bills. Still, she *enjoyed* working. Taryn had never been a lazy person, never felt entitled. Her art was an integral part of who she was. She wasn't going to give that up.

But Matt was right. She was probably nuts for inching up the graveled incline, on her way to see the woman who was, by most accounts, a cold-blooded killer.

When she'd left that morning the reporters in the parking lot had not even cast her a second look. "Slow day," she'd heard one of them say. "Nobody's talking."

"Getting sick of this Podunk place," another had complained. "You know I had to drive out to the highway to get reception earlier?"

"I hope they find her guilty and hang her soon. These people are clammed up tighter than a–"

Taryn had closed her car door then, wearing a secret smile. If only they'd known where she was going.

"Is it just curiosity?" Matt had asked.

"Yes, a little," Taryn had admitted. And it was, to an extent. Taryn had a voyeuristic aspect about her—not something she was always proud of. It was the same trait that had her glued to the bad reality television shows, watching episodes of "Teen Mom" and "The Real Housewives Atlanta" and getting as involved as if she actually knew those people. It was true that part of her was excited and had a bit of pride that, out of the hundreds of reporters trying to snag a story with the murderess, she'd actually been extended a real invitation.

"But I am also intrigued. I want to know what she wants," she'd gone on to explain. "To see what she thinks I can bring to the table."

"I meditated on this," Matt said. "Last night, before bed. I took a good, long look at the situation. It doesn't look like she has ill intentions towards you. So *today* should be fine anyway."

Taryn was moved. In his own, weird, way Matt took care of her. He was never going to be the macho type, preferring his incense and candles to a bloody fist or gun, but he protected her. And she'd always watched out for him, going back to the time when she was twelve years old and had beat up Jerry Fischer for calling Matt a "pansy" in gym.

"Hey, just think about it," she'd teased him right before hanging up the phone. "All the attempted murder stuff on me kind of came out of the blue, you know? None of the killers actually sent me an invitation..."

"Uh," Matt had replied slowly, "remember that party? The one I attended with you?"

"Oh." Oops. Well, at least *most* of the times she'd almost been killed had come out of the blue. But, to be fair to the person who'd tried to kill her that night, things had kind of fallen apart at the last minute. Taryn could take partial responsibility for that one.

She ruminated over her conversation with Matt, and Lucy's letter, as the trees closed in around her. Patti Griffin sang quietly, the religious tune not out-of-place in the cathedral of the forest. The sky, gray and brooding, was barely able to poke through the lofty trees towering above, their shadows engulfing the mountainside in hushed stillness. Dense underbrush filled in the spots between the soaring pines, maples, and oaks that seemed to reach towards Taryn and watch her from behind.

As Taryn studied the undergrowth, skinny saplings, lush kudzu, and thorny bushes she had a brief idea of how tough the original settlers would've had it. Most of the state parks she'd been to were fairly antiseptic—manicured and clean and easily navigable. This, however, was wild. She tried to imagine slogging around the mountains with a knife; thorns and branches cutting into her thighs and stomach, getting tangled in her hair.

Taryn quivered, suddenly feeling as though she'd stumbled back in time.

* * *

-

"I'D INVITE YOU INSIDE, but the house is a mess," Lucy explained to her guest. "I'm not used to company."

"It's okay," Taryn shrugged. "It's nice out here."

Thought the front porch was cluttered and full of furniture and ceramic flower pots, Taryn was enjoying herself sitting outside. The log cabin was old but appeared to be in good condition. The view from the porch was the sloping mountainside; an ethereal view of the colorful canopy spread out before them.

Lucy sat beside Taryn in an old metal chair. The white paint had chipped and flaked over the years, the silver metal that peaked out in bare spots was rusted. Taryn rocked back in forth in a creaky swing. Somewhere behind the house a dog barked. Other than the squeak, the barking was the only sound that interrupted the otherwise quietness.

"Bet you're wondering what all this is about," Lucy said. Her large bifocals took up most of her face. Her brown hair, streaked with the silver, hovered on her head in a messy bun. The paisley skirt and striped nautical shirt didn't come close to matching. Still, there was a stately air about her that was almost regal. She commanded Taryn's presence without saying a word, and it wasn't just because of who she was. Taryn was, in fact, a little in awe of being in the presence of such a famous person, but it was the woman herself that Taryn was now finding intriguing. Lucy sat erect, her back as straight as a steel rod. Her voice carried the mountain lull, a melodic accent Taryn had always loved. But her grammar was impeccable.

Taryn tried to imagine her putting together a homemade bomb and setting it off, killing those she'd grown up with in cold blood, and couldn't.

"I read your note," Taryn replied. "But, yes, I *am* curious."

Lucy pursed her lips and looked over Taryn's head. Her attention was fixated on something Taryn couldn't hear or see and for a few minutes Taryn thought that might be the end of their visit. Then Lucy spoke again.

"I know about your dinner with Jamey and Heather." At Taryn's look of surprise, Lucy laughed. "I might not get out much anymore, but that doesn't mean I am not in the loop. I do still have some eyes and ears around town."

Taryn wanted to know why and how, but decided to leave her questions for later. If there *was* a later.

"I attended school with Jamey, you know," Lucy continued. "For a time, as children, we knew each other."

Not that they were friends, or even acquaintances, but that they "knew each other." An odd turn of phrase. Since there was only one middle and one high school in the county, most of the children probably at least knew of one another. Still, Lucy looked a good ten to fifteen years older than the youthful principal.

"Are you not friends anymore?" Taryn ventured, unable to help herself.

"Not for a very long time," Lucy said. Her voice remained calm and even but Taryn detected a glimmer of sadness in her eyes that stung a little.

"People seem to start changing in middle school," Taryn offered lamely. Her own middle school years had been disastrous and would've been downright traumatic if not for her friendship with Matt.

"People change for a lot of reasons," Lucy replied vaguely.

"What, exactly, is it that you want to talk about? Is there something you want me to do?" Taryn asked.

"I know about *you*. I know what you do. What you can do," Lucy added.

Taryn nodded. That was beginning to happen more and more on her jobsites. She could no longer keep her skills a secret. Beside her, in her backpack, Miss Dixie was a solid reminder.

"I was wondering if..." Lucy hesitated now, blushing with embarrassment. Then she straightened again and smoothed down her skirt. "I was wondering if you'd *seen* anything. Heard anything while you were at the school."

Taryn paused, not knowing how to answer. By continuing with the conversation, was she somehow becoming a part of the court case? Was she getting too involved? What if Lucy was hoping that her victims were still stuck in the school and using Taryn as proof that her diabolical revenge had worked?

Nah, she thought. Nobody with bifocals that big could be that malevolent.

Still, she needed to feel her out. "What do you mean?"

"I've lived here all my life," Lucy explained. "I grew up around the school. When I was a child and attending school we used to tell stories about ghosts and 'haints' in there. We tried Bloody Mary during basketball games. I was a cheerleader, you know."

Taryn smiled. She'd also played Bloody Mary as a child. "Did you ever see anything?"

"Once a toilet flushed on its own," Lucy laughed. She looked much younger when she smiled. "We never tried it again after that. We decided the devil was in there with us. Ran out of there screaming like a bunch of banshees."

Taryn laughed along with her.

"Later, much later, I began hearing things. *Real* things. I didn't sleep well starting as a teenager. I'd go for these long walks late at night. I know these hills like the back of my hand. They've always made me feel safe. Prefer my mountains to people," Lucy said, her eyes dull.

Taryn, herself, felt closed in and claustrophobic. It was difficult to see how another person could see the same thing and feel comforted.

"What kinds of things did you see and hear?" Taryn prodded.

"Crying. Talking. Children, mostly."

Taryn remembered the wailing; even now the tiny hairs on her arms stood up as she sound echoed in her mind.

"I know from your face that you know what I am talking about," Lucy said.

Taryn wondered if she were really that transparent. Lucy did not push, however.

"It makes me feel a little better, to be perfectly honest, to know that I am not alone in this." The words dangled between them, heavy in the air. Taryn wasn't sure if the double meaning was intended.

"Is there anything you want me to do?"

Lucy hesitated before answering. "Y–yes. If you see or hear anything, I'd like to know. Please."

Taryn nodded. "I can do that."

"It's important to me," Lucy said suddenly, her face alight with desperation. "This old heart has hardened a lot over the years but the children...children. I just, I just *need* to know. Please."

"I'll do that," Taryn promised her. "Anything I hear or see."

Lucy nodded, her face grim. "It's the most important thing to me, you know."

Taryn leaned back against the swing, the wooden slats cutting into her back. Ironic. Lucy was on trial for murder. In a time when she, Taryn, would've been up to her eyeballs in depositions and lawyer meetings and studying every episode of "Law & Order" like it was her new job, Lucy was asking for ghost stories.

People shocked the hell out of her.

TEN

O n a quest for linseed oil, Taryn maneuvered the streets of Huntington, searching for the craft supply store she'd found online.

"And she sounded normal?" Matt pressed.

"Totally," Taryn replied. "Well, sort of. There were a few weird moments. But she definitely didn't act like she was going to break out the revolver and take me down. Or blow me up."

"I'd still be careful," he cautioned her. "I don't get a great feeling about this. Something's bothering me."

Taryn nodded. "You know, the weird thing is that she's not that much older than me. Maybe ten years? I can't really tell. Maybe less. And yet she seems, I don't know, so much older. Like she's from another time period. It's odd."

"So where are you now?"

"Huntington. Looking for a store. Kind of nice to get out of town for a day," Taryn confided. "I've even thought about getting a motel room for the night. Maybe you and I can do that when you come up?"

"Oh, yeah, sorry about that..."

Taryn's chest heaved with disappointment. She knew that tone. "What's up?"

"Work. You know we got that new grant? There's a lot of preliminary reports to file. I'm afraid I'm going to have to stick around and make sure they get gone properly."

You mean to make sure they get done the way you'd do them, Taryn retorted in her mind. Being involved in a relationship with someone who worked for NASA–an organization that required detail-orientated obsessiveness to successfully put people in a small tube and blast them into the stratosphere using highly unstable and dangerous chemicals and bring them back again safely– wasn't all it was cracked up to be.

"Sorry to hear that, Matt. I was looking forward to it," she said instead.

"I think I can get some things moved around and come up next weekend, though," he said cheerfully. "I'll fly in and maybe we can get that hotel room after all."

"Sounds good. I'm looking forward to showing you around Muddy Creek."

"Or," he said slowly, "we could just stay in the motel room..."

Taryn snorted, but laughed. She remembered a time when a thirteen-year-old Matt had balked at the idea of ever having a girlfriend. He'd been a late bloomer but when he'd bloomed he'd bloomed.

"So Huntington, eh? My parents took me up there when I was a kid. Dad had family there at one time. We went to an amusement park," Matt mused.

"An amusement park? You?" Taryn grinned. Matt did occasionally make a trip to Disney World, but it was more for the giant turkey legs and science stuff at Epcot than it was for Space Mountain.

"It was during the days of trying to convince them that I was a normal eight-year-old and not a freak," Matt sighed. "I still get nauseous thinking about the Big Dipper."

"Was it Camden Park?"

"Yeah, that's it. How'd you know?"

"I saw the signs for it on the way in. I think it's the same place that some of the country music singers used to play at in the 1980s when they were still getting their start," Taryn said. Her third talent: she had a penchant for country music trivia. She couldn't tell you a thing she learned in high school Algebra but could literally tell you every artist that had won Entertainer of the Year at the last twenty Country Music Association Awards.

"It was. When we were there we saw Vince Gill. It was raining and they'd pushed all these picnic tables together under a pavilion. We only stayed for a few minutes. Mother sorted, called him 'whiney', and said he'd never make it. Clearly, Mother knew what she was talking about."

Taryn laughed along with him as she pulled into the big box parking lot. After the week she'd had, it was good to talk to someone about inane things. It made her feel normal.

* * *

"I'D JUST LOVE to come and watch you paint." The woman before her wore black yoga pants, sported an orange bottled tan, and sipped on a gas station Slurpee. Upon meeting Taryn, she'd engulfed her in a bear hug, spilling some of the icy red liquid down the front of Taryn's white T-shirt.

"Well, I don't normally work around other people but–"

"Oh, well, you won't mind *me*," the woman screeched, slinging her bleached-blond hair back from her shoulders. "After all, I was the one responsible for bringing you here."

And you'll be the reason I leave if you keep it up missy, she wanted to reply. The truth was, she was not at ease working with someone hanging over her shoulder. It usually led to "advice" and while Taryn's temper was usually controlled, nothing pissed her off more than someone obnoxiously critiquing her. It's why she worked for herself.

"Louellen, leave the poor girl alone." The other woman who sat on the other side of Taryn was tall and thin with hands that shook every time she spoke. Her muddy brown hair was chopped off crudely at her ears, like she'd taken pinking shears to her head. Unlike the other women at the PTA meeting, she was not outspoken or quick to offer her opinion. Taryn had barely heard her speak. She still didn't know her name.

"Well I'm just glad you were able to join us today," Louellen declared, clapping her hands together. The multiple rings on her fingers sparkled in the incandescent lights of the school cafeteria. The other dozen or so women nodded their approval.

Taryn offered a thin smiled and told them she was happy to be there. The truth was, however, it made her nervous to be back inside a school. The familiar cafeteria smell, the scent of floor cleaner, the bright lights, the stragglers that continued to pass by with their backpacks slung over one shoulder...it was too close to feeling like she was back in school herself. And Taryn had not been a fan of school, at least not until college. She'd been picked on, ignored, and generally made to feel like there was something wrong with her. She wouldn't go back to being a teenager for anything.

Ironic how she could enjoy being around an abandoned schoolhouse and had no trouble visualizing the past, but had fits of anxiety for the fully-functioning ones in the present.

"It would have been nice, though, if you'd brought your canvases with you," Louellen said. She offered a pleasant, toothy smile but there was steel behind it. She wasn't joking.

"Sorry about that," Taryn replied. She toyed with the print outs of the images she'd brought with her. Expecting that question she'd printed off some of the pictures she'd taken with Miss Dixie, an offering of what was to come. "I usually just spend the first week taking photos and getting to know the place first."

"Perfectly understandable," an overweight woman in a blue jean skirt that hit her ankles declared. Her long, stick-straight hair fell to her waist in split ends. It didn't appear as though it had ever been cut. Her face, though pretty, was devoid of makeup. Taryn had immediately stamped her with "Holy Roller", though she didn't do it with maliciousness. The woman, in fact, had been nothing but pleasant to her. So what if she carried around a Bible and didn't believe in musical instruments at church?

"Just remember, we're paying you by the job and not by the *day*," Louellen laughed thinly. None of the other women of the PTA joined her.

"Don't worry," Taryn said. "I've never missed a deadline."

An awkward silence followed. Some of the women glanced down at their hands and fiddled with notes or cookies. Others pulled out their phones and pretended to be focused on important messages (Facebooking, most likely). Finally, when Taryn didn't think the air could get any thicker, someone slapped the table and told everyone to cut out for a ten-minute "refreshment and potty break."

The other women, and the lone man in attendance, shot up in tandem, scattering from the room in a race. Taryn was left sitting at the table next to the quiet woman with the short hair.

"Don't worry about her," the woman smiled softly. "She's always like that. I don't think she means to be rude. You know she's not even the president? She just takes over. A lot."

Taryn laughed. "It's okay. I get it."

"My son goes here. My daughter will next year," the woman said. "I went here myself. It's a good school. I only belong to this so that I know what's going on. He doesn't tell me a thing. And it gets me out of the house."

"I know what you mean. If it weren't for work I'd rarely leave myself anymore," Taryn said.

"A lot of us went to Muddy Creek. So we have, I guess you'd call it, an emotional investment in what you're doing."

"It's definitely an interesting place."

The other woman sighed and pushed back a lock of hair from her eyes. "When Lucy destroyed it, well, I about died. So sad to treat a building like that."

Taryn had trouble keeping the surprise from her face. Had it not registered that they'd actually let the building deteriorate even before Lucy had decided to become a pyromaniac?

Could the woman before her actually have more sympathy for the building than for the people who'd died? People she'd almost certainly known?

"So were they your teachers? I mean, the ones who died?"

"Yes," she nodded, eyes wide. "I had them all. I loved them. I loved it there."

Confused, Taryn wanted to press on but she was cut off when Louellen approached her from behind. Sharp fingernails dug into Taryn's shoulder; she didn't think it was unintentional.

"Listen, I just wanted to throw something your way," Louellen hissed.

Taryn turned and looked at her, trying to shrug her hand off her shoulder. "What's up?"

"It's just that we heard about your little visit," Louellen said, her eyes bright. Although she put on the illusion of keeping her voice down and things private between them, it still reverberated through the room. Others who were filing back into the cafeteria stopped talking and paused to listen.

"My visit?" Taryn asked innocently.

How could they know, she asked herself. She guessed there really were no secrets in a small town.

"With Lucy Dawson," Louellen whispered theatrically. When Taryn didn't react, she forged ahead. "I just wanted to let you know that there are certain things people here aren't doing right now. Because of legal issues, you see?"

Taryn nodded. Yeah, she "saw."

"I just don't want people to get the wrong idea of you."

"But she hasn't been found guilty yet, right?" Taryn prodded, feeling contrary.

True, Lucy had been recorded on an iPhone by a firefighter holding a can of gasoline in her hand as she watched the flames rip through the building. The video of her, with blank eyes, watching the inferno had been viewed more than one million times on You Tube. Frieda Bowen played a snippet of it at least once a day on her show. She'd gone willingly with the police, even waited for them on the embankment, without any trouble. She'd all but admitted to setting the fire and not calling for help.

But Taryn didn't like where *this* conversation was heading. Nobody told her who she could or could not talk to. She didn't need the job that badly.

"Well, of course she hasn't been found guilty yet..." Louellen blushed, feeling the piercing eyes of those around her.

"I always liked Lucy." The voice came from the other side of the room and Taryn was surprised to look up and see Jamey standing in a doorway, arms folded across his chest. "Most of us did at one time or another," he reminded them.

Some looked down at their feet, out of embarrassment Taryn imagined. She caught Jamey's eye and sent him a grateful smile. Still, she remembered Lucy's words about knowing each other and felt sad. What had happened? Everyone started out as friends in elementary school. Then things changed along the way. Had the social awkwardness of the teen years split them apart?

"I liked her," the quiet woman next to her all but whispered. "We were friends in elementary school. She thought the school was haunted. We all did. Don't you remember playing Bloody Mary in the bathroom?" She directed this to Louellen.

"Yeah. A long time ago. Before she started killing people," Louellen retorted.

Before things got out of hand, Taryn stood and picked up her photos. "Look, I realize this is a sensitive topic. I don't know the full story. But my visit with her had nothing to do with the case. And it was kind of private. I've been an adult for a long time. A long time." She tried not to let the tears sting her eyes, an old habit when she got upset or frustrated, but she could already feel her face turning hot.

"Of course," Jamey said soothingly, walking towards her. She felt comforted by his gentle smile. "We're all adults here. Want me to walk you out?"

Taryn managed to send a polite smile to the rest of the group before Jamey took her arm in a companionable movement. She could feel the group's eyes on her back the whole walk across the linoleum floor.

Man, it really was like being back in school. Back in school with the mean girls.

ELEVEN

*H*ey Sandy," *Taryn smiled* as she walked through the dusty doors of the front office.

The receptionist glanced up and offered a small smile, something between boredom and frustration at being interrupted from the tablet she poked at. "Hey."

"I need to mail something," Taryn began, "but I haven't been able to find the post office. Can you point me in the right direction?"

"Sure," Sandy nodded. "It's in the grocery store."

"Huh?"

"The grocery store at the end of Main Street? The post office is connected to it, at the end."

Taryn laughed. She'd been in that store three times already, stocking up on snack food. She hadn't once noticed a post office. "Thanks. I guess I missed it."

"Easy to do," Sandy nodded. "The sign's itty bitty."

Taryn offered a "Thanks" and turned to go.

"Hey, wait a sec," Sandy called.

Taryn paused and turned. "Yeah?"

"So you, like, seen any ghosts around the school or anything?"

Startled, Taryn creased her forehead, a nervous habit, and chewed on her bottom lip. "Well, uh...why do you ask?"

Sandy held up a hand and shrugged again. "I dunno. My mom always said that people thought the school was haunted. That some girl had hung herself in the bathroom. Or something like that. And that you can hear her crying."

Taryn started to remind Sandy that Muddy Creek had always been an elementary school and that it was highly unlikely that an eight-year-old would commit suicide. Knowing that facts and logic had no place in a good ghost story, however, she kept the thought to herself.

"Haven't really seen anything out there," Taryn said at last. "But I'll let you know when I do."

Sandy's eyes brightened. "Awesome. My friends and I used to go out there before it burned down. We'd party and stuff behind the school, crawl in through the windows and shit. Dare each other to stay inside alone. Never saw anything myself but my ex said he heard something weird one night. I don't know, though. He was probably high."

Taryn laughed. "Yeah, that might do it."

"But if you see something, please tell me. It's, like, totally boring here all day. I don't get to talk to nobody much. Everyone just gets up in the morning and leaves. You're the only one who's stuck around and talked."

"I'll be back," Taryn promised her. "And hopefully I'll have some stories for you."

As she pulled out of the overgrown parking lot, Taryn couldn't help but laugh. She had to be the only person in town that wasn't hoping she'd see a ghost.

* * *

"WELL THAT WAS PAINFUL."

A year ago, the majority of Taryn's bills were household expenses: rent, utilities, groceries for when she was home, internet, and cable. She had two credit cards and student loans that she'd been steadily chipping away at over the past seven years. Her car was finally paid off.

Then her health went downhill.

Now she found herself paying on medical bills for everything from her CT scans and MRIs to her chronic pain treatments. She had a total of six medical specialists, including a neurologist, gastroenterologist, orthopedist, pain management specialist, and allergist. She saw all of them regularly and they all regularly sent her bills. She could have used her settlement and paid all of them off, but then she wouldn't have been left with much to live on. Instead, she'd worked out payment plans for the biggest bills and sent each of them a small amount each month. It was painful to see the money go, especially since none of the doctor visits ever resulted in any changes.

"I'd rather be shopping," Taryn muttered as she pulled over the embankment and dove towards the school. "Mama needs new boots."

She didn't, of course. Taryn could have opened a thrift store with all the clothes she had stuffed away back in her Nashville apartment.

"Hello Pepto," Taryn spoke to the sad-looking building in front of her. She'd decided that it needed a nickname. It made her feel closer to it.

The school did not reply. A good sign.

"Last day for you and me," Taryn told Miss Dixie as she slung her around her neck. After today she'd start her sketching and then it would be on to the painting.

She might still use her camera from time to time, but the rest of the job would be all on her. Miss Dixie had done her work, it would now be up to Taryn to do the rest.

The sun had almost disappeared entirely. She could see it trying to poke through the steely sky, but it was only a shadow, a brilliant shadow whose glare barely reached the earth. The sky held no color at all, but thanks to the heavy rain the week had seen, a few orange and red leaves were peeking through the trees. Taryn could only imagine how beautiful the area would look when the hills were alive with fall colors and sunshine. She knew that people flocked to the New England states for fall foliage tours but she'd yet to see a place that did autumn like Appalachia.

"I like to be in on the secret," Taryn sighed aloud.

"Looks good now," she'd overheard one of the reporters say at the post office. She was now able to tell the reporters apart from the locals. They were the ones with the inferior smirks and cell phones visibly strapped to their belts or hanging out their shirt pockets. "Just wait 'til all these leaves are gone, though."

"Yeah, then the trash will really shine through," his companion had sneered with a nasty laugh.

"The armpit of America," the first one laughed along with him. "Jesus H. Christ I'll be glad to blow this dump."

It angered Taryn, their obnoxious behavior. It also embarrassed her. They'd had no consideration for the people standing around them at the time. For all they knew, she was a local herself. Sure, the reporters had zero problems showing up and exploiting a story for their own gain and using the resources at their disposal but God forbid they lower themselves to treat it with any kind of respect.

"This is the twenty-first century, right?" Taryn muttered. She stood in the middle of what had once been the driveway, her hands on her hips. The region had been exploited for decades. The so-called "War on Poverty" had done little to help the area's image of poor white trash, steeped in illiteracy, garbage, and dirt. Even now she occasionally ran into people in Nashville who still looked down their noses at their eastern neighbors, joking about their outhouses and lack of shoes. At what point had it become socially acceptable to make fun of the region and why was it still considered tolerable to demonize and belittle the "hillbillies" and "rednecks" when other groups had somehow earned the right to demand respect?

Taryn shook her head. It wasn't her fight, after all. She was not from Appalachia and had no real ties to it. But in her somewhat nomadic life she'd garnered respect for every place she visited. Taryn found beauty in everything, even in the bad.

It was no wonder the people were mistrustful of outsiders, however. From so-called "documentaries" that showed the burned-out trailers with a dozen cars littering the lawn while ignoring the McMansion next door to the Hollywood movies that portrayed the region's inhabitants as toothless inbreeds, she'd be cautious of strangers as well.

"Nobody cared about Lucy Dawson until she killed someone." Taryn said it quietly, a statement that didn't *need* to be spoken aloud yet somehow felt compulsory. Somewhere, inside the building, something crashed. The sound echoed, a tuneless blast that startled Taryn and had her flinching.

She was standing at the good end of the school, the part that was damaged by neglect and not by fire. Taryn walked to it and, brushing aside the tall daisies that grew in clumps, and placed her hand on the concrete wall. She expected it to be cold so she was surprised by the warmth that spread under her fingers. For a moment she held her breath, as though waiting for something. Then she laughed.

"You're freaking yourself out," Taryn scolded herself. "All those talks of Bloody Mary and ghosts."

As though in reply, her fingers quivered and all but lifted from the wall. Something under her hand pulsated. It was as though the building was breathing, taking a breath. She might have imagined the sigh that followed but that didn't make it any less real.

Disconcerted, Taryn hopped back and stared at the place where her hand had just rested. "Well that was a surprise," she said, her voice trembling a little. "Can you hear me?"

A sparkle came from the window above her, a mischievous wink. Taryn turned and looked behind her, but the sun had disappeared back behind a cloud again.

"You want something from me, too, don't you?" Taryn asked.

The music from her dream began to play inside. It began softly, barely discernible notes. She pressed her head to the wall, trying hard to hear what was playing. The same line, the one about the haunting, about the blue eyes, filtered outwards. Taryn closed her eyes and bit her lip even as her heart began to beat wildly inside her chest. Someone was in there, someone was singing, and the school wanted Taryn to hear it.

"BOOM!" She ducked and flinched, feeling as though something had been thrown at her.

"Oh!" Taryn yelped. "Geeze."

The clamor had her grabbing her ears and wincing in fear and pain. It was the sound of someone deliberately causing a ruckus, of anger. Although she stood a few feet back from the building now, she could feel the fury radiating through the layers of concrete and wrapping itself around her.

As quickly as it came, the rage dissipated. The clouds parted and the sun remerged. The air was quiet and still again. Taryn closed her eyes and exhaled. "I'm getting too old for this," she whispered.

Miss Dixie, quiet against her chest, bounced as though in agreement.

"I've got a job to do, though, and I am going to do it." Unlike the reporters, the vultures as she was starting to think of them as, she was going to do her job and do it with integrity. The PTA deserved it. The school deserved it.

She wasn't yet sure what Lucy Dawson deserved.

TWELVE

It was late, even for Taryn. She was used to carrying on at odd hours of the night, sometimes not going to bed until dawn when she was in a groove, but it was rare for her to stay up just to be awake. She just couldn't sleep. She'd flipped through every television channel at least three times, pausing on shows for a few minutes at a time before losing interest and moving on. She'd listened as the reporters gathered outside to head off for dinner then listened again as they all filed back, some clearly intoxicated (despite the fact the county was dry). She'd listened to the late-night talk shows with half an ear as she fell down a few rabbit holes on the internet. She'd started researching the history of the county and had somehow ended up looking at vintage rabbit fur coats.

Taryn couldn't sleep.

Miss Dixie rested beside her, watching her with disapproval.

"Yeah, yeah, yeah. I know," Taryn said, shooting her camera a withering glance. She'd yet to remove the memory card and take a look at the shots she'd taken that afternoon. She was uneasy, afraid of what she might have captured.

"Aren't you worried about getting involved?" But whatever Miss Dixie was feeling, she was keeping mum.

There was something in her shots, Taryn knew it. Once she looked, however, she'd be stuck. She would be as sucked into the story as those reporters strolling outside her door, their shadows passing over her window as they made their way to and from the ancient vending machines.

"See," she began, almost pleading with her camera, "it's not too late now. I can start painting right this minute. Not even look at the images until after the job's finished. Just do my work and go home." Taryn deserved that, right? Maybe, but that wasn't who she was.

Outside, howls of laughter rang out like a shot in the dark. It was Friday night. The reporters had apparently found a way to entertain themselves.

"How many times have I become involved when it wasn't any of my business?" she demanded. "And almost been killed for it?"

The lamp on the bedside table flickered then, a quick flash that dimmed the room for a moment, leaving her with nothing but the glare of the television screen. It could have been a short. Or a bad bulb. For most people, anyway. For Taryn it was a sign.

She was already involved. Ignoring her pictures would not change that.

"Well, damn," she sighed, blowing a clump of stringy hair from her eyes. "Let's see what we've got."

She'd taken twenty-nine photos that day. They were the last of what she needed. She'd visit the library on Monday and do some research, see if she could get ahold of some images of the school before it was destroyed. She'd already planned on taking the weekend off, on doing some local sightseeing to get out of her own head. But the pictures, they were finished. That part of the job was done.

The first eighteen looked exactly as they should. Nothing was out of place; the school looked as sad and deserted as it did in person.

And then she arrived at #19.

"Of course," Taryn said, shooting Miss Dixie a look after she'd glanced at the image. "Did *you* know about this?"

She could have sworn her camera winked at her.

There was the school, pale green and full of life. Gone were the invasive climbers, the holes in the roof, and the blackened concrete. Windows so clean they glistened looked at Taryn smugly. The driveway, *not* full of potholes and overgrown with weeds, was freshly paved. Four vehicles were pulled up to the building, all parked in a neat little row. The front door, whose color was now indeterminable thanks to the fire, was a hunter green and wore a big "Welcome Back, Students" sign. A playground, now almost completely camouflaged by the overgrowth, held fresh mulch on the ground. A tall slide, towering jungle gym, and two sets of swings patiently waited to be filled with tiny bodies.

If not for her own car, parked at an angle like a drunk after a bender, she might as well have been looking at a picture taken by a proud parent on the first day of school. The first day of school, twenty years ago.

* * *

"WHAT CAN I DO TO HELP?"

Matt lived in his own little world, oftentimes spending hours and even days within his head. "Cerebral" was a term often used to describe him.

"Weird" was another.

When it came to Taryn, however, he'd always been as focused as he could be. Although there were times she'd had to rope him back down to Earth and snap her fingers to get his attention, when she really needed something he was there.

"I don't know where to start," Taryn admitted.

She sat in her car, the driver's door open and her feet resting on the window. The view before her was something out of a picture. Although new mining efforts had presented the region with the unsightly mountaintop removal, the line of mountains that spread out for miles were all still intact. And they were on fire. Fall had arrived in all its full glory and it was a beauty. Taryn might as well have been sitting in a sea of crimson. She was glad Sandy had told her about the off-the-beaten-track side road that led up to what was known locally as "The Ledge."

"Well, we definitely know it has something to do with the school," Matt said, all business like.

Taryn smiled and felt her heart skip a beat. "We." With Matt everything was a "we" for him. Even when he felt that logic dictated she step away from whatever she was involved in, whenever she committed to something he was right there with her, 100%. It was one of the reasons why she'd hung onto the relationship for so long. She wasn't always certain that they worked as a couple, but as a team in general they were fantastic. She, herself, would've walked barefoot through hell or high water for him.

"Right," she agreed. "But we don't know what I am working with here, or what I am meant to do with the little material I have been given."

"So let's go over what we know. One, we know the school has a history of being haunted."

"Not necessarily," Taryn interjected. "What we have is some kids who talk about it in an urban legend kind of way. Nothing truly concrete. We can't ignore the fact that the spirits, if these are really spirits, are most likely from the school's recent events."

"Well, that gives me something to do. I can do some research, find out if there is any history of other deaths, local tragedies connected to the building, etc." Taryn could hear Matt making notes as he talked. She might ask for them later. One of them had to be the organized one after all.

"While you're at it, it wouldn't hurt to get a general history of the area," she pointed out. "If you can give me kind of the Cliffs' Notes version of that, I'll also do some man-on-the-street interviews and see what I can find out."

"Got it. So what else? Ah yes. We know that the school was abandoned for almost twenty years. We need to figure out if it was used for anything during that time period. Clubs? Organization? Devil worshipping rituals?"

Taryn laughed. It wouldn't be a small town in the south with at least one devil worshipping rumor.

"There's something else I want to know," she said. "We have to figure out why Lucy Dawson is so curious about the happenings there. I swear, I've seen her in a few news footage type thingies and I didn't see nearly the animation on her face as I did the other day when she was asking me about ghosts. I mean, Sandy I can understand. She's a kid, you know? Of course she's going to want to know what's going on. I would've too, at her age. But why Lucy?"

"Good thinking." Matt paused and when he began speaking again his voice was softer, gentler. "There is another elephant in the room, and one we're going to have to address."

"And that is?"

"Lucy Dawson. Why did she do it? Was it an accident? Did she mean to kill those people? Was she trying to do something else? Is there remorse? What's her motivation?"

"Damn, Matt, you missed your calling as a prosecutor."

"Yeah, well, since being with you I've been watching a lot of Dateline and the Investigation Discovery Channel."

The last few rays of the light disappeared from the sky. Like a ball of flames, the sun slid over the mountains in the distance, leaving nothing behind but streaks of pink and deep purple. A slight wind blew, making it nippy. It would be nightfall soon. Dusk came quickly there. She didn't want to be driving back the side of that mountain with it too dark so she'd need to go soon. It wasn't just the lack of sunlight causing her to chill, however. The mere mention of Lucy's deed troubled her.

"Yeah, I know. I've been thinking about it." In her mind, Taryn tried to reconcile the mild-mannered woman she'd talked to on the porch with the woman she'd seen online—the wild looking woman with the blank eyes and impassive face that barely reacted to the mayhem she'd caused.

"What kind of feeling did you get from her? Anything?"

"Nothing," Taryn sputtered, annoyed with herself. "Not a thing. It was hard to even remember that I was sitting with the same person. I tried to tune in, but she must have a brick wall built around her. I got nothing back whatsoever."

"Hmmm," Matt mused thoughtfully. "Might have to bring in some bigger guns for that. Would you be open to visiting her again, this time using a little extra help?"

"As long as it isn't something that's going to freak her out," Taryn replied, envisioning her walking up the path carrying a bag full of voodoo implements and waving incense everywhere.

"I'll think of something," he promised her. "So we've got a game plan anyway. We look at the history of the town, the history of the school—"

"The history of the people who died," Taryn interrupted him.

"Yeah, you think?"

"I do. I don't know why, but they're a part of this. They're either innocent bystanders or..."

"Or what?"

"Or there was a reason," Taryn whispered.

Suddenly, she felt very alone up there on The Ledge. Without a single soul to be seen, she felt vulnerable. Taryn pulled in her legs and began rolling up her window. It was time to go.

"There's something bothering you," Matt prompted her.

"Yes."

"Better tell me now."

Taryn sighed. "The picture I sent you, the one of the school? The building wasn't neglected. The picture was taken before the explosion, but long before it happened. Not just a few days or even a few months before."

"So you think we might be barking up the wrong tree?"

"I'm thinking people need to start talking."

THIRTEEN

*T*he attorney's words replayed through her mind* as Taryn wandered up the crowded sidewalk, making her way to the public library. It was only a few blocks away, the WPA-era building, but the walk was taking longer thanks to the reporters who totally ignored her and refused to move out of her way. Still, it gave her time to think.

"Work's going fine," he'd told her on the phone that morning. "I've emailed you a breakdown on the roofing and electrical work they finished."

Taryn hadn't opened that up yet. Why ruin a perfectly pleasant morning by looking at her finances?

Taryn's Aunt Sarah had passed away almost two years earlier. As her only surviving relative, the old New Hampshire farmhouse was left to Taryn. Still, it was a surprise when she'd received the news–both of her aunt's death and of the bequeathal.

Her death had been a blow to Taryn. Although she hadn't seen her aunt in years, as a child she'd been as close to her as she was her own mother, in many ways closer. A former principal, Sarah herself had loved and related to children in a way that her sister, Taryn's mother, never had. She'd never had any children of her own, however, and whatever maternal feelings she'd held she'd given to her niece and students.

Taryn missed her. Some of her most treasured childhood memories were of visiting the big, rambling house in the woods. Of waking up next to her aunt in the big, four-poster bed with the wood crackling in the fireplace and the smell of sausage and eggs drifting up from the old kitchen. Of canoeing around the deep, shadowy pond with the woman who'd been a hippie as a young woman. Going on nature walks through the woods, looking for bear scat and moose.

She'd gone up there a lot as a young child. Something had changed along the way and either the invitations had stopped coming as frequently or Taryn herself had grown up and found other interests. Either way, she didn't visit as often as a teenager and young woman. Her aunt had spent the last few years of her life as a veritable recluse. Taryn hadn't even known she'd been battling cancer. The fact that Sarah had fought the disease, and ultimately died, alone was something that ate at Taryn on a daily basis.

She would never forgive herself for it.

The old house needed a ton of work. Everyone had tried to talk her into selling it. She'd certainly needed the money. That house was as much of her as it had been of her aunt, though. She couldn't let it go. When the settlement had come through, she'd used a chunk of it to go towards restoration. Taryn had no idea what she was going to do with the house once it was finished but there was still time to think about it.

"Dude, *really?*" Taryn stopped in the middle of the sidewalk and glared at the heavyset reporter who had just nonchalantly tossed his Styrofoam coffee cup to the ground. The brown liquid remaining inside sloshed out, splattering the concrete and speckling Taryn's boots.

"Oops," he grinned, but didn't over to do anything about his litter.

Taryn remained where she stood, her hands on her hips. Several others paused and were now watching the little scene unfold. "You are going to get that, right?"

The man shrugged. He could've been anywhere from twenty-five to forty. With his stubble, jeans, microphone, and camera man in tow there was little to set him apart from the others. They were all starting to look alike.

"What do you mean?"

"Pick it up," Taryn said slowly, enunciating each word. "Why should someone else do it?"

Not to mention the fact that the garbage can was literally only five steps away.

Now, with a slightly red face, the man bent over and grabbed it. What was left of the coffee spilled onto his hand. It was his turn to glare at Taryn as the little rivets ran down his fingers. "Happy?"

"Sure."

"What do you care, anyway? You're not from here. I've seen you at the motel."

Taryn shrugged. "I'm a human being. Geeze, dude. Have a little respect for the place."

He snorted, an ugly sound that made his troll-like face even more unattractive. "Ha! Have you seen the amount of garbage they got up and down the roads, lady? The burnt out trailers and broken cars they use as yard art? Good damn. I ain't having no respect for any place until they start respecting themselves!"

Several around him nodded their approval, although a few managed to look somewhat ashamed. Still, he walked the short distance to the garbage can and tossed the cup.

"I ought to have earned some kind of karma for that," Taryn muttered to herself as she quickened her pace. Some cat calls followed her as she left the scene and continued to the library.

She really ought not to be allowed out in public sometimes.

* * *

"TWO BIRDS, ONE STONE," Taryn whispered to herself, flipping through the microfiche. She'd be able to look up the old school to get some ideas of what it had looked like intact and carry out research for her other project at the same time.

What set this job apart from a lot of her others was the relative newness of the building itself. Most of the time her paintings were the only true representations of the buildings she recreated; either they'd been built and destroyed before photographs were popular or the original ones had been lost. Muddy Creek Elementary, however, had no shortage of images to peruse.

This was, after all, more of an emotional hire than anything else. They had hired her to create a painting of a place many in the county viewed with nostalgia. The painting, if she'd understood the debate at the PTA meeting right, would hang in the library until the community center could be built. It served no real purpose, however, other than sentimentality. Any number of people in the county almost certainly had a picture good enough to be blown up and used for the same purpose. Sometimes people just liked something a little different.

(Good for her, of course, or else she'd be out of a job.)

From 1986 until 1989 she'd found no less than fifteen articles featuring helpful photos of the school. All sides were represented. It would undoubtedly be the easiest job she'd ever had. Even an amateur could print off any of those pictures, study it, and paint a decent recreation by using it as a template.

Fortunately, Taryn's talents were a little extra special. When she was finished anyone looking at the painting would feel as though they could walk right on inside and make their way to their desk. She didn't just paint what she saw, she painted what she felt.

"'Muddy Creek Cardinals Win County Tournament'," Taryn read aloud. "Coach LeRoy Marcum led the Cardinals in a win against the Turkey Falcons 44-32 for the trophy. 'My boys had a good season,' he said after the game. 'They worked real hard and we're ready to come back even stronger next year.'"

The coach and his team stood outside the gym, their red uniforms clean and straightened by worried mothers. They smiled proudly at the camera as the tallest stood in the middle and held the trophy up over his head. It was nearly as big as he was. They couldn't have been more than ten, eleven years old.

Taryn's heard melted a little at the sight of the sweet, young faces that beamed out at her. She wondered if Jamey was amongst the group.

Another picture, six months later in 1988, showed two boys and two girls sitting at a table in front of a shelf full of books. In their hands were what looked like pieces of plywood with lightbulbs screwed into the middle. Taryn leaned in closer, trying to figure out what she was looking at. When she realized what they were, she laughed.

"Muddy Creek Academic Team prepares for regionals," she giggled. They were buzzers, antiquated ones of course. She'd been on the academic team in high school but their buzzers had looked like little black flashlights and fit in the palms of their hands.

She paused briefly on a picture of a young girl, perhaps eight or nine, that stood under the letters on the front of the school. She wore a pink frilly dress, complete with layers of ruffles, and had a headband adorned with lacy pink flowers. "My, my. They sure did dress for school here."

Her name was Jenny McPhee and she had apparently been traveling to Charleston that day to collect an award for the school. Muddy Creek had the highest test scores in the state that year. It was 1989. The young girl was beaming, her wide smile revealing a row of crooked teeth.

Over the next hour Taryn went through dozens more. She read stories about cheerleaders, basketball players, the enrichment group, a field day... She especially enjoyed the shots of the mock Olympics. A young, good-looking male teacher stood behind a finish line, fists pumped into the air and mouth open in a "whoop" as he cheered his students forward. All in all it looked like Muddy Creek had been a nice little school. Everyone appeared happy in the shots but then, of course, they would have knowing that they were going to be in the paper.

With her eyes starting to hurt and a headache forming, Taryn was about to call it a day when one last picture caught her eye. A rather plain-looking little girl gazed solemnly at the readers. Through the black and white it was hard to tell what shade her hair was, but it looked brown. She stood next to an older woman perched on a stool. They were in the gym and the rest of the students were gathered around, sitting cross-legged on the floor. Taryn couldn't see their faces. The little girl wore overalls and a flannel shirt. Her hair hung down in messy braids; her knee was ripped and stained. The woman beside her held a guitar, her head tilted back and eyes closed.

"Ten-year-old Lucy Dawson sings with Marilu Evans at Muddy Creek's annual talent show." Taryn read it aloud then moved her face closer to the screen, to where her nose was almost touching it. The young girl glowered back at her. Something about her eyes, the way they focused dead straight ahead of her, made Taryn shudder. It was as though she was looking at Taryn nearly thirty years into the future.

"Well, hello there Lucy," Taryn whispered, not caring if the other patrons could hear her. "It's nice to see you again."

FOURTEEN

*T*aryn *was feeling good about her day.* She'd organized her supplies, put in a good morning of research, and fought with a reporter. Not too shabby.

Now, sitting in her car, she looked over the stack of brochures she'd picked up at the West Virginia Welcome Center on her drive up. There had to be things to do in the area. She'd find them.

"Wild & Wonderful West Virginia," Taryn read aloud. "Let's see...hiking, kayaking, rollercoasters, Museum of Art, bowling..."

Suddenly, Taryn felt very tired.

"The Huntington Mall?" Remembering her overflowing closet back home, the one she kept promising herself she'd purge, she shook her head. "Can't do it."

Then, something else caught her eye. "Oh my God!" Taryn squealed, as excited as she'd ever been. "Van Lear!"

It wasn't nearby, or even in West Virginia at all, but according to her GPS it was less than an hour and a half away. That settled it. Fifteen minutes later she'd filled up her car with gas and her stomach with a Hershey and Mountain Dew and was on her way to Butcher Holler.

"I'm coming Loretty!" Taryn sang as she sped out of town, leaving Muddy Creek behind. "This is the best day of my life." To commemorate the occasion, she popped in a CD and cranked up "Van Lear Rose," the rocking duet between Jack Black and Loretta Lynn. As a southern girl and traditional country music lover, it would've been downright embarrassing to have been so close and not visit the Old Homestead.

Taryn always liked her life, but sometimes she downright loved it.

* * *

ALTHOUGH SHE'D BEEN DISAPPOINTED that Loretta Lynn's brother was ill and unable to give her a tour of the old log cabin, she was excited about the fact that, in the late afternoon hour, she was the only one wandering around.

"Huh, I thought it would be more isolated," Taryn mused as she walked around the little house, the soft grass moist under her boots. She laughed at her complaint, and at herself. Although the house was fairly close to the road, that road was barely more than one lane and from where she stood she saw nothing but towering mountains and a deep valley. There wasn't another building, car, or person in sight.

She'd seen "Coal Miner's Daughter" more than a dozen times. Now, as she and Miss Dixie explored the grounds of her idol's house, she found herself quoting random lines from the film.

"I didn't know it was dirty. I thought 'horny' meant cuttin' up and actin' silly." Taryn giggled aloud, her laughter echoing off the side of the mountain. "'And come off of that dumb hillbilly act.' 'If you knew Loretta you'd know that ain't no act.'"

Taryn laughed again. After bouncing over the boundary, she now stood on the front porch, holding her breath in reverence. The acoustics were terrific and for a moment she considered singing a few lines from "You Ain't Woman Enough to Take My Man" or "One's On the Way." When she opened her mouth to sing, however, it didn't feel right. It was too sacrilegious; this was hallowed ground, after all.

"Country music is my church," Taryn declared reverently, stroking a wood beam.

The feeling of just being there, of exploring the old homestead and seeing something for the first time in person that she'd only read about or seen on television was overwhelming. "It's like a hillbilly Mecca," she'd tried to explain to Matt once. "Loretta and Dolly are like our leaders."

"You're not a hillbilly, though," Matt had pointed out. "You were born in downtown Nashville. You grew up mostly in a subdivision."

Taryn had rolled her eyes at him. Sometimes the truth had no place in her fantasies. Besides, she might not have been born at the end of an old dirt road or spent her childhood cutting tobacco but the honesty of the music and integrity of the artists had always spoken to her. That had to count for something.

She was born not only in the wrong time period, but in the wrong part of the country.

Somewhere out there was a thirtysomething woman, sitting in an old farm house and staring out the window at the mountains, feeling like she was missing her place in the crowds of the city.

Taryn filled up the rest of her memory card with pictures of Butcher Holler and Van Lear, a picturesque mining community that was interesting in its own right. She stopped every so often and checked her LCD screen, hoping that Miss Dixie had caught something from Loretta's life. The shots were all normal, though.

"Damn. What's the use of being able to do this if I can't pick up on the cool stuff?"

On the way back out she stopped at the old country store, filled to the brim with concert shots and family pictures, and dutifully bought a T-shirt that she promptly slipped on.

"I needed that," Taryn smiled when she was back on the main road, heading back to Muddy Creek. She tried to sightsee when she could. It helped to get to know the place. And today had been worth it in other ways. She was now feeling more peaceful, more motivated.

"Dang," Taryn shook her head as the road widened and the sky blackened. "An hour and a half to get back and this is a good road."

She tried to imagine what it had been like even fifteen years earlier, back when the "new road" had felt like a pipedream. Heather had told her that before the new one came in, it had taken almost an hour to get to the nearest big grocery store– located in the county seat in the next county over. Now it took less than half that. Back in Nashville people were always righteously complaining about the coal mines and coal companies. So far in Muddy Creek she'd been surprised to hear the opposite–to hear some downright praising going on, which went against everything she'd been taught. There were lots of bad things that could be said about the coal mining industry, but some good things could be said about it as well. If not for the coal company, that road wouldn't exist.

Taryn thought about that as she drove along, traveling deeper and deeper into the mountains. She liked being out in the middle of nowhere, but she also liked to get out when she needed to.

*　*　*

"SO YOU ENJOYED YOUR DAY?"

Taryn juggled her phone from shoulder to shoulder as she tugged at her jeans and kicked off her boots. "Yep! I went to Van Lear, to Butcher Holler."

"I didn't know that was in West Virginia," Matt said.

"It's not. I drove over the state line to Kentucky," Taryn replied. "Oh, and I also spent the morning at the library. Saw a lot of pictures of the school from back in the 1980s. So that was cool. I didn't really find anything that stood out, though. The biggest tragedy seemed to be the high teacher turnover rate and the school's closing."

"So nothing to attribute any urban legends to?" Matt asked.

"Nah. Not that I could see. I don't know. Maybe I wasn't on the right track at all. You do anything?"

She could hear Matt shuffling papers on the other side of the phone. She figured he'd been busy. When Matt had a project, he committed. Matt enjoyed having projects. It made him feel useful.

"Nothing about the school, per se, but I did find out something interesting about the town," he began.

"Yeah? Devil worshipping center? The lost colony of Roanoke end up here?"

"Not that interesting, unfortunately," he laughed. "Actually, some of this is kind of morbid."

"Do tell!"

"Okay, so let's get the mundane out of the way...The county's primary industry is coal mining, which we already knew. Strip mining and mountaintop removal are the preferred forms of extraction today, and have been since the 1980s. Second biggest industry is education, followed by healthcare."

"Kind of funny, considering the county doesn't even have a hospital," Taryn smiled.

"It's rated the third poorest county in the state. Unemployment rate is a staggering 43%."

"Damn!" Taryn was impressed. It made sense, though. There wasn't much there. "So the unofficial top industry is the–"

"Welfare system," Matt supplied.

"Well, I was going to say government assistance programs. The U.S doesn't have welfare anymore, not the way we had it before. President Clinton eradicated it. Now, in order to receive assistance, you either have to apply for disability or go through the program that makes you have to work, go to school, or volunteer a certain number of hours a week."

"Huh, I didn't know that."

Taryn shrugged. "I watch a lot of TV. So what else?"

"Okay, here's the sad thing. Have you heard of, or has anyone mentioned, a kid by the name of Lukas Monroe?"

Taryn ran the name through her mind and ruminated on it for a moment before answering. "Nope. Not ringing a bell."

"Well, his story isn't exactly a heartwarming one. He was abused, basically tortured, by his family back in the early 1990s. Happened right there on Main Street where you're at."

Taryn looked around the motel room, half expecting this Lukas to pop out at her and say "boo". "Geeze. That's awful. What happened?"

"I have some links. I'll send them to you," Matt said, his voice somber. "It's not really something I want to talk about just yet. I read through a lot of stories about it and I am still trying to process."

"No, that's fine. Just send them to me. I can take the heavy stuff."

"Taryn, it's some pretty horrific stuff. You might want to pace yourself," Matt warned her. Taryn promised him she would.

Once she'd hung up she settled back on the bed and snuggled into her pillow. With the lamp and television on the room was almost cozy. She would wait until tomorrow to read Matt's message. She hadn't heard the kid's name, or knew anything about the story. She couldn't see how it might be connected to what she was doing, but she'd been surprised before.

The sounds of the reporters outside were almost soothing. She was getting used to them. "You can't change shit around here," one of them was saying now. "It's a piss-ant town with sloppy rednecks," another one agreed. They shared a spiteful laugh, like a Greek chorus in the background of her night.

Suddenly, the television flickered off. Before Taryn could reach for the remote, the lamp beside her flashed dead as well, going out with a "clink" and a small puff of smoke. The pale streetlamp from outside filtering in around her thick, smoke-filled curtains was the only light she was left with.

"Uh..." Taryn sat up and perched on her knees, looking around the murky room. The noises continued outside around her. If anyone else's power had gone out, they weren't complaining.

Just as she was about to get up and try the overhead light, she was struck by a repugnant scent and movement from the corner of her eye. When she turned, there, against the wall across from her, stood a man. In the dimness she could just barely make out the outline of his body—stocky and hunched over, and definitely male.

He stood there quietly, watching her. Taryn felt the blood drain from her face. For a second she had a horrible thought that someone had been in there with her the whole time, hiding behind the shower curtain or under the bed. And now they were there to do terrible things to her.

With mounting terror, she panicked, casting a glance at the door and quickly trying to calculate the amount of time it would take her to reach it without the figure overcoming her.

She'd risk it.

In one fell swoop, Taryn had pounced from the bed, the box springs protesting under her weight, and was to the door without her feet barely touching the floor. With trembling figures she swiped back the chain and yanked the door open, imagining the feel of his meaty hands on her neck as he dragged her back into the room.

But then she was outside. Nobody had touched her or prevented her from leaving.

She stood there now, outside her door, panting with wide eyes. A group of men and one lone woman stood just feet away and turned to look at her now, eyes amused.

"What's the matter? Devil after you?"

"T-there," Taryn panted, pointing inside. "There's a man in my room!"

The men weren't laughing now, but none offered to move. They all appeared frozen in place.

"Oh, for Christ's sake," the woman hissed. Handing her to purse to the man standing next to her, she marched past Taryn and pushed everyone else aside as she charged in, fists up and face excited with the threat of danger. With someone else taking the initiative, two other men in her part followed suit, feeling braver in a crowd. Taryn, feeling somewhat safer now that others were involved, stood outside, her bare feet now cold from the late-night air.

When they reemerged, however, all three looked confused.

"Maybe you were just having a bad dream?" one of them suggested. "Or something on the TV?"

"No," Taryn shook her head. "There was someone there. I saw him. And the TV wasn't even on."

"Well, it's on now," the man in the middle pointed out. "And there's nobody there, ma'am."

Intent on proving them wrong, with fear pushed aside Taryn stomped back into her room. The lamp was back on, the television was blaring an episode of "Sex and the City" and nothing was out of order. Too confused to be embarrassed, Taryn poked her head back outside.

"I don't know, then," she shrugged. "Maybe it was just a dream. I'm sorry."

The men walked away but the woman drew closer to Taryn.

"You okay, honey?" she asked. The woman's sweaty, wet hair was hanging limply in her face. Black eyeliner and mascara was smudged on her hollow cheeks. She looked like she'd been up for days. She'd had red lipstick on at one point, but she'd eaten most of it off and the rest was stuck to her front teeth.

In short, she looked the way Taryn felt. Still, her face looked concerned and she was the only one speaking to Taryn.

"I don't know," Taryn replied truthfully. "I know I saw someone there."

The other woman nodded. "I believe you. I've had a few experiences like that here myself. I can tell you this, I'll be glad when all this is over and I can get back home. There is something here, something I don't like."

"You and me both, sister," Taryn agreed.

The women laughed and Taryn returned to her room.

With her door closed and the chain back on, she stood in the middle of the floor and looked at the spot where the man had stood. He'd definitely been there, she'd seen him. But who was he? And what did he want?

"Maybe I was on the right track today," Taryn murmured as she did one last check around her space. "But which part do I need to revisit?"

Sighing, she turned back to her television. She wasn't in the mood for a comedy. Instead, she picked up the remote and began flipping through the channels. When she landed on the late news, she paused. Frieda Bowen was on, a repeat from her earlier show. She was in the process of yelling at her guest, both arguing over whether or not there was any scenario in which Lucy Dawson could have been justified in her actions.

Despite the heated shouting match going on before her, Taryn began laughing. Of course, on the screen Frieda's lipstick was on her mouth, and not on her teeth. And her eyeliner wasn't running.

Other than that, though, she'd looked exactly the same in person.

FIFTEEN

With *sleep impossible to achieve after what she'd see that night,* Taryn stayed up until daylight, poring over the links to the newspaper articles Matt had sent her.

It was no wonder he'd asked her to look at them herself and didn't want to talk about what he'd found. He was right; the story was pretty horrific.

From what she'd learned, Lukas Monroe had seen more by the time he was fourteen than most people would ever have to in a lifetime.

His father had not only been the owner of one of the pizza places (now closed), but had sat on the school board. (So Lucy's explosion definitely wasn't the first sordid affair the local system had been indirectly involved in.) At the age of fourteen he was visiting a friend and the friend's mother had apparently called the police–Lukas was covered in bruises. He was also missing five teeth, limping on an ankle that turned out to be broken, and had three dislocated ribs. Police were shocked to discover that he was severely malnourished, battling MRSA thanks to an infected wound on his back, and about twenty pounds underweight.

The entire *town* was shocked when they found out what had really been happening...

For the past three years Lukas' father, respected town citizen, had been chaining little Lukas to the family's toilet at night. In the beginning he would sometimes be left there for eight or nine hours at a time. In the past five months, however, he hadn't been let go at all. The school had not reported his truancy. He'd finally broken free, thanks to the help of a sibling, and escaped to the friend's house.

Lukas had been whipped with chains and belts, starved, burned with cigarettes, humiliated, and suffered severe emotional and physical trauma. Both of his parents were arrested and held on $500,000 bonds. Although she would sometimes sneak scraps of food to him when his father wasn't looking, his mother had done nothing to stop the abuse. During the trial, Lukas had even claimed that she would sometimes go in to use the toilet and, despite his pleading, not even acknowledge that he was there.

Taryn had read through the interviews growing more and more stunned with each passing one. Then she'd broken down in tears. The capacity of human cruelty was unfathomable to her.

"The fact that the little fellar was right here the whole time, right on Main Street, and nobody knew was a real injustice," one arresting officer had told the local paper.

In a twist of cruel irony, Lukas' house had been next door to the county jail.

After that, Taryn eventually stressed herself to sleep once daylight trickled in through the curtains. It had not been a restful slumber, though. The picture of his sweet face, with broken teeth and big, brown eyes, haunted her. She thought it always would.

Lukas had *not* attended Muddy Creek Elementary. He'd gone to the city school, and then to the middle school. As far as she could tell, his family didn't have any ties to her school at all. She didn't think his experience, as awful as it was, had anything to do with what she was working with.

But it was still terrible all the same. Most every place had a dark, underlying secret that it hides from the world. When you started peeling back the layers, you didn't always like what you found.

* * *

SHE WAS PREPARING TO WALK out her door when an unexpected knock came from the other side. The reporters had already filed out for the day; she knew it wasn't any of them. When Taryn opened the door Sandy stood on the other side, a hair dryer in hand.

"Here," she said proudly, thrusting the Conair towards Taryn. "Got one for you."

"Hey, thanks! So you found one around here?"

Taryn took it from her and welcomed the girl inside.

"Nah, didn't find one here. That one there's my mom's. She got her a new one for her birthday so she don't need it no more," Sandy shrugged.

Taryn appreciated this kind of hospitality–the kind one didn't exactly get from the Ritz Carlton.

Exhibiting no shyness, Sandy began walking around Taryn's room, peering at her stacks of canvases and tubes of oil paints. She even bent over and looked at her laptop, but the screensaver was on. She thought she caught a look of disappointment on Sandy's face.

"Oh, hey," Taryn said, suddenly remembering. "While you're here...You said your mother went to school with Lucy Dawson?"

"At Muddy Creek, yeah," Sandy nodded.

"She wouldn't have any pictures or anything from those days would she?"

Sandy shrugged. "Yeah, probably. I can ask. What for?"

"It helps me," Taryn explained. "I went to the library yesterday and found a few but I'd love to see more of the kids. To, you know, get a feel for what kind of school it was."

"Yeah, yeah, I'll ask her. She likes talking about the 'good old days,'" Sandy laughed. "She'd probably get a kick out of having a new person to tell her stories to."

"Tell her I'd be happy to meet with her at any time."

"Sure. She don't work no more, not since she got the fibro. So she's home all the time. Except on Monday nights and Thursday nights," Sandy said. "She goes to Bingo at the church then."

Taryn considered asking her about Lukas Monroe, ask what happened to him and if he was still around, but the story was still too fresh for her. Like Matt, she wanted to process more. Or perhaps she needed to put poor Lukas and his trials to rest. She wasn't one of the bloodthirsty reporters, after all. Just that morning she'd gone online and seen a scathing interview with a guy Lucy Dawson had dated for three weeks in college. They were getting desperate for information. Maybe she didn't need to be digging any of that up where Lukas was concerned. He'd probably moved on a long time ago. It was none of her business.

* * *

THE LOCAL HIGH SCHOOL was only one story, but it was sprawling. The visitor's parking lot was at the very back. It took Taryn a good ten minutes to walk the length of it and then around the building to get to the front door. She was surprised that there wasn't anyone waiting at the front, any security of any sort. She was able to stroll right on in and look for the principal's office on her own.

"I don't often get visitors of the good kind," Jamey laughed as he led her past his secretary's desk to his private office.

"I don't often visit the principal's office," Taryn laughed. "Or I didn't."

"So to what do I owe the pleasure?" When he settled back into his chair Taryn thought he posed a striking figure–a well-dressed, well-groomed man with a movie star face and kind eyes. She wondered how many teenage girls found reasons to get sent to his office.

"Well, sorry to just bust in on you like this, but I was on my way out to the school and this was on my way," Taryn apologized.

"No, no, that's fine. In fact, Heather will be here in just a minute. She was just asking about you, too."

Taryn took a seat across from him. "I was actually wondering if you had any pictures of the school from when you attended it," she began. "I am starting to sketch today and really wanted to kind of get a feel for the student life." After talking to Sandy that morning, the idea of asking Jamey had seemed like an even better one.

Jamey folded his hands under his chin and closed his eyes. When he opened them, they were as clear as a bell. "You know, I don't think I do. I mean, I *did* have some but they're all gone."

"Oh," Taryn said. "What happened?"

Yeah, like it's any of my business, she thought to herself. *God, I am so nosey.*

"There was a fire at my mother's trailer about ten years ago," he explained. "You ever see one of those go up in flames? There's no real way of saving it. You're lucky to just get yourself out alive. They were all destroyed."

"Oh, geeze," Taryn cringed. So much for her not bringing up anything traumatic today. "I didn't know. I'm sorry. I wouldn't have asked."

Just then his door opened and Heather breezed through it and made for her husband, the scent of apples and vanilla trailing in her wake.

"Hello baby," she cooed, leaning down to kiss him on the forehead. He preened upwards for it and gave her a genuine smile, one that caused a twinge of jealousy in Taryn. She missed that—the ability to touch her loved one whenever she wanted. Her fiancé, Andrew, had died in a fiery car crash several years before. She'd never really had that daily closeness since. Just being able to reach out and physically feel the person beside you whenever you so desired was what she missed the most.

The old adage "they still live on in your heart" was a crock. What good was his memory when they'd never make new ones, when she could never touch him again?

"Hello Heather," Taryn smiled, plastering on a polite smile. "Sorry to butt in on your visit."

"Oh sweetie, that's okay," Heather laughed. "I always stop in right before lunch. You're not intruding at all!"

The fact that Heather was beautiful and nice was just a little much for Taryn. She had a hard time trusting that particular combination.

"Taryn was just asking if I had any pictures from my old school days," Jamey told her.

"Oh, well, we've got your old basketball pictures at the house. And your graduation..."

"She means older, dear," Jamey teased her, pulling at her long, blond hair. "From Muddy Creek."

Heather frowned and scratched at her cheek. "Oh, yeah, well that's going to be a problem."

"He told me about the fire at his mother's," Taryn explained. "I'm so sorry. I didn't know about it or I wouldn't have asked."

Heather pooh-pooed the idea off with a wave of long, elegant fingers. "No worries. The good thing was that she wasn't home at the time. We knew that place was a deathtrap, a fire hazard. Those wires had bothered Jamey for years. But, she wouldn't leave. She'd lived there all of Jamey's life. His father died when he was eight and Carmie always said that she still felt him there. She wouldn't leave him." Heather rolled her eyes as she said this, as though the whole thing was ridiculous, but Jamey looked down at his desk and frowned.

Taryn felt her face growing warm. She hadn't meant to open up a big old can of worms. She just spreading cheer and bringing up all kinds of stuff today. Good going.

"Well, now that I've dredged up the past, I think I'll head on out to the school," Taryn said as she rose to her feet. "And I'll let you all enjoy your time together."

"Sorry we couldn't help," Heather apologized. "But if there's anything else you need, anything then please let me know."

SIXTEEN

*T*he sketching was going well. Her hands were black from the charcoal, but Taryn was in her element, sitting outside on a blanket in the fresh air. Her iPod was tuned to her favorite sketching mix (not to be confused with her painting mix, photography mix, or editing mix) and from time to time she bopped her head along with Shooter Jennings' "Fourth of July." The upbeat melody with the crisp chill, gray sky, and scent of dead leaves gave her an extra shot of energy.

If only the stench of the stagnant water didn't keep trickling in. At times it was nauseating, causing her to wrinkle her nose in disgust. She hadn't found the source of the water yet, since the creek behind the school seemed to be flowing fine, but she could certainly smell it.

When she heard the roar of Lucy's truck, she looked up and watched the Jeep as it attacked the gravel road with purpose. The small woman at the wheel's face was hardened, her mouth set in a grim line. When she saw Taryn she slowed down to a roll and Taryn thought she might stop altogether but then she offered a slight wave of her hand and Lucy laid on the gas again, sending the gravel flying.

"Bad day in court I guess," Taryn murmured to herself. Of course, she guessed that if you were on trial for murder then every day was a bad day in court. In fact, it was likely that most good days involved not being in court at all.

Sandy's mother had claimed Lucy was "weird" in school, at least according to Sandy. Taryn found herself wondering what constituted as "weird" in Muddy Creek. Was it her music choices? The movies she'd watched? Did she eat her own hair? Talk to her imaginary dragon during class? (To be fair, that last one was all Taryn. Only it had been an imaginary Chinese girl. Taryn herself had also been a little weird.)

She wanted to know more about Lucy, wanted to know more about the school.

She wanted to know why Lucy had killed those people.

"I can't believe she's a cold-blooded murderer that wanted to kill *anyone*," Taryn muttered. "I just refuse to believe it."

The crashing sound came from within again, a reply to Taryn's spoken thoughts. It wasn't the first time she'd heard it, of course, and the last incident had left her with a picture from the past. Now, with curiosity piqued, Taryn stood and gazed at the school, wondering what she should do next.

"Well, I'm here..."

It might have sounded crazy, that she would be frightened so badly frightened the night before over a ghost and yet was now contemplating going in search of one...but this was different. For one thing, it was daylight. For another, it the difference between being the hunter and the hunted that mattered. Getting caught off guard was usually the scary part. Taryn liked to be in control; she liked to know what was going on. If she knew what she was getting herself into, she could handle it a lot better.

* * *

IT DIDN'T TAKE LONG for her to find an entrance. After all, the building had no working doors at this point. The county had made a feeble attempt to keep trespassers out by leaning a board over the front, but considering the fact that there were three more in the back and a gaping hole at the top that didn't have any coverings at all, it was almost laughable.

She was glad she'd worn long sleeves and pants. As a teenager she and Matt had explored many an old, abandoned building around Nashville. She'd even belonged to an urban exploring group for awhile—a group of young people that got together on Saturday nights to drive around town, armed with camera, hoping to find a vacant place to check out and photo document before the authorities ran them off.

Taryn was an old pro at finding her way in and around places she had no business being inside.

She choose to enter through the back. After carefully checking them to ensure she wasn't in a batch of poison ivy, Taryn gingerly pushed the Virginia Creeper aside and let herself in. As she moved, broken glass crackled under her heavy boots—another smart decision, fashion-wise.

The small room she stepped into was dimly lit and smelled of stale sweat and rotten food. An old metal table was pushed against the wall; ancient cigarette butts and piles of ashes littered the top. Several dusty Styrofoam cups held the dredges of liquid that had dried up long ago. Taryn was in a teacher's lounge of sorts.

Before her was an open door. The poorly lit hallway beyond beckoned. Taking a deep breath, she ran her hand over Miss Dixie for luck and forged ahead.

SEVENTEE

Now *that she was inside*, the scent of stagnant water was even stronger. Tiny gnats, fierce and intrusive, swarmed her head and stuck to the nervous sweat on her face. Luckily, it was deep enough into the season that whatever copperheads she was sure lived inside were probably long gone. Gnats she could deal with. Taryn didn't do snakes.

Cobwebs draped from the ceiling, covering the puffs of spongey insulation that exploded from the holes in the cardboard tiles above her. The ceiling literally hung down in some places and brushed the top of her head. She proceeded cautiously, taking careful steps and hoping the rest of the building didn't collapse down upon her. If it did, she might not be found for days.

Taryn was surprised by the darkness; considering the massive amount of roof damage from the explosion, she'd been expecting it to be lighter inside. It was then that she realized she was at the opposite end of the building from where the roof had caved. In this part, the building was still mostly intact. With the windows boarded up and the electricity out, there wasn't anything to provide a light source. Taryn stopped and pulled out her cellphone. The small flashlight didn't do much, but it gave her morale a boost.

The starkness of the interior and sheer absence of light were unnerving. Every few steps Taryn stopped and collected her bearings, trying to adjust her eyes. The floor was strewn with soda cans, cigarette butts and what looked like joints, fractured beer bottles, and other undeterminable scraps of trash. The smell was rank and she gagged, the acid rising quickly into her throat and burning her mouth.

"Shake it off, girlfriend," she muttered shakily. "Shake it off."

When she found herself standing in front of two bathrooms she stopped and considered them, then shook her head. That was too much even for her. She was brave, but she wasn't stupid. The idea of going into the dismal, airless room and getting trapped was a nightmare waiting to happen.

Taryn was no dummy.

If Bloody Mary lived in one of them, she'd just have to stay there.

A few lonely chairs, small with orange plastic backs, were turned on their sides and distributed up and down the length of the hallway. Taryn remembered sitting in similar ones when she was younger. Part of her wanted to walk over to one, upright it, and try it out. The thought of what had once slept on it, thrown up on it, or used it for less-than-honorable intentions had her hesitating. She settled on taking pictures.

"Okay, now what do we have?" she asked as she took stock of her surroundings. Her voice echoed in the stillness; the reverb took her aback. With the split second delay it had almost sounded like someone else was in the building with her, mocking her.

Dang, she was getting skittish. Maybe it was all the medication she was on.

Taryn saw four doors to her left and twice as many to her right. She turned right and began walking. She wanted to see everything, if she could.

"Need a game plan," she declared, her boots thumping on the old, filthy tiles. She tried to see past the broken-down mess, tried envisioning children lining up outside classroom doors, preparing for recess. Tried to see teachers scurrying straight ahead, a stack of papers they'd just xeroxed in hand.

It wasn't easy. Her imagination was good, but this was almost asking too much. Abandoned factories and train terminals were one thing; an abandoned building that had once catered to children had a certain despondency to it that she felt deep in her bones.

"I'm getting soft," she muttered.

As Taryn walked she sang to herself, Alabama's "Song of the South." She thought something uplifting might be helpful. The sound of her own voice might not have been great company, but it was better than nothing. When she was scared, singing made her feel better.

The room at the very end was the library. Taryn presented the school with her first genuine smile since entering the building when she saw it for what it was. After seeing pictures of the library online, she almost felt as though she was entering an iconic site. Taryn loved visiting places she'd only seen in pictures or movies. For her, it made no difference whether it was the Eiffel Tower or an old mill in Central Kentucky. Being able to look at something in 3D that she had only previously been aware of as a static image tickled her.

That was part of who Taryn was—someone that genuinely delighted in seeing things come alive.

Well, except for the ghosts. She didn't always delight in seeing the dead come to life.

So far, however, if there were any ghosts in the building they were keeping to themselves. Somewhere behind her came the faint drip of water, but she tucked the sound away and ignored it. It had nothing to do with her or why she was there. Things had been still since she'd found her way inside.

Almost *too* still.

The library had seen better days, of course. With the windows boarded up and the roof still intact she had to scan her flashlight around the room to be able to see much at all.

"Huh. I'll be damned," Taryn mumbled. The shelves were still lined with books, their spines mildewing and molding from the dampness and neglect. "They couldn't have done anything with them?"

Surely a thrift store, another school, or a nearby community center could have used them? Or hell, they could've just opened the building and told people to come in and take whatever they wanted or needed. That was one thing Taryn didn't understand about abandoned places—why just let everything rot? Things that could be used by people who would appreciate them...why didn't they let them *have* them? Was it really that much better to just let it all sit there and go to waste?

Making her way across the chaotic floor, Taryn began perusing the shelf closest to her. The sign above her simply read "Mysteries." Right away, she was delighted to discover a row of Nancy Drew novels, all the original hardcover editions. Taryn picked up a copy of the *Mystery at Lilac Inn*, her favorite, and flipped through the pages. Although the cover was soft with dampness and stained with yellow mildew, the pages were still in good shape. She'd loved that series as a child. In fact, when she was in third grade her teacher had taken them to the library and allowed them to pick out any book they wanted and that was the one she'd chosen. She'd been so *proud* of it, the first book she had ever picked out. They'd learned about the Dewy Decimal System that day and how to use the card catalogue. When they first entered the room she'd gone straight to the old wooden box in the center of the floor, opened one of the skinny drawers, and searched through the little notecards until she'd found the word "ghost." The book had been the result of that search.

Taryn looked around her now, half expecting someone to be watching her, but she was alone. And although she felt guilty and hated herself just a little for it, she slipped the book into her backpack. Nobody would miss just one.

Heck, nobody would miss *any* of them.

She decided to think of it more as a search and rescue than a theft.

Standing in the middle of the room, Taryn turned in a little circle and took pictures as she slowly moved 360 degrees. After each shot she checked the playback. Nothing.

"Okay, let's move on. And no more stalling or stealing," she promised herself.

Yeah, like she'd be able to keep to *that*. Stalling was her thing. (And apparently stealing was now, too.)

Next door, Taryn found a supply closet and didn't even waste her time with that. There was nothing to see beyond a bunch of old brooms and mops and, besides, who knew what lived back in the dark recesses? Forget that. She was adventurous. She wasn't stupid. Usually.

The next door was locked. From her frequent walks around the exterior she knew it was a classroom. "Well, I hope what I need isn't in there," she said, shaking her head. She hadn't come prepared to pick a lock.

The next three doors revealed additional classrooms of varying sizes. They all maintained their chalkboards, tables, and a few of their desks. In the last classroom, Taryn walked up to the chalkboard and marveled at what would now be considered old-fashioned or passé. Kids today would never know the joy of being chosen to take the erasers outside and pound them on the concrete to clean them. They'd never squeal as the chalk dust floated up around them, colorful little clouds that made them cough and sneeze. They'd never know what it was like to grip a tiny piece of white chalk, getting the last few bits out of a piece that the economical teacher was determined to use until the bitter end.

Aw, hell. Now she was depressed.

Up ahead she could see blessed daylight emptying through the roof but first she made a stop at the main office. It was the second principal's office she'd been in that week.

There were two rooms, one presumably for a secretary, and both had been ransacked. The dented and dusty filing cabinets were on their sides, drawers open and papers spread all over the floor. Taryn wondered if the vandalism had been for fun or from someone looking for something valuable. She bent down and picked up a folder on top of the pile and was surprised to see that she was holding a student's file. Did those not get transferred when the new school opened?

It was all so peculiar, though; as though once Muddy Creek closed everyone just got up, walked away, and washed their hands of the place. They'd closed the doors without ever looking back. The new school was a new start, not just physically but mentally as well. Apparently, even the pieces of chalk and attendance records had been left behind.

After taking a few pictures, Taryn turned and set out for the hallway again. A flash of color on the wall caught her eye, however, and she paused.

She hadn't seen it when she'd first walked through the door; she'd been too intent on the mess in the floor. Now she didn't know how she'd missed it. In crimson spray paint above the principal's desk "LOOK AWAY" was scrawled in big, loopy cursive letters. The paint had run before drying; now the words appeared to be melting towards the floor, the red droplets sliding down the wall like blood.

Taryn took a step backwards and winced at the sight. Her immediate reaction was to do exactly what the wall ordered her to do—she looked away. But then she looked back.

"Interesting choice of words," she whispered with a nervous laugh as she snapped a picture. She pondered on the meaning, and if it had one at all, as she flipped Miss Dixie over.

The office was in perfect condition, not a thing was out of place. Piles of papers were stacked neatly on the desk; the frothy yellow curtains that blew out from the open window were cheerful; framed pictures of lighthouses and country gardens hung from the walls; and the beige, touch-tone, corded desk phone waited for action.

"Huh. Guess it *does* mean something," Taryn laughed weakly.

Knowing she might be on the right track for something, she turned around and took a closer look at the office. Short of going through all the discarded files on the floor and shuffling through the mess, she didn't know where to start. She started to squat down and begin picking things up from the ground, but then hesitated, a manila file folder in hand.

"No, wait, this is *wrong!*"

Paying no mind to the mess, she plopped down on the floor and turned her camera back on. Once again, she took a good look at the photo she'd just taken. Something about it had flipped a switch in her mind, but she couldn't figure out what. Surely the standard, mass-produced artwork couldn't mean anything...

Then her focus turned back to the neatly organized desk. The phone.

"Ah! That's it," she smiled, nodding her head. She'd recognized that phone. Her aunt Sarah had one just like it. She'd kept it all the way through the mid-1990s, when she'd finally been talked into getting a cordless and chucking the rotary. Though the one she was presently looking at was a touch tone, it was virtually the same model.

Taryn was looking at a scene from the 1980s, she'd bet money on it. Even if the school had suffered from lack of budget, and she was sure it had, they would've updated eventually.

There was no need to go through any of the paperwork in that room. The school had only been closed for the past twenty years. The picture was pointing out a scene from the 1980s. Whatever was left was sure to have been from the last few years it was open. Still, she opened the file in her hand and checked, just to make sure.

Sure enough, it was a memo dated 1995.

"Okay, I won't waste time with that, then."

Before she closed the folder, however, she noted the name stamped on the bottom: Principal Julia Mockbee.

Taryn shuddered and closed her eyes. Julia Mockbee had been one of the victims of the explosion. She'd died, along with the others.

"I'm going to need to know how long she was there," Taryn said aloud as she rose to her feet. "When she started her job, if she was here back in the 80's. I'll ask Matt."

Daylight wouldn't last much longer and she'd only been through half of the school. She was going to need to pick up the pace.

As Taryn left the room, the writing on the wall caught her eye again. *Look away.*

She was certain she felt a cold wind spread through her, a sickly and vile gust that turned her stomach. Taryn's enthusiasm for her exploration was beginning to wane.

There was a small room directly across the hall from the office. The door was off its hinges. As Taryn stepped towards it, a clatter rang from inside, a shifting similar to the sounds she'd heard on the outside.

Taryn stood in the hall and studied the closet, wondering if it was worth exploring since it was really more of a storage room than a cupboard, when the clatter came again. As she watched in sheer fascination, a yellow, squishy ball leisurely rolled from the room and made its way directly to her. Taryn gasped and jumped backwards and to the side, out of the way of the oncoming intruder, but it rolled to an abrupt about a foot from where she had stood and waited. Telling her it was her turn.

The two of them were alone in the quiet again. The clatter had stopped; now it was just her and the ball. Taryn viewed it with a combination of fear and fascinated curiosity. The ball was soft, like a rubber toy you might throw to a dog. A deep hole had been drilled into the top and pale yellow foam peeked out. She figured it to be about the size of a soccer ball, but she'd never seen one like this before.

"Oh, what's it going to do to me?" she laughed nervously as she moved forward, still ready to bolt if she must.

From what she assumed was years of grubby little hands and dirty gym floors, the ball was stained with dirt and grime. When she finally got up the nerve to touch it, she bent over and picked it up with care. Biting her lip, Taryn turned and surveyed the area around her. Nothing else had moved, nothing was out of the ordinary. Perhaps it had been a mouse or possum inside, shifting things around.

The ball was extremely lightweight. It barely felt as though she was holding anything at all. It was spongey in her hands, squishy enough that she could squeeze it flat with little effort. "What kind of game were *you* for?"

At that point, she wouldn't have been surprised to receive an answer.

Still holding the unexpected gift, Taryn commenced her walk towards the small room again. From where she stood she could see deflated basketballs, old metal baseball bats, an orange roadworks' cone, and a ratty net. It was a PE room, or sports' storage. She imagined it had been picked clean over the years; there wasn't much left. The yellow ball she was holding appeared to be the only one of its kind.

"Then where did that noise come from?" Taryn suddenly realized there wasn't a single thing in that room that should have caused the racket she'd just heard. "Huh."

Now she turned back to her ball and studied it again. There was something about the texture, the feel to it that was distracting. She didn't like it. Feeling dirty holding it, Taryn suddenly didn't want to be in her hands any longer.

Like a hot potato, she let it go and watched it drop to the ground and bounce away from her. And then, as though driven to a magnet, it dove back towards the little room. Right before it turned the corner and went back inside she caught the fingerprint stains she'd missed while holding it. An entire handprint revealed itself just before it rolled into the shadows and disappeared into obscurity.

"Oh shit," Taryn mumbled. She allowed Miss Dixie to do her thing, but this was one shot she didn't care to look at right away. She'd wait until she was back outside. Maybe in her motel room. Far away.

The good thing was that Taryn had made her way to the other end of the school, the end with the fire and collapsed ceiling. It was a lot lighter down there and Taryn wasn't sorry to leave the darkness behind.

"Let's just get this over with," she sighed, stepping into the first classroom. It was the one where she'd seen the figure, heard the noises. She'd known all along that if there was anything going on inside the school, it might be in this room.

"Room Five," she read aloud the number hanging over the doorway.

She'd seen the damage from the outside, but it was a lot different being on the other side of the window. The large, gaping hole that allowed the sky to poke through above her looked like a portal into another room. The charred walls, black ashes leaving the floor covered in a black snow, and the leftover furniture tossed around haphazardly, were a contrast to the almost whiteness of the sky above. She'd seen little sunshine since arriving.

Taryn started to lift Miss Dixie then abruptly came to a halt. "Oh!" she cried with a stark realization.

This was the room of impact, the place where the explosion had gone off. And she was standing in the very location where the pipe bomb had been placed and sent fiery waves throughout the building.

The nefarious circle around her feet was eerily perfect. Long, black streaks led out from it, fanning towards the desks and tables like sunrays. By the door a stain remained, a blemish so red it was almost black. Taryn had walked right over it without noticing it and now she gasped. Someone's blood...There were no remnants of the homemade bomb, they'd been taken away as evidence, but nobody had done anything to clean up the mess it had left behind. Why would they?

Taryn closed her eyes and bit her lips. People had died in that room. It wasn't the first time she'd been in a room with a known death. She'd spent many hours in the hotel room where a famous musician had died years ago. She knew many of the places she'd worked at had their own sordid stories.

But this was different. For one thing, it was *recent*.

Now, as she looked at the desks and chairs turned on their sides, some of them missing pieces, she appreciated what she was *really* looking at. This wasn't evidence of neglect and abandonment, not like the rest of the school. This disarray had happened during the explosion.

One of the teachers had been blown right out of the classroom. Their body was found down the hall, which meant it had soared from the room and actually turned the corner. Another was discovered on the roof.

She'd been doing more research on the incident, despite the fact that she had hoped to come in with impartial eyes.

"So, this is it...," Taryn said weakly. "This is where it all went down. Where the magic happened."

Unable to take the creep factor of standing in the explosion's home, she stepped from the circle and strode to the row of windows on the other side of the room. Now, looking out, she was able to see the embankment where Lucy had been found standing. Lucy hadn't just placed the explosion, after all, she'd stood back and watched the action as she detonated it.

"Damn. People are *crazy.*"

Most of the walls were discolored. What was left of them anyway. Big chunks were missing in places–another reason the room was lighter than the others.

As Taryn carefully took in the scene before her, however, her eyes focused in on the far wall, the one that would have been at the back of the classroom. Above the coat rack and shelves that would have served as storage, she saw the same blue spray paint she'd seen in the principal's office.

"Haunting Me," she read, intently focusing and trying to make out the letters that were warped and smeared from the flames and firemen's water. "Haunting Me? *Apparently.*"

There was another one on the wall opposite of her too, though. It was much clearer. "Friend," she read. "Friend? What does any of this mean?"

Look away from the friend? Don't look at what's about to happen? Was a friend haunting someone? Was it a warning to those who had died, an attempt to provide a puzzle that could've saved their lives, if it had been solved in time? Had Lucy been playing games with them?

From the condition of the paint, it was clear that they'd been created *before* the blast, not after. She couldn't exactly see Lucy hanging around at the school after she'd been arrested. But, then again, she did just live up the road from it and could have easily sneaked back in any time she wanted. Taryn had been there for almost two weeks and rarely saw any vehicles of any kind drive by. Even the reporters had better things to do and those guys would jump at just about any story lead.

She had work to do, however, and her heart and mind had had just about had enough. For the next twenty minutes Taryn wandered around the room, taking extra care not to disturb anything. The police tape that had once existed was wadded up in the floor. Police weren't doing much, if anything, to keep it secured. Still, she didn't want to be responsible for contaminating the crime scene.

Again, Taryn resisted the lure to look at her camera's screen. Quite frankly, she was scared. If she saw something that distressed her, she was likely to make a run for it and fly right out that window behind her. She'd done a lot of crazy things in her life, but this set the bar at a new high.

When she was finished she stood back in the middle of the room, did a little bow, and offered a "thanks" to the remaining energy. Despite the opening and fresh air, the room was still stuffy and a little claustrophobic. She was happy to depart, but wanted to leave behind good vibes in case she had to return.

There were only a few more rooms left, including the gym. Taryn could see it from where she stood. She could have been in and out in another half hour, tops.

"Might as well do it while I'm here," she sighed. "Get it all done at once."

As Taryn began walking back down the hallway, though, she was abruptly struck by the feeling that someone was watching her. She paused, turned, and looked behind her, half expecting to see another interloper like herself striding through the wreckage.

Nobody was there. The hallway had grown so dark, however, that she was unable to see the library end now. The blackness was opaque, thickening near the principal's office then, in a hombre, slowly building upon itself as it traveled down the tile, until it became thicker and denser. It was almost solid, an idea that Taryn found uneasy.

"It's just the sun," she said aloud, her voice echoing around her. "The sun just dipped behind the mountains."

The cry came then, the wretched howl that shook her to the core. It came from the gym. The sound, simultaneously seductive and menacing, flicked its invisible tongue and licked at her, tempting her to turn and march onwards.

But Taryn wasn't playing. She'd had enough.

Although it meant running towards the darkness, Taryn held onto Miss Dixie to steady her and began to take off at a frenzied pace, her backpack slapping her with each step. As she ran, felt something from the gym watching her, following her, and quickening its pace.

The fear eating at her was all-consuming. The quicker Taryn moved, the thicker the sticky quicksand she was traveling through grew. She might have been in a dream, distances distorted and geography skewed. The short expanse of hallway that logically should have existed between where she'd been and where she was headed stretched on for miles. She could feel the ice-cold fingers reaching out for her, grabbing her hand and stroking the nape of her neck. She could feel and smell its bitter, fetid breath.

"Oh God," Taryn croaked, hot tears streaming down her face. "Don't fall, don't fall!"

When she reached the principal's office, rather than continue on to the storage room in which she'd entered, she made a sharp turn and aimed for the front entrance. The board was inches away from her now and with one mighty kick Taryn had it pushed aside and was rocketing out the door, safely received by the welcoming daylight.

Taryn didn't stop until she reached the embankment, the same one Lucy had stood on and waited, watching.

Whatever had been behind her was gone, of course. If it had ever been there at all.

She'd done enough.

EIGHTEEN

Still shaking two hours later, Taryn had yet to return to her motel room. First, she'd driven around town, going down side streets and traveling out into the hollers that branched out from the main street like long, skinny arms. The driving, and especially the music she played while doing it, helped clear her mind.

There was a strange juxtaposition of dwellings in Venters County. If she'd felt like stopping or even slowing down in the middle of the road, she could have taken some great shots. She was looking at a mixture of old and new, of wealthy and poor.

Down one holler (the street sign read Cresty Hollow), she'd been surprised to see new constructions stacked side-by-side at the beginning of the road. The small, brick houses were mostly ranch-style. Each one had about half an acre with it. Small vegetable gardens grew in the backs and on the sides, wicker furniture graced the front porches, and gravel driveways housed trucks, campers, and the occasional motorcycle. The same kind of place could be found just about anywhere in the country.

Further down the road, however, things changed.

A mile into Cresty, Taryn found herself facing much older homes. The material changed from brick to wood, even to veneer in some of them. Gray, cheerless houses sat back from the road, hiding behind clumps of trees. Chicken coops and garden sheds housed geese, roosters, and goats. Dilapidated roofs slanted over sagging porches filled with big, plastic children's toys that had faded from the sun. Windows were covered with garbage bags or aluminum foil. Chimneys expectorated black, sooty smoke.

Taryn didn't want to gawk or be disrespectful, but the change was fascinating.

On another road, this one without a name, she dipped over the side of a hill and found herself in what felt like a hole, surrounded on all sides by sloping banks. A young boy in jeans and boots, but no shirt, stood above her and watched as on her radio Patty Loveless wondered if her lover still missed her when she was gone. The house behind him was small enough to have fit in her motel room. The porch was covered with lawn mowers and engines. The oil had spilled from many of them, leaving shiny puddles dotting the gray, concrete floor. The sad-looking yard was bare of grass, save a few straggling weeds that came to the boy's waist. Scattered around were children's toys: a mechanical car big enough for two children to ride in, a plastic shopping cart holding a headless doll, bicycles, basketballs, neon green plastic machine guns, a child's kitchen set with stove...They were dirty, dented, and damaged in a number of ways.

In the side yard she saw an above-ground swimming pool, partially caved in. With the slight breeze, leaves were blowing off a nearby tree and gently landing in what she imagined to be murky, fetid water. A brand new Ford Explorer gleamed in the driveway.

Around the corner she saw something else that nearly made her do a double take. A large, brick, three-story house rose from a hilltop. Its expansive yard was well-manicured and unnaturally green. Wrought iron outdoor furniture flanked both sides of the front door. A gazebo to the side held an outdoor kitchen that cost more than her vehicle.

There was no one real "style" to the architecture of Venters County. As Taryn explored more and more she learned that there were an equal number of ranch houses, bungalows, Craftsman, trailers, modular homes, farm houses, and McMansions. They came in all shapes, sizes, and colors.

There was great wealth and great squalor around Muddy Creek. Piles of garbage towered by $50,000 vehicles. Tiny, windowless houses that didn't look bigger than chicken coops boasted high-quality RVs in the driveways. Corroded, single-wide trailers had exotic in-ground swimming pools. Miniature mansions with rusted out pick-up trucks on their last legs. They were all mixed together in some sort of abnormal pattern. She'd never seen anything like it.

For awhile the exploration took Taryn's mind off what had happened at the school. But then it grew too dark to see and she was tired. Supper took care of another hour. She ate in a small restaurant that served fried chicken and mashed potatoes out of little cast iron skillets. The noise of the jukebox and pool players in the game room adjacent to the dining area was comforting; she could be alone without being by herself.

Eventually, though, Taryn had to retire.

"I will be there in two days," Matt promised. She kept him on speaker phone as she drove back to her room. "Is there anything you want me to bring?"

"Just you," Taryn answered. "It will be good to see you. All this is getting to me."

"The job?"

"The job, the trial, the reporters, the school...I guess I'm just not as adventurous as I used to be," she laughed weakly.

"You're plenty adventurous to me," he assured her. "Do you want to go ahead and send me some of the pictures you took today now or wait and let me look at them when I get there?"

"I haven't even looked at them myself, yet," Taryn admitted. "But if it's okay, I'd like to go ahead and send them to you. Then we can talk about them when you get here."

"Sure, just upload them to Dropbox and I'll take a look. Give me something to do on the flight up there."

Taryn still had him on the phone when she parked the car and began walking towards her room.

"Well, shit," she whimpered, stopping in her tracks a few feet from her door.

"What's wrong? Everything okay?"

"No," Taryn seethed. "Looks like the maid didn't shut my door to when she left."

"You have maid service there?" Which was beside the point yet surprisingly relevant.

"Sort of. They bring towels. Great. There better not be anything missing," Taryn said as she resumed her pace and hurried towards her door.

Sure enough, it was standing wide open. Nobody else was milling around. She figured they were all out to dinner. The lightbulb outside her door was stark yellow, casting an orange glow on the door. She hadn't left a light on inside, since she hadn't intended on returning so late.

"Keep me on here," Matt said, "just in case."

Knowing him, he'd probably already picked up his other phone and was prepared to dial 911 if he heard anything he didn't like on her end.

Taryn flicked on the light inside the door with a flourish. Then she gasped.

Her room had been vandalized. It looked like a tornado had gone through it and taken no prisoners. Paints were squeezed out and left in globs on the carpet. Linseed oil made an oily trail around her bed. Three of her canvases were in the middle of the floor, holes punched through their centers. Extra charcoal pencils were broken in half and left in a pile on the little table. Articles of clothing had been snatched from the tiny closet and were dispersed around the room; some had been dipped into the oil and paint, others were torn or hacked with scissors or knives. She was suddenly very glad she'd been wearing her favorite boots. At least *they* weren't damaged.

Furious, Taryn stomped into the bathroom and flipped that light on, too.

"Oh, man, not my makeup," she groaned as she scanned the small space. Her Kat von D foundation had all been poured out. The thick, creamy liquid oozed down the sink even now as she watched in anger. Lipsticks were pushed all the way to the tops of their tubes and then smashed by their lids.

"What happened? Everything okay?"

"Someone came in here and destroyed all my stuff," Taryn cried. "My *makeup*! They destroyed all my makeup! Can you believe that?"

"Make sure they're not still there. Hurry, look around!" She could hear Matt's concern but brushed it aside.

"They're not here, dude. I just stood in the middle of the room and saw everything. There's nowhere to hide. *Damn* it."

Fire in her eyes, Taryn turned and marched towards the main office. Someone was going to pay for what they'd done. That was the nicest makeup she'd ever had. It had been a birthday present. And nobody messed with her clothes. *Nobody.*

* * *

LATER, AS TARYN sprawled on out the bed in her new room, she continued to feed her anger and throw herself a pity party. Of course the maid hadn't even been working that day. Whoever had done it to her room had taken their own initiative to welcome themselves inside. The lock had been broken.

The manager offered to refund the rest of her stay, another three weeks, but that did *her* little good. She wasn't paying for it in the first place. He then offered her a check for $300 "as our sincerest apology."

In other words, "please take this money and don't sue us."

She'd settled for $500. They could afford it. They were charging those reporters a fortune.

Still, there was at least four times that much damage done to her art supplies alone.

Luckily, she'd had her most important possessions with her at the time. Miss Dixie, for one, was with her. Taryn never went anywhere without her. Her laptop was in her trunk; she traveled with it as well, just in case she got a wild hair while she was out and decided to some photo editing. She had extra canvases and brushes with her as well.

Another piece of luck on her part was that the intruder had not been able to open one of the storage tubs Taryn had unloaded into her room the night before. The lid always stuck on her. Sometimes she had to use a knife. It contained more paint, a sketchpad, and oil. So she really didn't need to buy anything at the moment, although a few extra shirts wouldn't hurt.

And her makeup, she thought sadly. She was actually grieving for a tube of lipstick she already missed.

Now, as she had time to stew on it, Taryn wondered if the reason the tub hadn't been opened was because the intruder couldn't open it or had run out of time.

She wasn't surprised they'd been able to do the amount of damage they did. During the daytime there was hardly anyone around the motel. The motel guests were there to work—they all left early in the morning and most came home after dark. Of course, they did pop in and out during the day as they returned for things they needed or took breaks, but in general the place was pretty quiet.

"Who's mad at me *now*?" Taryn grunted. She always seemed to be pissing someone off.

But, although she was feeling a significant amount of rage, there was also another thought running through her head: this might have been a break for her. If she was making someone angry, or uncomfortable, then she was close to something that someone didn't like.

So what had she done? What had she said?

She'd talk about it when she saw Matt. They'd figure it out together.

* * *

SINCE SHE'D HAVE TO DO IT eventually anyway, Taryn forged ahead with the next activity of the day: going through her pictures. She stocked up on Cokes and candy bars from the vending machines (now two doors closer) and found a Rom Com on television. Then, with her favorite blanket spread over her legs (they'd missed it under the pillow) and her back up against the flimsy headboard, she opened her laptop and braced herself for what she might find.

"Bring it on," she whispered, but her smile wavered. There was a reason she was keeping all the lights on and the volume loud.

But what could go wrong when Kate Hudson was making eyes at Matthew McConaughey?

As silly as it might sound, Taryn found herself slightly disappointed in the first ten shots she flipped through. Oh, they were spooky to be sure. The hallway looked even gloomier than she'd remembered. Possum and bird carcasses littered the floor in the library—something she had not noticed while she'd been too excited about the Nancy Drew books. Now, in her pictures, their glassy eyes looked up at her with desperation while their bodies lay flat.

"Sail possums," she whispered, referring to the flat sail-shapes their bodies took on postmortem.

Then there was the graffiti, writing only illuminated by the flash of her camera. Curse words were intermixed with song lyrics and crude drawings. Uninformed vandals, confused by what they'd probably seen on television, had left pentagrams in hopes of signifying a satanic presence.

But these things, though jolting, were typical.

"Maybe there's nothing there after all," Taryn shrugged, popping a bit of chocolate into her mouth.

And then the lights went out.

Taryn sat up straighter and looked around, half expecting to see the shadowy figure again. Unable to see beyond the glare of her computer screen, she settled back against her headboard and gripped her blanket, pulling it up to her neck.

"Ghosts can't hurt you, ghosts can't hurt you," she chanted, willing herself to believe it. A ghost had not hurt her yet, anyway.

She made a feeble attempt to tug on the lamp's string, but nothing happened. She knew it wouldn't. Apparently, the show was just getting started.

"Focus, focus," Taryn reminded herself. "You'll be okay."

Resigned to what was going on around her, and choking back her fear, she returned to her pictures. The ones taken in the principal's office were next. There were ten in all. The first few were not exceptional in any way.

However, as she found herself peering closer to the screen, once again lingering on the words "Look Away," she paused.

"From what?" she asked the dark room. "Are you telling me not to look? Or am I barking up the wrong tree?"

"Watch."

The single word, spoken at barely more than a whisper, had Taryn bolting upright in the bed, frantically scanning the room in panic. "Hello?" she croaked. "Wha–"

"Taryn, watch."

The command was clear and close; the person speaking could have been sitting on the bed next to her. Indeed, as Taryn held her breath and turned to her left, a faint misty white cloud began to materialize in the air beside her. It was fresh, sweet-smelling, and almost comforting. The sheet under her bottom shifted, as though the person next to her had lowered themselves down and disturbed the bed. She might as well have been hanging out with a friend, going through the pictures together. She could feel their breath on her cheek, sense their nearness.

The deep familiarity of the floral perfume, the faint whiff of cigarette smoke, and talcum powder was overwhelming.

Only, her Aunt Sarah had been gone for nearly two years. She couldn't have possibly been there with her.

"Aunt Sarah?" Taryn whispered, humbled that her human response was hopefulness, and not fear. "Is that you?"

"Watch," the voice demanded again. She'd never heard her aunt speak in such an authoritative tone. She'd never seen her in action on her job, though. Perhaps there had been a side to her aunt she hadn't known. Everyone had such a side. "Look."

In obedience, Taryn turned back to her screen, resisting the urge to dive into the empty space beside her and engulf herself in the last bit of residue left of her entire family.

"I'm looking, I'm watching," she muttered. The coolness around her shifted in approval.

But there was nothing new in the picture of the office. The image had not changed; Taryn did not see anything suspicious or questionable in the shot aside from the scrawling on the wall that might even simply be more graffiti.

"Moving on then," Taryn said. She waited for some show of authorization, but when nothing came, she shrugged again and went to the next shot.

She was inside the classroom, the room where the explosive detonated.

Taryn had taken the first picture from right inside the doorway. The next had been taken while she was standing in the center of the room, inside the circle of blackness, facing the line of windows. Once again Taryn felt chilled by the implication of where she'd been and what she'd seen, but if she was expecting some overwhelming sense of clarity to occur, she was to be disappointed. Nothing happened.

For the third picture, she'd stood at the front of the room, her back to the chalkboard. She faced the room, stood before where the students would have most likely been seated. The desks and tables were no longer in any order but she could use her imagination to envision what they must have once looked like: little desks and orange plastic chairs, all line up in neat rows facing the teacher like tiny soldiers.

Only now, that wasn't what she saw at all.

As Taryn watched in fascination, the glare of her screen grew brighter and brighter until she could barely stand to look at it. Beams of light zoomed towards her in even sheets; she was reminded of being in a movie theater and looking up at the projection booth—the dusty beams of light soaring towards the big, white screen.

Shielding her eyes, Taryn rose to her knees and moved the computer off her lap. She placed it several feet down the bed from her and watched as the shaft of light grew more brilliant, momentarily forgetting about her guest.

Then she looked behind her.

In its brightness, her computer had turned into a projector of sorts and now it was facing her pressed-wood headboard. The image transposed before her was the same room as in the picture, but the scene was not the picture she'd taken.

Taryn sat back on her heels and cocked her head to the side, studying the scene with critical eyes. There were the desks, all neatly lined up as she'd expected. Only now they were full of students. The children appeared to be about nine or ten years old, an equal number of girls and boys. All but one of the seats were filled.

The classroom was a cheerful place, full of the fun, exciting things any child at that age appreciates. A "Ghostbusters" movie poster was tacked on the back wall by the coat rack next to a poster of a kitten holding a pencil and large, pink eraser. Childish, handmade lanterns dangled from the ceiling. Orange pumpkins, fat and smiling jack-o-lanterns, lined the ledge below the windows. They looked like papier-mâché. The walls were covered with printouts of everything from superheroes with spelling words to barnyard animals holding onto long-division charts. Books were lined neatly on shelves.

It was the scene of an ordinary classroom, the kind in which she had once sat.

She could not see the front of the room, of course. That's where she, Taryn, had been standing. Whatever the class was looking at she, herself, was obscuring.

But there were the students.

Some were engaged in their reading. These were intent on staring at their pages, noses pressed almost all the way to the paper, not lifting their eyes. But others were—what were they doing?

Several little girls were looking at one another, sharing muffled giggles behind their hands. A small boy with bright, red hair looked into a faraway distance, his face nearly as red as the top of his head. Some children covered their faces, only revealing their eyes. They looked on the verge of tears.

And then there was the awkward looking child in slick pigtails and big, thick glasses. She sat in the front row closest to the door. Although she had an open book in front of her, and her fingers had carefully marked her place, she wasn't reading. Unlike the others, she wasn't smiling or laughing or embarrassed. But she was looking forward.

Looking straight at Taryn.

Their eyes met through the decades and locked. Taryn didn't dare to breathe. She and the young girl watched one another with grave interest, unmoving until the child cocked her head to the side and gave her counterpart the nod.

Taryn gasped and fell backward as the headboard went black.

NINETEEN

*T*aryn *wore a navy blue skirt* with a white, buttoned-up blouse. Both had been found at one of the local thrift stores early that morning. She hadn't had time to do any real shopping since the majority of her clothes were destroyed.

Still reeling from the last night's events, she marched down the sidewalk with purpose, quickening her pace after glancing at her watch and noticing the time.

"Hello there," the woman who held the double doors of the courthouse open for her was the same one that had gone in and checked her room a few nights earlier. "You joinin' us today?"

Taryn nodded, feeling surreal at the fact that not only was Frieda Bowen holding the door open for her but that she looked shy about it. Taryn returned her friendly smile with politeness. "Yes. Just for today, though."

She laughed. "Wanted to see what this circus was all about?"

"I'm a glutton for punishment," she said drily.

"Well, it's an interesting case for sure. Just make sure you don't make a lot of noise or draw attention to yourself. Judge doesn't like any distractions. He threatens to throw us all out just about every day." Frieda rolled her eyes.

Taryn highly doubted she'd do anything to draw any attention to herself. As she took her seat on a padded bench behind the defense's table, she wondered again about her decision to join the courtroom antics. So far she'd had little interest in actually watching the proceedings; seeing the highlights on television each night had been more than enough.

But that was before Lucy Dawson had nodded at her through twenty-five years and a camera.

The Lucy that walked out with her attorney looked vastly different from the one in pigtails, or even the one Taryn had sat with on the porch. This one wore her hair in a tight bun, modeled a navy blue business suit, and carried an expensive-looking leather briefcase under her arm.

Of course, the thick glasses were still perched on her nose, the suit was already wrinkled, and the briefcase was scuffed with a broken strap. To Taryn, it looked as though Lucy had an awareness of what "normal" people might wear for such an occasion, but hadn't quite been able to replicate it.

"How were they even able to hold the case here?" Taryn whispered to Frieda. Perhaps feeling as though they'd bonded back at the motel, the celebrity reporter had followed her in and taken the seat beside her. She guessed that, since she'd been looking for scary people in her room and they were staying at the same place, they were kind of buds now. "Doesn't everyone in town know her?"

Frieda shrugged and rolled her eyes again. She looked much more like the person on television today. Like the shark she was often called. "We've been playing that game for months. Her attorney didn't even ask for a change of venue. Can you believe it?"

"So this local woman can kill half a dozen other local people in a county where everyone is related to everyone else and they thought they could still find a fair jury?" Taryn tried wrapping her head around that logic and failed.

"You're telling me. Just wait until you see how some of this unfolds. Better than most TV I've watched," she whispered with a grin. "Or hosted."

Lucy's attorney was a tall woman with blond, frizzy hair. Taryn had seen her on television as well and recognized her right away. She wore an ill-fitting black dress that showed off multiple layers of blubber on her stomach and hunched over a cane when she walked. She didn't look more than fifty-years-old. Taryn hoped she was good, but after taking a quick glance at the prosecutor, with his tailored suit, Mac unfolded on the table before him, and youthful (and hungry) looking face, her expectations fell short.

It was going to be a long afternoon.

* * *

"CAN YOU GIVE US A GENERAL SENSE of Ms. Dawson's well-being at the time you knew her?"

"Objection." Lucy's attorney struggled to rise to her feet and wobbled once she'd made it. "Calls for speculation. Mr. Winston here is not a healthcare worker."

"Sustained."

The prosecutor shuffled through a stack of papers on his desk shrugged his shoulders. "Can you recall any altercations between Ms. Dawson and anyone else from that time period?"

The middle-aged man on the hot seat had what Taryn thought of like a hipster beard—it fell to the middle of his chest. He'd chosen a flannel shirt and gray corduroys for his courtroom debut. Between his heavy, brown work boots, facial hair, and little horn-rimmed glasses he looked like a nerdy lumberjack.

Granted, Taryn didn't know a lot about legal proceedings, just what she'd seen on "Law & Order," but she found it outrageous that a man Lucy Dawson had dated in high school was testifying against her. As what? A character witness? Prosecution couldn't do that, could they? Well, they were. So far he'd told them that she'd had a volatile temper, difficulty making friends, and was prone to erratic phone calls in the middle of the night, calling him over to sit with her when she couldn't sleep.

Taryn's heart went out to Lucy. She, herself, would've been mortified to have that dragged through the community (not to mention the rest of the world). Most people would be. Who the hell wanted their high school loves to get up and talk about them twenty years later? Like they couldn't change? And what a weeny he was to get up and talk.

"Well, yes I can in fact," the man, this "Mr. Winston", replied. He said it with such a smile that Taryn shrank back against her seat in disgust.

As the witness answered, he spoke not actually to the prosecutor but the entire courtroom. His eyes traveled from one side to the other as his hand gestures became elaborate and his voice rose and fell with great reverb.

Why, Taryn thought, he's putting on a show! What a joke!

She could almost hear him ask, "Am I projecting enough for those in the back?"

Weeny.

"I do recall one particular incident in which we'd been to a party after a basketball game. She was speaking to one of our acquaintances, she and Lucy were not really friends but knew each other, and the other girl became extremely emotional."

"Can you elaborate?"

"Yes, she began crying, wailing really, and then she reached out and struck Lucy."

"Did anyone else there draw any conclusions from this?"

"Yes," the witness nodded. "It looked as though Lucy had provoked her. She was asked to leave the party."

He spat out that last part, as though he still carried around the anger with him— anger that he'd had to leave thanks to her antics.

"Did she say what that altercation involved?"

"No," he shook his head. "Just said that it was personal and that the other girl, her name was Wendy."

"Can you clarify what you mean by 'was'?"

"Yes sir. Wendy committed suicide the next day." He said it dramatically, eyes widened to the room.

"Oh, come on," Taryn seethed quietly. "What does that have to do with anything? Are they seriously trying to say that Lucy had something to do with that as well?"

She waited, with baited breath, for the objection that was sure to follow but none came.

The woman beside her sympathetically patted her on the hand. "It's been like this for almost two weeks," she whispered. "You can't even imagine. Best stuff I've had in years."

Taryn looked at her from the corner of her eye. She was both disgusted and drained by her presence. In one sense, she was just doing her job, just like Taryn was. In another, she didn't have to be so gleeful about it.

"Did Ms. Dawson ever mention her years at Muddy Creek Elementary?"

The witness shook his head "no." "No. Not in any extraordinary way. She would occasionally talk about it in reference to things she'd learned, but didn't offer any anecdotes about her time there."

"Did she seem to hold any animosity towards anyone from her past?"

Taryn thought there might be an objection in that, too. How could this dude know who Lucy was angry at? More so, just because she was mad at someone when she was sixteen didn't mean it held any relevance today.

"When Lucy turned seventeen I took her out for a birthday dinner over in Huntington. We went to the Red Lobster. It was a nice meal for a birthday, an expensive one."

Well, pin a rose on your nose, Taryn thought.

"She wasn't happy that night, though. Nothing I could do would make her happy," Mr. Winston complained. Taryn bet that he could still quote the exact amount he'd spent that night, right down to the change. "When I was taking her home I asked her what was wrong. She said that there were people in her life she'd just like to see gone. I didn't think anything of it, but later she asked me if I ever thought about things being better if 'certain people' disappeared. I had no idea what she was talking about, so I asked her who she wanted to see go. She said, 'All the people I knew in elementary school.' Just like that."

Taryn was glad she wasn't being questioned about the number of people she'd wished dead over the years. Of course, Lucy had gone through with her death-wish.

When it was Lucy's attorney's time to question the witness, Taryn had a momentary spark of hope. She didn't know the man sitting before her, but she could spot a slime ball and media whore when she saw one. She bet that he, like half the reporters in the room, was probably already working on a book.

When Taryn was trying to let off steam, she occasionally visited a forum for fans of reality television programs. Everyone had a username and, depending on the number of replies they made, a scale of "desperate attention-seeking whore" status points. Taryn, with around two hundred replies, was rated "a Bachelor All-Stars Contestant." She was almost certain that Mr. Winston's DAW status in life would be that of "Playboy Centerfold."

Glancing to her side, she saw Frieda scribbling song lyrics on the back of his notebook. She apparently had an affinity for Poison. Taryn imagined that even celebrity journalists got bored after awhile.

"Mr. Winston," Lucy's attorney began as she hobbled up to the witness box, "did you ever hear Lucy Dawson say that she wished to kill anyone?"

"Well, no," he grinned. "Not straight out like that."

"Uh huh. And did she ever tell you exactly which person or persons from her elementary school she wanted to see dead?"

His smile faltered for a second, but he continued to look around the room, playing to the audience. "Well, not specifically by name, but it seemed pretty clear to me."

"Ah, then, you're a mind reader! Congratulations!"

"Objection!"

"Sustained."

"The teenage girl, Wendy, that died when we you were a child, can you recall the circumstances around her death?"

Now he didn't look so cocky. In fact, by the way he squirmed in the seat and pulled at his collar, he looked downright uncomfortable. Taryn wondered if his flannel was starting to get to him. She hoped so.

"Well, um, yes. Her boyfriend at the time was first charged with manslaughter. She'd hung herself, and it appeared as though he'd helped her do it. She left behind a note. He was only given tampering with evidence later."

"Uh huh. Thank you very much. No further questions."

As the crowd shuffled out of the room half an hour later, Taryn let herself get caught up in the sea of arms and legs.

"What the hell was that all about?" she demanded, once outside the courthouse. The lawn erupted in an uproar as phones were whipped out, microphones turned on, and people could finally express themselves outside the stuffy confines of the legal system.

The reporter strolled up beside her and patted her on the shoulder. "My name is Frieda, by the way, and you're not asking anything we haven't all been asking ourselves. I came down from New York, you know, and I've never seen anything like this before in my life. It's a great story. I mean, you've got murder, small town politics, the seedy underbelly of Mayberry...But the human side of me if a little disgusted at the farce this trial is. Fair justice my ass. I used to be a prosecutor, you know. Lucy Dawson is not getting a fair trial."

Taryn was shocked. The barracuda on television had been crucifying Lucy on her show every night. But this woman was a completely different person. She was honestly disgusted by the miscarriage of justice and didn't sound so sure that Lucy was getting what she deserved.

Taryn felt the delicate hand on her arm before anything else. When she turned, she was facing the same woman she'd sat next to at the PTA meeting. The quiet one she hadn't minded.

"Hi," Taryn said as she leaned over and gave the other woman a brief hug. Luckily, she'd also been raised in a Southern, we-hug-everyone-whether-we-know-them-or-not household and embraced her back. "What are you doing here?"

"I come here sometimes to listen. Not every day; I couldn't handle that."

Taryn smiled. "I know what you mean. I couldn't either."

"I'm Naomi, by the way. I don't remember if I introduced myself the other night." Naomi's eyes were wide and red, as though she might have been recently crying. They were still glassy. In her loose dress that swept the ground and her hair slicked back from her head she looked thin, almost gaunt. Her face was pale. Taryn imagined that the trial was taking a lot out of people. She was dealing with ghosts of another kind, but she could commiserate.

"This is Frieda," Taryn gestured. "She works for the news."

"But don't hold that against me," she joked. When she shook Naomi's hand, her small fingers disappeared inside Frieda's big grip. Taryn hoped she wouldn't squeeze too hard.

"I'm going to have to head back to the motel," Taryn apologized. "I have some painting to do today. Do you think they'll bring Lucy out this way?"

She didn't know what she would say to her, but Taryn was struck by the urge of wanting to see her face again, to make eye contact.

"Nah. They'll slip her out the back," Frieda told her.

When Naomi excused herself and walked away, Taryn turned back to Frieda and raised her eyebrows. "Hands off of that one," she warned her. "I don't think she could take a barracuda throwing questions at her."

"I agree," she replied jovially. "Looks like a stiff breeze would blow her over. And anyway, we're not total monsters. I just play one on TV." They both turned and watched as a handful of the reporters turned and ran towards the back of the building, where Lucy's truck was pulling away.

"Well, most of us anyway."

With a flood of emotions she neither understood nor was ready to process, Taryn began her walk back down the sidewalk. She stopped a few feet past the courthouse, though, and looked across the street. The jail set directly before her; its orange bricks dull in the hazy, afternoon sky. Beside it was a two-story white house. A yellow condemned sign was tacked to the front door. A maple tree grew through the porch.

Lukas Monroe had spent far too much of his young life chained to a toilet in that house. Right there in the middle of town, out in the open, where any number of people could have saved him. Taryn shuddered and shook her head sadly. To think he'd been tied in there, unable to escape, and yet still had to hear familiar voices out on the street.

How many times had his hopes lifted as someone knocked on the door or clumped their heavy boots on the floorboards inside? How many times had he thought someone was there to rescue him, only to have those hopes dashed?

In the end, he'd had to save himself. Nobody had come for him.

Taryn loved old houses. She saw potential in everything. She often felt more connected to the past than any present she'd been a part of.

But some things just needed to go. Sometimes the simple physical reminder of them was too much to bear. For one of the first times ever, she was looking at a house she hoped would someday fall to the ground.

* * *

TARYN SAT FACING the other children in the classroom. Their desks had been arranged in a circle. She sat with her back to the door with her head bowed down. She could feel the presence of another girl close to her. It was comforting, though they did not look at one another. Neither moved.

Hot, biting tears shamed her. She sniffed then immediately tried to cover it up with a cough. Taryn was acutely aware of her pride, more so than she'd ever been in her life.

Little baby, she sang tunelessly to herself, *little baby gonna be okay. I'll take care of you, it's gonna be okay.* Though she felt completely alone she pretended someone was there with her, their arms wrapped around her, smoothing her hair back and holding her close.

Someone said something but their voice was muzzy and distorted. When she looked up a figure reared in the center of the ring, their outline hazy and wavy, like a hologram. They flickered in and out of her sight, a clumsy spirit pirouetting across the tiles.

The sea of children's faces all became a blur, with one another's until she faced a sea of headless, featureless monsters. Taryn caught her breath and collapsed within herself, drawing her scrawny knees up to her chest and whimpering.

The room was spinning, whirling around and around until Taryn thought she might throw up. Then a face broke through, a sweet, golden face of a young boy across from her. Through the sea of monsters he was the only one with a smile, the only one that *looked* at her. Their eyes met across the space for a brief second and then the monster was back, re-materializing between them.

A blast of fire and bright light, and then darkness.

TWENTY

*F*or one of the first times ever, I'm afraid to go to my jobsite."

Matt leaned over and patted her on the knee. "No wonder. I wouldn't be thrilled to return, either."

"I spent all night sitting at the little table outside my room painting," she complained. "At least until it got too dark to see. I'd normally be *there*, at the place."

"It would be difficult for me to return as well."

Taryn glanced over at him while she drove towards Venters County. The plan had been for him to fly into Huntington and rent a car. The car rental had fallen through, however, and without a public transportation system she'd had to fetch him. She didn't mind. She was enjoying the outing and it meant she got to see him that much faster.

His mix of Native American and Italian heritage gave Matt a smooth, olive complexion she envied. He spent far too much time indoors, which could sometimes make him appear pale, but he'd been working in his garden that fall and now his face was full of color. His long, thick eyelashes were things of beauty—even the girls who'd refused to date him in high school because he was "weird" had fawned over *those*. And his thick, glossy black hair fell across his head as an ebony cap. He was a beautiful man.

"Are you sure that was Sarah there with you?" he asked.

Taryn nodded. "I could smell her. And I definitely wasn't scared. I kind of wanted to savor the moment, if you know what I mean."

She could feel him frowning beside her. "I don't know, Taryn. I think I'd be careful about that."

"What do you mean?"

They had turned off the main highway and were now making their way across the last five miles of winding road. She was taking him to town the back way, through Muddy Creek. He wanted to see the school before she took him to the room.

"You don't know what you're dealing with here," he reminded her. "And from what I've read about this stuff, since you've been experiencing it anyway, is that things aren't always what they seem."

"You think something was pretending to be Sarah?"

"You can't rule it out."

And while Taryn did give it some serious consideration over the next few miles, she wasn't convinced. The spirit had done nothing to hurt her; it had simply wanted her to watch the scene unfold before her. She didn't think it was a malevolent ghost.

"There's still something I don't understand," Taryn admitted as they pulled over the side of the hill and dipped into the school's parking lot.

"What's that?"

Taryn put the car in park and turned around in her seat. "Andrew. I don't get it. What about Andrew?"

As he was always capable of doing, Matt temporarily put his own romantic feelings aside and, for a moment at least, turned into her friend. "Why hasn't he contacted you? Why can't you see *him*?"

She nodded miserably, embarrassed by the tears that threatened to fall. Miserable at the idea of making Matt feel bad.

Matt, for his part, appeared unfazed. Instead, he leaned over and brought her face close to his. Without kissing her, he gently tilted her head up until the curve at the top of her nose fit securely into the rise of his forehead. It was a perfect fit, and always had been.

"I don't know," he said at last. "I wish it worked that way. I wish you could see him. I don't know why *any* of this is happening."

"I have something important to tell you," he whispered.

"What?" she replied, keeping her voice at the same level.

Barely moving, Matt leaned down to the backpack at his feet. He slowly removed a small bag and brought it up between them. "I didn't know how to say this," he began seriously, "so I thought I'd..."

Taryn reached her hand into the bag and then squealed when her fingers touched something familiar. The mood already broken, she jumped back and laughed in delight.

It was full of makeup.

"I didn't know what to get you, so I went to Sephora and told them stock you up."

It was the first time she'd been at Muddy Creek and felt any sense of peace.

* * *

"SO GIVE ME ANOTHER RUNDOWN on what happened the last time you were here."

They'd been walking around the building for an hour. In that time Taryn had been able to separate her emotions and memories from her actual job at hand and had acted tour guide, giving Matt a decent walk-through of the school's history and interesting architectural features.

"I gotta tell you," she laughed. "It's not a walk in the park in there. It's creepy, even by our standards."

Matt grinned and slipped his hand into hers. It was cool on her warm, clammy skin. "As bad as that distillery in Tennessee?"

"Oh Lord," Taryn pretended to groan. "Okay, maybe not *that* bad, but bad in a different way."

The distillery had since been cleaned up, though it was still empty. When she and Matt had explored it however, on a weekend trip during college, vagrants had apparently been calling it "home" for awhile. The neat, yet towering, piles of excrement served as evidence.

"Okay, well, so no poop. I can live with creepy-sans-poopy places," Matt said.

"This is creepy in a way that I've seen before. It's just so...sad. Why let this happen to a school anyway? It could've been used for something."

"You think everything can be used for something," Matt pointed out.

"Well, not *everything*," Taryn replied, thinking of Lukas Monroe's white house on Main Street.

"There's an old school down in Benham, Kentucky," Matt began, "in Harlan County, that's been turned into a motel. It wasn't that much bigger than this one. I saw it on the internet. Looked like your kind of place."

"Some schools have been turned into flea markets and stuff," Taryn said. "Things *can* be done."

"Oh, I didn't realize when I first made the travel arrangements that Huntington was where that plane crash killed the football team." Matt paused, pulling Taryn to a stop beside him. "I'd seen the movie but for some reason didn't put it together."

"And about ten miles from here was where that big flood happened that killed a lot of people," Taryn added. "Right now they're battling a major heroin epidemic. Dozens of people overdosing a day. And across the state line, over in Martin County, was where something happened to that coal slurry pond and it spilled however many thousands of tons on the community below."

"Geeze," Matt shook his head, trying to process the information. "Lots of bad history here."

"Lots of *good* things, too," Taryn conceded. "It's a beautiful place. I hear the reporters talking about how worse it looks in the winter, with all the leaves off the trees. They say that the foliage is covering the trash."

"People will always find a reason to complain about something."

They now stood before the entrance to the teacher's lounge. Even then, in broad daylight with Matt beside her, Taryn was distrustful. She knew she had to go back inside at some point, but the dream from the night before still haunted her.

"You can stay if you want," Matt said. "I can go alone."

"No, I'll go," she sighed. "It's better that I do this now, with you, while I can. Ready?"

* * *

TARYN KNEW MATT would go nuts over the books in the library, just as she had, but they didn't have a lot of time. Her tummy growled from hunger; he was tired from his flight (it had taken two changes to get there), and she didn't have much time before the sun set. They had to go straight to the action.

"I didn't hit the gym last time," Taryn laughed. "Wanna start there?"

So when they stepped inside, she turned him to the left and they made the short walk to that end of the building. She couldn't help but notice how much faster it took them to walk it at a reasonable pace–much quicker than it had taken her to run it a couple of days before.

The double doors leading into the cavernous room were propped open. Nothing to have to jiggle around to break into it.

Inside, it appeared as ordinary as any other school gymnasium. Well, aside from the garbage blowing across the floor and the vermin excrement scattered about. "Look, Matt, there's your poop!" He sent her a nasty look, but then winked.

"You okay if I take a look around?" he asked.

She nodded. "Yep. I'm going to take some pictures anyway. Knock yourself out."

Taryn avoided the kitchen in the back. Instead, she walked around the perimeter and focused on getting a feel for what the space had once meant to the children who'd played in it.

Cafeteria during the morning and noon and big playroom for the rest of the time, it served the same purpose as many other small-town school gyms did. Even now she could see tables standing upright on their wheels, pushed back against a wall, ready to be rolled back out in time for the next meal.

Thinking of the yellow foam ball she'd seen in the closet by the principal's office, Taryn snapped a few pictures of the middle of the floor, wondering what rainy day games had been played in there. The school had had a successful basketball team, at least for some time. They'd won the county tournament. It was hard to imagine the room full of spectators, pushed up against the walls in plastic chairs (since there weren't any bleachers) and the smell of hot dogs and sweat in the air.

She stopped moving and looked across the floor at Matt, who stood on the other side of the room. With something akin to despondency she raised her shoulders then let them fall back down. He nodded his agreement.

They began making their way across the floor to one another when a sound had them both stopping in their tracks. "Is that—" Matt started.

"Singing," Taryn finished.

The shadows of the gym obscured his features, but Taryn still made out the anxiety. She scurried across the floor and broke the distance between, reaching for his hand. "Wanna go?" she asked hopefully.

"Just a second," he whispered. "You have Miss D ready?"

Together, holding hands, they crept to the doors. Taryn didn't feel right about having the vast room to her back, but with Matt there it didn't feel as foreboding.

The tinny music that rolled down the hall was familiar. Taryn recognized it right away.

"James Taylor," she quipped, still looking straight ahead.

"That was two notes," Matt hissed.

She squeezed his hand. "I know my music."

As they listened, neither one daring to breathe very hard for fear of making whatever was happening stop, Taryn attempted to determine where the voice was coming from. It was a good, loud clear voice. Female, with a deep reverb.

At first, she thought it might be coming from a radio. It was almost too good to be live. (Well, "live" in whatever sense you wanted to make of it.) But as the music grew louder, and the words became clearer, the single backing keyboard became more prominent. It was live; someone was in the school, singing "You've Got a Friend."

Or had been there, singing it a very long time ago.

"Let's follow it," Taryn mouthed quietly.

Matt sent her an "are you crazy" look but Taryn merely shrugged. Her mettle hardened when she was with him; nothing bad could possibly happen when the two of them were together.

With her taking the lead, Matt and Taryn crept down the hallway, sidestepping plastic wrappers and Coke cans as they went, trying to make as little noise as possible. They didn't want to spook the spooks.

There was little doubt where the singing was coming from—it was Classroom Number 5, explosion site. When they neared the door, Taryn paused and pointed to the cardboard sign hanging skewed from the knob. Half of it was gone, torn from the blast, but it clearly read "Welcome to Mrs. Evans' Class." Mrs. Evans. The teacher that, according to Jamey, had scared the bejesus out of everyone. Taryn wondered how she'd missed the sign the first time. She'd been too intent on taking her photos.

Inside, the musician continued to pound on the keyboard as their voice rang out clear and strong. Even though the music was very clear, Taryn felt very far removed from the sound. When she peeked into the classroom, with Matt on her heels, she saw nothing. There were no students, no musical instruments, and no musically-inclined instructor.

Matt peered in over her head and she could feel his sharp intake of breath.

The song was a happy one, a hopeful single that had played incessantly on the radio for several decades. The singer was emoting, doing their best to belt it out. The musical notes traveled straight through the walls and leveled over Taryn's head, wrapped around her and squeezed. Taryn was a huge music lover; she loved music almost as she loved painting. She could get lost in a tune and completely forget where she was; music had the ability to make everything better for her and always had.

This was not uplifting in any way. Instead, she felt sick to her stomach just listening to it. If Matt hadn't been with her, she might have covered her ears and screamed, probably as she ran from the building. Her reaction was utterly confusing; the fact that she wanted to pull her hair and cry out baffled her.

Matt coughed then, a faint sound, but the interruption was enough to cause the song to come to a sudden stop. A single note lingered in the air, before fading away with a harmonic resonance.

Taryn tugged on Matt's hand, slowly pulling him inside the classroom.

And then all hell broke loose.

The desk at the front of the classroom was covered with ashes, burnt-out cans and paper cups, insulation, and shards of glass from the windows. All of this went rocketing through the air, as though given a mighty shove by an irate set of hands. The debris shot off the desk like a terrible gunshot and though Taryn and Matt were not in the direct line of fire, they both ducked and made to cover their heads.

Before she even had time to process what had just happened, a chair by the door flew from the ground and hurtled towards the line of windows. Taryn watched in horror as it landed against the wall and shattered into pieces, the wood breaking as easily as if someone had snapped a twig.

Then, for the second time in less than a week, Taryn found herself running down the dark hallway, looking for a way out.

TWENTY-ONE

So when did ghosts start throwing stuff at us?" Matt still couldn't wrap his head around what had happened earlier. She'd taken him to dinner, after stopping at a yard sale on the side of the road to pick up a few more pieces of clothing, and now they were heading back to her room. Neither one had spoken much of Muddy Creek and the events that had transpired there. Taryn didn't even know where to start.

"They don't *normally* do that," she replied. "Like I said, there's something different about that place. I can't even begin to figure out what happened there. But it was obviously something not good."

"I didn't uncover a single murder there. No tragedy that caused a death. Nothing negative about the school at all," Matt grumbled.

Taryn couldn't help but smile. There they were, complaining that nobody had died or suffered a terrible fate.

"Then it's obviously something that nobody knew about," Taryn said. "Something that was hidden or covered up. Only a few knew, and that's why the ghosts are irritated. They want their stories told."

"Do you think Lucy has anything to do with it?"

"I don't know," Taryn replied. "Probably. But we need to go visit her now. Well, not like right now, but soon. I hate to bother her with everything that's going on with the trial, but she did ask."

"That teacher, Mrs. Evans. That's whose room we were in, right?"

Taryn shook her head. "Yeah. The one nobody liked."

"You think she could've had something to do with it? She was one of the ones killed that night," Matt pointed out.

Taryn pulled into the parking lot and turned off the engine. "Possibly. And maybe that's what the words on the wall in there meant. 'Look Away.' That Mrs. Evans did something awful, and nobody knew about it. Now her ghost is still there, still angry, and the student she did whatever to still haunts the building because that's where they knew her from."

Matt sent Taryn a satisfied smile. "You're so good at this. That has to be what happened. But what makes you think there are two spirits?"

"The one we dealt with today is obviously an adult. That singing voice did not belong to a child. The angry ghost, that's the adult. That's the one who did, well, whatever happened. But the wailing, the crying, the specter in the window? I think that's something completely different. I don't want to make this too complicated, but I don't want to write it all off as the same thing just yet."

"So what did you make of the bouquet of flowers on the desk? That's the image that's been bothering me," Matt said. He'd tugged his suitcase from her trunk and was pulling it towards her door as he spoke.

"What flowers?"

"The big bouquet of flowers. On her desk. Daffodils and something else. Hard to see. Pretty arrangement, though," Matt added. "But completely out of place to see all this black debris and a pristine floral arrangement right in the middle of it."

Taryn stopped walking and stared at him. "What flowers?"

Matt turned and looked at her. "In the classroom? The classroom we were just in?"

"Just now? I didn't see any flowers. I saw all that stuff fly off the desk, but not any flowers."

"No, not today. From the pictures. I thought you would've brought it up now, to be honest."

As it registered, Taryn slapped her forehead. "Oh my God. With what happened with the makeshift photo projector that night I totally forgot to look at the rest of the images. I just..."

"You have a lot going on," Matt reminded her gently.

She knew what they'd be doing that night. Well, some of the evening anyway...

"Hey Taryn, I'm glad I caught you!"

Taryn turned and saw Sandy jogging towards her, a barefoot toddler with sticky fingers waddling in tow.

"Hi Sandy, what's up?"

By the time Sandy made it to Taryn's door, she was red and panting. The little girl, eating an ice cream sandwich, had spilled most of the vanilla down the front of her Dora the Explorer t-shirt.

"Come on Neveah," Sandy snapped, blowing a piece of hair from her eyes.

"Everything okay?"

Sandy nodded and bent over at her waist, trying to catch her breath. When she raised back up, her gaze landed straight on Matt. And didn't move. "Yeah, sorry. Just out of shape. That's my daughter, Neveah. Anyway, I talked to my mom. She wants to meet with you. Tomorrow if that's okay."

Taryn looked at Matt and he shrugged in return. It was okay with him.

"Yeah, that would be great. Where does she want to meet?"

"She said at the restaurant around the corner, maybe at eight?"

Taryn gulped. "A.M.?"

Sandy snickered. "Yeah. She has to be to work at noon."

"Well, if we must," Taryn sighed with disappointment. She'd been planning on making it a long night.

"Oh, and she said she'd bring her pictures with her, if you want to see them."

Well, that was something.

"Thanks, Sandy. We'll look forward to seeing her in the morning then."

Sandy sent them another smile and with one movement bent over, scooped a messy Neveah up in her arms, and sauntered on down the sidewalk.

"You're my good luck charm," Taryn teased Matt as she opened her door. "I've been waiting for that invitation. And she was totally checking you out."

"Oh, I don't think so." But the tips of his ears were red.

"We'll be doing ghost stuff all night. Let's try something else first," Taryn told him, slamming the door shut behind her.

She'd been lonesome for awhile.

* * *

"ARE YOU GOING WITH ME?" Taryn asked. She'd overslept and was meant to be meeting Sandy's mother in less than fifteen minutes. As she frantically ran around the room, trying to piece an outfit together and find her new makeup, Matt stirred in the bed.

"Ohhhh," he moaned. He sat up and looked around sleepily, trying to adjust his eyes. "Yeah, I will. I guess if you can get up."

Taryn laughed and tossed his pants to him. "Come on, we don't have long."

By the time she reemerged from the bathroom he was dressed and standing by the door. In his hand he held what looked like a notecard. He studied it intently, as though trying to decipher a foreign language.

"What you got there?" Taryn asked as she walked up behind him.

"This," he said, handing it to her. "It was here in the floor, like someone slid it under the door."

It was a plain notecard, available at just about any discount store. And though it only included one line of text, it was enough to have Taryn momentarily forgetting her promptness:

Ask Heather about that fire.

* * *

THE WOMAN WAITING FOR HER donned bright-red hair with black roots, a t-shirt with fake dollar bills sewn onto it, and stretch pants. She probably weighed around three-hundred pounds and wasn't much over five feet. Her face was lined with wrinkles, despite the fact she wasn't that much older than Taryn, and her blue eyeshadow had creased and flaked. But she smiled warmly when Taryn walked in.

"Hello there," she called from across the room. "Saving you a seat over here!"

Matt excused himself to place their order while Taryn made her way over to where Sandy's mother, Misty, was seated.

"So how did you know it was me?"

"Oh honey. You live here as long as I do and you know everyone in town," she cackled. Taryn noticed she was missing two teeth, yet the others were as straight and pearly white as could be. For some reason, this fascinated her. She needed to get out more.

"And how did you know I wasn't a reporter?"

Misty rolled her eyes. "You don't have that sliminess clinging to you like *they* do."

When Matt joined them, Taryn slid over in the booth. "I hope it's okay. I brought my boyfriend with me." She rarely referred to Matt as anything other than "my Matt" but, in this case, she thought it would be less awkward if her hostess realized he was more or less part of her family.

"Oh, I don't mind having a good-looking man sittin' across from me," Misty beamed. "Misty might not be a spring chicken no more, but she's no *fool*."

Matt laughed, obviously enjoying her.

"So we were hoping to ask you some questions about your time at Muddy Creek," Taryn began once their drinks arrived. "If you could tell us anything about what it was like to go there, that would be great."

"Oh," Misty smiled, "I loved being little and going there. It was a good school. All the teachers really cared about you. Not like these days where they's all runnin' out before the students at the end of the day and don't even try to get to know their names."

Taryn nodded. "I know what you mean. Times have changed."

"I don't know if you seen it, but there's a path that runs up the mountain behind the school. We used to go for walks up there sometimes, as a class. 'Nature walks' we called 'em. There were some old coal ponds and whatnot. Real scenic like. I remember Miss Adair bringing her dog with her ever time. He'd run off the snakes, you know? Why, they wouldn't let a dog come to school for nothing these days!"

115

Or let teachers wander around a mountainside with snakes and a bunch of students, Taryn thought to herself.

"I saw pictures of the basketball tournaments and stuff. Looked like you had some good teams," Taryn prodded.

"Yep. I weren't no cheerleader or nothin', but I went to those games plenty. High school and middle school, too. Man, I had me some times. If I'd known then what I know now, I'd a had me even more fun, too!" She chortled after just about everything she said.

"So can you tell me anything about the teachers there?"

Misty took a sip of her coffee then closed her eyes. "Well, let's see. There was that one that was always falling asleep in class. We'd toss water on her head, trying to wake her up. That was fun. And then Miss Adair. Mr. Scott."

"You remember a Mrs. Evans?"

Misty's eyes popped open then glassed over. "I do. Lordy, ain't nobody gonna forget her. That woman was meaner than a snake. I hated her."

"What did she do?" Matt asked.

"What *didn't* she do? She yelled, put kids down. You couldn't do nothing right. You'd work so hard on something and then she'd come along and just about call you stupid to your face. You know, I came to school once and in the middle of class she walked right up to me, bent down and sniffed my hair, and said, 'Misty, you don't smell good today.' Lordy, I was mortified." Misty shivered at the memory. "When I left that school I didn't care if I ever saw that old cow again."

Taryn had a faint memory of seeing Mrs. Evans' sister in a television interview, talking about how much she'd loved her students, how she'd considered them part of her family. Her students had clearly formed other opinions.

"And Mr. Scott?"

Misty ran her tongue over her lips and offered another toothy/toothless grin. "Never saw a teacher love his students more. He'd bend over backwards for them. You know, he is the one that taught me about music. He and Mrs. Evans was the only ones that had music classes back then. And he made the best art projects with us. You shoulda seen these punkins we made out of balloons one time. And these little Christmas trees out of pinecones. I still have mine somewheres. You know he bought ever student in his class a Christmas present one year? Went to the thrifty store and bought toys, books, clothes, and shoes. Some of them kids, I bet them's the only gifts they got that year."

"I'd also like to know about Lucy Dawson. Were you friends with her?"

"Well," Misty started, "I *knew* her of course. We was in the same grade. But we weren't friends, not like that. Just acquaintances I'd guess you would say. She wasn't a very likable girl. Not even back then."

"Oh yeah? Why not?"

Misty grimaced. "A shit stirrer is what we'd call her today. Always up in everyone's business, trying to cause trouble." She leaned in closer and lowered her voice, despite the fact that everyone else in the restaurant had cleared out. "You know, I weren't no surprised none when I learnt about what she done. No I wasn't. I always knew that girl would do something like that. *Always*."

Taryn exchanged looks with Matt and then turned back to Misty. "Are those your photos there?"

Misty nodded and slid the album over to Taryn. "Yeah. A little bit of scrapbooking, too. I bought me some of them crazy scissors and a few years ago I tried being creative with them. You wanna take them with you? You can just send them back with Sandy tomorrow or something. I don't mind."

With the thick photo book under her hand Taryn's heart began beating quickly. There was something in these pictures, she was sure of it. She just hoped she wasn't opening as big a can of worms as she had in the past.

* * *

"I JUST CAN'T BELIEVE I didn't see those flowers," Taryn complained for the tenth time. "Or that I didn't even go through those pictures after what happened."

"Well, you're doing it now," Matt told her. "And, besides, it doesn't really bring us any closer to where we need to be."

They'd spread a blanket under a weeping willow tree behind the motel. A small stream flowed there and the water was unexpectedly pure. With the melodious splashes and gently falling leaves around them, they could have been on a movie set: Small Town America, Lot B. Matt had flopped on his stomach and was flipping through the pictures in the album again while Taryn once again scrolled their her pictures, trying to find something she hadn't already seen.

"Getting anything out of those?" she asked.

"I don't know what I am meant to be looking for," he admitted.

"Neither do I."

"Hey, does it seem weird to you that so many people didn't like Lucy when she was younger? I mean, she was a kid, right?" Taryn was still chewing on the idea of having so many enemies. So far she hadn't met a single person who'd actually been a fan of Lucy's. Then or now.

"For a famous author, her hometown sure doesn't show her any love," Matt agreed. "Wonder why she stayed around?"

"No idea. I wouldn't have."

"Nor I."

117

That reminded Taryn. She kept meaning to order some of Lucy's books online. She wanted to give them a re-read, now that she'd met her and become involved. Taryn had to face it, however; she was searching for clues in whatever manner she could.

"So is there anywhere around here I can take you on a date?" Matt asked, giving her ankle a tug.

"Aw, you wanna date me now? After twenty-something years? That's sweet."

Matt leered at her and slapped her bottom. "I treat my woman *well*."

Taryn laughed and lunged at him then, rolling him over until he was on his back and she straddled his waist. She'd always been able to pin him down easily. "You wanna take a lady to the Red Lobster in Huntington?"

"Huh?"

Taryn leaned down and snuggled into his chest. "Just a joke. I'll explain later."

Sometimes it was nice to forget about the ghosts, even if just for a little while.

TWENTY-TWO

*S*he'd told Matt that she needed to do this one by herself. Taryn had no idea how Lucy would feel, her bringing a man along with her, and she didn't want to impose. She was already feeling uncomfortable with showing up unannounced. But then, Lucy had her phone turned off. There was no other way to get in touch with her.

It was Saturday, so court was not in session. Taryn spent the morning painting in front of the school, somehow managing to both look at the building and not really see it at the same time. When she was finished, and had wrapped everything up, she got into her car and drove on up to the log cabin. Matt, meanwhile, was meant to be doing his own kind of work in the library. She hoped he'd have better luck than she'd had.

The first thing Taryn noticed upon pulling into Lucy's driveway was the burn pile. It was stacked high, taller than she was, and seemed to contain mostly weeds. Taryn smiled with irony. It was a wonder the county was letting her anywhere near matches.

Lucy's front porch was full of furniture. It literally held everything but the kitchen sink. Except, since it did have one of those old wash stands on it, even that old cliché didn't apply in this case. It wasn't just junk cluttering Lucy's porch–the wardrobe, wash stand, twin headboard, cedar trunk, and chest of drawers were all antiques. And worth money. A shower curtain Taryn herself had coveted from Macy's, but been unable to afford because it cost more than $100, was casually tossed over a stack of pots and pans, growing mold.

Taryn could hear her mother, even after all these years, snapping, "That's not an antique–that's just old."

Taryn liked the "old" stuff as much as she did the antiques. In Lucy's situation, though, she had both, and both were valuable.

Lucy came to the door at the first knock. She looked different outside of the courtroom. Her long hair swished around her as she woke the long, white nightgown she wore made her look like she'd stepped out of another time period. Her face, sans makeup, looked older and sadder. Her glasses fell down her nose and stayed there as she peered through the screen door and contemplated Taryn's presence. Finally, she nodded and smiled grimly.

"You saw something, then," she murmured.

Taryn bobbed her head and waited as Lucy wordlessly opened the door and allowed her to enter.

The interior of Lucy's house was a sight to behold. Although her own parents would've been shocked at its disorganization and the amount of stuff she'd been able to pack into it, Taryn couldn't keep herself from looking around and marveling. Yes, there was a lot, and Lucy might have been a few untidy days away from being classified a hoarder, but there were so many interesting things to see. The small child's chair, for instance, holding silk flowers in an antique vase and nailed to the wall. The corner full of metal and aluminum buckets of many sizes, intermixed with old-fashioned washboards. The rolling pins attached to the wall above the couch, there must have been more than two dozen. Their red handles were dusty and caked with grease, but Taryn could immediately imagine the stories of pies and biscuits they could tell.

"I've got a lot of stuff, I know," Lucy said as she motioned Taryn to take a seat.

She settled into a chair covered in multi-colored afghans while Lucy took her seat across from her on a stately red, velvet settee. Next to her was a state-of-the-art stereo system, out of place amongst the rest. Country music was playing now.

"I like it," Taryn replied in all honesty. "It's homey."

"I don't see many people anymore, so my stuff keeps me company," Lucy said. "I like being surrounded by things. I know we're not supposed to say that, or mean it, but I don't care anymore. It's my money, and I don't answer to anyone else."

"I don't blame you."

Lucy sat back against the settee and studied Taryn. Taryn watched as her hostess' bare feet swung back and forth beneath her, her toes barely brushing the floor. She was a small woman. An old Restless Heart song, "The Bluest Eyes in Texas" began playing through the speakers and despite the brevity of the situation, Taryn smiled. She loved that song; it was one of her favorites. The haunting melody had always touched something inside of her. She started to remark on it, to kind of cut the ice and make light of the mood, but then Lucy straightened, looked around the room as though she'd seen a ghost, and closed her eyes in panic.

"Lucy?" Taryn asked, worried.

Lucy clutched her arms tightly to her chest and began rocking back and forth, muttering words to herself Taryn couldn't hear.

"Are you okay?" Taryn asked. She quickly rose to her feet and walked to the other woman. Lucy did not appear to recognize that Taryn was there.

She couldn't hear what she was saying, so Taryn fiddled with the button on the stereo until she'd turned the volume down. Lucy continued to rock, to mumble to herself, and then (even worse) to emit a high-pitched whinnying sound that shook Taryn.

"Please, are you okay?"

And then she stopped. As though it had not happened at all, Lucy opened her eyes and shook her head. Her color had returned to normal. She was all right. "I'm sorry," she apologized, clearly embarrassed. "It happens sometimes. Please, take a seat."

Taryn returned to her chair, afraid and bewildered.

"So, what have you seen? I know it's something, or else you wouldn't be here."

"I don't know what I've seen," Taryn answered, still nervous about what had just happened, "but I can tell you what I've heard."

For the next several minutes it was Taryn's turn to study Lucy as she told her about the singing, the objects flying around the room, the clattering of objects in the storage closet. When she'd finished with that, she thought for a second about omitting what she'd seen in her pictures but then gave in and told her about those as well.

Lucy listened with eyes closed, only opening them when Taryn mentioned the flowers. For the slightest moment, Taryn thought she saw Lucy's eyes widen with something akin to fear, but it might have been sadness. It was gone before she could register or understand it.

"I don't know what any of that means, you know," Taryn said. She hoped her voice didn't hold accusation.

Lucy opened her eyes again. "I don't know what to tell you. I don't know what some of it means myself."

"But you know who's doing it, what it's all about," Taryn pressed.

Lucy nodded. "I do."

"Then does it matter if I do anything or not?" Taryn asked, confused. "I mean, I guess I thought I was helping. But if you don't want to talk about it..."

Lucy rose and began pacing back and forth across the floor, her nightgown dragging the ground behind her. "I don't know what to tell you. There are some things that deserve to be buried. Gone and buried. Don't you ever feel like that?"

"I don't think these things are, though," Taryn protested. "And now I am involved. I can't say for sure that they won't follow me. They followed me to my motel room."

"Oh, honey. That motel has its own ghosts to worry about," Lucy laughed.

"So I should just walk away?"

Lucy stopped and sent Taryn a withering look. "You can do what you want."

Taryn felt her temper rising. "Look, I thought I was here for a reason. And I see and hear these things for a reason. You can't just ask me to, well, you know, tell you stuff and then not tell me what it means."

"Humph," Lucy sighed. Then, "Has there ever been a song in your life that you just hated? A song that everyone else loved? It comes on, and they all want to turn it up and sing along with it but all you can do is cover your ears and try not to scream."

Taryn nodded. There were songs she actively disliked. Only, she was sure they weren't talking about music here.

"At first, when people see your reaction, they want to know why you're acting like that. Why you hate it. So, you try to explain it to them. Only they still don't get it. In fact, they get angry at you. Now they want to change your mind. They won't accept the fact that you have the right to dislike it, that you don't have to go along with what they want. And soon," Lucy finished as she continued her pacing, "you just stop telling them altogether. There's no purpose."

"I want to know what song you hate," Taryn pleaded.

Lucy smiled at her, a gentle one this time. "You know, I believe you do. But this time, you're just going to have to figure it out alone. I don't have any more explanations left within me. I can't talk about that song anymore. I just have to let it play."

Lucy followed Taryn out the front door and stood on her porch as she walked down to her car. At the burn pile. Taryn paused and pointed. "You cleaning?"

Lucy nodded. "Man up the road does that for me once a week. Poison ivy. I am deathly allergic to it. Don't even have to touch it to catch it. He burns it while I'm gone so that I don't have to be here and breathe it in."

Taryn, also highly allergic to the awful weed, shuddered. "I don't blame you. I hate that stuff."

"Oh, Taryn!" Lucy called as Taryn started to slide into the driver's seat. "The dream about the hallway? I have that one, too. I don't know what it means. And that's the God's truth."

TWENTY-THREE

*A*ny luck?" From the grim look on Matt's face, Taryn wasn't hopeful.

She'd been sitting outside at the small table for the past hour, waiting for him to return. He didn't have a vehicle so he was limited to where he could travel by foot. And, frankly, there weren't that many places to go to downtown–four restaurants, the library, and a gas station. Still, Taryn had felt his absence in an almost painful way, and she worried. It was funny how he could be several states away, and she could literally go for days without having more than a passing thought about wishing to be with him nonstop (yeah, it was a problem she was trying to sort out). Yet, get him in the same room with her, and she didn't want to let him go.

Now, as he ambled up to her and pulled out the other chair, she felt guilty for having sent him to work. They always spent their time together working on one project or another. They were never able to simply sit back, relax, and be.

"You go first," Matt sighed as he rubbed at his eyes.

Taryn stretched her legs out under the table and rested them in his lap, where he immediately began working on her ankles.

"Well, my day was eventful. I worked on the painting this morning and then I went to visit Lucy."

"Yeah? How'd that go?"

"Well, I told her about what I'd seen, dreamed, and heard and she gave me..." Taryn paused for dramatic effect, "nothing."

"Nothing?"

"Nada."

"Damn," Matt said, shaking his head. Taryn laughed. She could count on one hand the number of times she'd heard Matt curse. He thought cursing showed a lack of imagination. Taryn herself liked a good "shit" or "damn" when the moment called for one.

"The fact that she's avoiding talking to me about it means that it was something bad, Matt," Taryn said. "I hate to push her, I do. She obviously doesn't want to talk about it."

"But it's affecting you now," he pointed out. "You can't just walk away. What if this follows you back to Nashville?"

"I know," Taryn agreed. "And I also feel like I have some sense of loyalty to the other people involved, too. Like Aunt Sarah. Sarah has nothing to do with Lucy; that's all with me. And if she wants me involved, then I am going to have to do something about it."

"And the child-ghost," Matt reminded her.

"Right," Taryn concurred. "So how did it go for you?"

"Ohhhh." Matt dropped her foot and groaned into his hands.

"That bad, huh?"

"Seriously, Taryn. Do you have any idea how many people have died here?"

"Well, I was just reading about the heroin epidemic in the area. Apparently, Huntington was hit hard by it, and they see something like twenty overdoses in a single day. Every day."

Matt shook his head. "That's not what I mean. I mean, the number of murders, suicides, and general random deaths. There has to be an above-average loss of life here."

"Here, listen to this..." He bent over and rummaged around in his backpack before extracting a navy blue notebook. "Ethan Wayne, death by self-inflicted gunshot wound. Wendy Spacke, death by hanging. Loyal Oswald, fatal overdose. Paul Jackson, jailed for first-degree murder. Travis Windsome, jailed for first-degree murder."

"Okay," Taryn said slowly. "But not all of those were deaths. And, of course, you're going to have that in any county. Unfortunately, these things happen."

"Ah!" Matt grinned, throwing her a wink. "But you don't know the connections to these, do you?"

"I recognize the name Wendy. That's the girl who killed herself. She was a classmate or friend of Lucy's, right?"

"They all were."

"Huh?"

"Taryn," Matt leaned forward and lowered his voice, "all of those people were classmates of Lucy's at Muddy Creek. And those aren't even all of the casualties."

Despite the somber information, Matt couldn't help but look pleased with himself. Taryn, for her part, was shocked.

"You're kidding me!"

"I'm not," he asserted vehemently. "I started seeing a trend early on, so I ran with it. I used to be a reference librarian, you know. I got skills."

"Good Lord. There weren't that many people in her class to begin with, were there?"

Matt waved his hand around. "Hard to say for sure, but my guess would be no. Muddy Creek Elementary only had one class per grade. Each year they had seventeen students 'graduate' so you can figure that's what their average was for each class, more or less."

"And how many kids were causalities of Lucy's class? And these are the ones from Muddy Creek, right, and not spillovers into Middle School?"

"Well, causalities from Middle School, and from outside of Lucy's class are also high. Abnormally so I'd say. But with Lucy's, there are only around four students in her class that 'made it out' or however you want to say it. That's her, Jamey-the-principal, and two other girls I lost track of."

Taryn laughed a little, though it wasn't funny. "Well, considering that she's on trial for murder..."

Matt closed his notebook and leaned back in his chair. "Taryn, I think something really, really bad happened there."

"Do you think Lucy..."

"Had something to do with it," he asked. "No, I don't."

"A paranormal thing?"

"Maybe," he replied. "This is one of those cases where I think it wouldn't be too farfetched to think the school or building or whatever is some kind of vortex. Maybe we're dealing with something way out of our league here."

Taryn slumped back in her seat as well and groaned. "Great. So now what?"

"I bought a pint of whiskey from a reporter in the parking lot. Want to drink?"

"You don't drink," Taryn protested.

"I think it might be time to start."

* * *

TARYN AND MATT stood over the sea of green felt and contemplated their next moves.

"See?" Matt said as the satisfying click of cue hitting ball rang out through the room. "I told you I'd get you on a date."

"I haven't played pool in forever," Taryn grumbled. "It's not fair. You're a math person."

"Don't let her fool ya, man," the guy at the next table over called. "I've been watching that one. She's better than she wants you to think she is."

Matt laughed and looked at Taryn with adoration. "Don't I know it. It's a game she plays."

Taryn rolled her eyes then blew both men a flirtatious kiss. Then, after prancing around the table on her tiptoes, she leaned backward, struck a pose, and got three balls in at once. "Ta da!"

The other man laughed and clapped Matt on the shoulder. "Good luck with that one, man."

Taryn laughed. "It's payback for my eleventh birthday party," she said as she sidled up next to Matt and nuzzled his shoulder.

"Are you still complaining about that?"

"Yep. And I'll continue to do so until," she pretended to ponder the question, "forever, really."

"Well, I've got time then." He fondly ruffled her hair.

She'd had her eleventh birthday party at a skating rink in Nashville. The manager had created all kinds of games for the kids to play, most including balls and strategy. Matt had won every single one of them. Of course, he'd taken his time playing them, had even gotten down on his hands and knees and measured distances with his fingers (much to the fascination of Taryn's girlfriends who already looked at him as an unidentified specimen), but he'd still won.

Incidentally, that had been her last birthday party. Her female friendships had steadily fallen apart over the course of the next year and she'd had trouble making close bonds since. But she still had Matt, at least.

While they waited for their pizzas, Taryn played around on the jukebox, delighting in the fact that it was the old-school kind without the moving CD covers. "Hey, you want to play anything," she called over to their table. "I put $5 in here and that apparently allows me to play all of them."

"You're the music person," Matt answered back. "I wouldn't know one from the other."

"Okey dokey then. Don't be surprised or irritated when they're all Garth Brooks and Shania." Of course, Taryn would never play all Garth or all Shania. Although a little of both never hurt anyone.

With "Honey I'm Home" blaring through the small room, Taryn danced back to their table, wiggling her hips and moving her arms until her tiny dress flew around her knees.

"That whiskey must have been good stuff," Matt remarked when she sat down.

"Actually, I didn't have any before we left. I am just glad to be out, to be doing something," she confessed. "You know, I don't mind this place so much. I mean, let's face it, there's almost nothing to do here but I am starting to recognize faces and getting this little groove going. I think maybe it's time to leave Nashville. It's just become a closet for me anyway. I'm having way more fun in other places."

Matt's eyes lit up as she reached over and took her hands. "I would love it if you came to Florida with me," he said.

Taryn squeezed his fingers back but looked down, unable to meet his eyes. "I don't know. I don't know that I am ready for that. I was thinking of going to New

Hampshire for awhile, staying in Sarah's house. It needs more work and I can't keep my eye on it from down here."

The color all but drained from Matt's face. She hated herself for the disappointment she'd caused. "But that's even farther away," he whispered.

"I know. But we fly to each other anyway. Once we're in the air, does it matter?"

Matt let go of her hand and cracked his knuckles. "Are you ever going to come to Florida? Be honest, Taryn."

She bit her lip and struggled to find the right words. "I want to," she began. "I really, really do. I want to be with you all the time but...I just don't think I am ready. I feel like..."

"There's someone else?" he asked gently.

Taryn shrugged her shoulders. "How could there be?"

Nobody was better for her than Matt. Nobody loved her more; she didn't love anyone more. And there was chemistry between them. It wasn't just a case of friendship. There were times when she thought she'd have trouble breathing without him near. She could not even stand the idea of a life that didn't involve him. Since Andrew had died...

And that was it. Since Andrew died. She'd been happy with Andrew. Happy in a different way than she was with Matt. She could never explain that to him. How could she tell him that she felt like someone else was out there, that her story was not meant to end with him? Her feelings were based on nothing rational. Every reasonable bone in her body screamed at her to drop everything and go with him, to run, run, RUN!

And then there was that one little fragment, that one tiny tinge, that told her to wait. It whispered it. Just wait.

"I know this song," Matt smiled abruptly, the clouds passing from his face. His ability to bounce back with ease was something Taryn envied. "It's Chicago. My mom had this album."

"Mine too," Taryn bobbed her head in agreement. "One of the few things that made my otherwise vanilla mother interesting. She used to play it in the car, on the cassette player. Do you think our kids will even know what a cassette is?"

They both ignored the fact that she'd used the hypothetical "our kids."

To her surprise, Matt began singing along with it, his baritone voice smooth and strong. He didn't sing often, but his voice was a nice one. But Taryn's face turned crimson when the irony of the lyrics struck her. A man and woman, going separate ways, trying to move on with their lives without each other...not wanting the other to see them upset.

Still, it was a catchy tune and Taryn hummed along with him until they were both smiling at each other and snickering, too caught in the silly moment of irony to be grieved.

All at once, the color drained from Matt's face. "Taryn–"

As though they shared the same mind, she was struck at once by the implication of his thoughts. "Oh my–"

"How did we–"

"Miss that?" she finished for him.

Both jumped up from the table and sprinted to the jukebox. Using her finger, Taryn eagerly scanned down the list of tracks until they found the one playing over the speakers.

"'Look Away,'" she read excitedly. "That is the title."

"The graffiti. They're song titles," Matt swore, slapping his thigh. "It's a song title."

"Oh my God," Taryn laughed, on the verge of mania. "Lucy stood there and talked to me about songs and had this big speech about if I'd ever hated one nobody else liked and–okay, it doesn't really matter. The fact is, I thought she was using some metaphor or something. She may have actually been talking about a song!"

"How literal of her," Matt beamed.

"We've got to reassess this," Taryn shouted out with excitement, slapping her hands together. "Let's get that pizza to go."

"Good thing you played that track," Matt proclaimed over his shoulder as he marched up to the register to change their order.

Taryn was left standing by the jukebox, her hand still flat on the glass.

"But I didn't," she whispered.

TWENTY-FOUR

"*So one more time,*" Taryn said before stuffing her mouth with another bite. "Tell me what we've got so far."

"Two song titles," Matt replied. "Maybe three. We have 'Friend,' which we determined is meant to be the James Taylor song. 'Look Away' which is, of course, the Chicago song. 'Haunting.' Which you think is from 'The Bluest Eyes in Texas', given Lucy's reaction to the song."

"And the fact that it says 'Haunting'. And I've heard it in the school. And in my dreams..."

"That first one doesn't make much sense in the context of everything else," Taryn pointed out through a mouthful of pepperoni.

"None of this makes sense in a context of anything. How can we be sure that these aren't just random song titles spray painted on the walls?" Matt muttered.

"We know they have to mean something," Taryn protested. "They're all from the same year, for one thing. And it's roughly the same year we've narrowed this bad thing down to."

"So who did this? Lucy? The ghosts?"

Matt shrugged in frustration. "Beats the hell out of me."

"Okay, so does anything stand out?"

"'You've Got a Friend.' That one was written on the floor. A little hard to make out."

Taryn nodded. "Yep. And it's the one written in the bright blue paint. The only one written in blue."

"So we have to consider the fact that these might not be drafted by the same person," Matt added.

"Why so?"

"All the others are painted on the wall, in red. This one is on the floor, in blue. And it's from an entirely different decade. So unless there is some symbolism there..."

"Ah, I got you! I am so glad you're here."

"Me too," Matt sent her an angelic smile from the other side of the bed.

"Let's do this full time," Taryn exclaimed, surprising herself. "Just quit your job at NASA, move up to New Hampshire with me, and we'll solve mysteries!"

"Just like Scooby and Shaggy," Matt grinned, giving her a wink.

"So what's our theme here?" Taryn asked. "Are these all songs that Lucy hates?"

"They're definitely a message," Matt said slowly. "Dang it. For a minute there something came to me, but then I lost it. Let me see that photo album again."

Taryn dug it out of the nightstand and crawled over to him with it. Sitting on his lap, they opened it together and began flipping through the pages for the umpteenth time.

"This one is cute," Taryn said, pointing to a shot of a young Jamey standing in the middle of the gym, holding onto a basketball. He looked about eight years old.

"And there's our criminal," Matt added, pointing to the picture right below it.

It was hard to believe that the young girl with pigtails, holding tightly to the red pompoms in her hands, would one day be on trial for murder. "Hard to believe Lucy Dawson was ever a cheerleader."

"You like her, don't you?" Matt asked.

Taryn nodded. "I do. I guess I see something of me in her. She's quiet; she keeps to herself. Didn't have a lot of friends when she was younger. Has lost most of the people in her life. I don't know. There's something there. Something almost maternal. You wouldn't know it right at first, but I get a good vibe."

"So you don't think she did it?"

"No," Taryn replied. "I believe she did it. I just don't think it's because she's a murderer."

"Do you know this game?" Matt asked. "I earmarked this because I wanted to ask you. I don't recognize it."

Taryn stretched her body out to get a better look. The children were lined up on one side of the gym. In their hands they held the yellow, Styrofoam balls. Their faces were gleeful, excited. Some had their arms raised, prepared for battle. She couldn't see what they were preparing to throw the balls at.

"A kind of Dodgeball I guess," she shrugged. "I don't recognize it but I did see one of those balls in the storage closet."

"The kids look so happy in these," Matt said, indicating a group shot of Mr. Scott's class on the playground. They all stood around a drawing on the concrete. The teacher himself was covered in multi-colored chalk dust, his tanned skin now gaudy rainbow streaks. The kids grouped around him and clung to him; some looked at him adoringly, and they all laughed like they were having the best times of their lives.

"As opposed to these kids," Taryn pointed to the next page, a picture of Mrs. Evan's class. She sat tall and erect on a stool in front of her classroom. The two small windows behind her held gingham curtains, one of the only spots of color in the room. She balanced a guitar in her lap and the photographer had caught her in mid-strum.

Although there were also children grouped around her, these kids wore scowls, not smiles. One was even glaring at his teacher, a far cry from the adoring smiles worn on the previous page. And yes, there was fear. You could almost smell it, even from where Taryn and Matt sat. The whole setup appeared very rigid, almost Victorian. Taryn laughed in spite of herself.

"Do you think she was really that bad?" Matt asked.

"Well, her reviews have not been stellar."

"What has Lucy said about her?"

Taryn thought about it before answering. "You know, Lucy actually hasn't said anything at all about the teachers. I don't know how I missed that. Oh well. I will go back. I am armed with much more information this time around."

"This little boy, right here," Matt indicated to a tow-headed kid sitting at a desk with a white, plastic recorder in his hand. "He reminds me of me a little bit."

The boy's somber expression, the tufts of hair hanging down into his eyes. He wasn't cracking a smile, but there was something going on behind his eyes, that was evident even from the camera. Taryn also thought of Matt when she looked at him.

"Aw, he's a cutie. Wonder who he is?"

Matt slipped his finger behind the plastic sheet and gently pulled the photo free. "Let's see..." Turning it over, he read the inscription aloud. "Ethan Wayne, October open house."

Matt turned the photo back over and carefully re-inserted it. Taryn could feel him shaking slightly. She leaned back into him and snuggled against his chest.

Ethan Wayne. Death by self-inflicted gunshot wound, only ten years after that photo.

These had been children, real children. And someone had failed them. Whether Lucy wanted her help or not, Taryn was going to find the answers.

* * *

THE FEAR THAT scorched through her body burned. She could actually feel her insides blister. She reached up and brushed a droplet of sweat from her forehead and was shocked at the heat on her face. She couldn't ever remember feeling that hot, not even when she had chicken pox as a little kid.

The hard chair under her was uncomfortable but she dared not wiggle and draw attention to herself. Instead, she brought the book in her hand closer to her face and stared intently at the words before her. She'd read them a dozen times already and hadn't retained a single sentence.

She *wanted* to look up. The last time she'd done it, however, a giggle had escaped. She didn't understand the giggle, was angry at herself for letting it bubble to her surface. She didn't find anything funny. Why was laughter swilling inside her, along with the anger and fear?

Nothing will happen to me; nothing will happen to me, she chanted inside. She knew that for a fact. It was a hard, cold truth that did little to soothe her. Indeed, it made her feel worse—if that was possible.

It would be lunchtime soon. From the corner of her eye she could glance down at her My Little Pony watch, a Christmas present from her granny, and see the time. In just two more minutes they'd all be lining up and filing away. Good girls and boys.

Stop it, she scolded herself. And then, *please don't laugh, please don't laugh...*

A sound then, a soft thud that caught her off guard. On reflex, she did look up now. The eyes that stared back at her were only a few feet away. Nothing came between the two of them. Dull, soulless eyes that didn't even see her.

The giggle did escape then. She hated herself for it.

If there was a God, then why wasn't she dead?

TWENTY-FIVE

aryn hated leaving Matt behind at the motel, especially considering there wasn't much for him to see or do there, but he'd been asleep when she left. Matt had tossed and turned all night; it was better to let him rest. He'd be leaving the next day. She didn't want to return him in worse shape than she'd collected him.

Still, Taryn wasn't thrilled at being at the school alone. The dream she'd had the night before was still with her, and it wasn't one she enjoyed hanging over her head.

"I can't make heads nor tails of what's going on here," she complained to Miss Dixie. "And the only person who could tell me won't."

She contemplated going to Jamey or back to Misty but didn't feel like either one of them would open up to her. Indeed, Misty appeared to have nothing but good memories of her time at Muddy Creek. She'd have to get through Heather to get to Jamey and Taryn couldn't be sure that gatekeeper would hand over the key. She knew a possessive, and protective, woman she saw one.

Taryn was one.

"Maybe it is a malice over the school," Taryn whispered as she set up her easel and started unpacking her paints. "Wickedness. It might not have anything to do with the school or the people, but the place."

So what had happened? Had Lucy been possessed to try to burn it down? Had she not known there were going to be people inside?

No, she'd known. The building had been empty for twenty years. She'd had plenty of opportunities to destroy it. She only lived a few hundred yards behind it. No, she'd waited until a homecoming, a school reunion.

Taryn hummed to herself. Haunted by the bluest eyes in Texas...She hummed as she walked, as she searched. What about that song had troubled Lucy? What about it was so significant that she, or someone, had taken the time to write it in the school?

It had been in the newspaper that former staff members would be taking a "field trip" from the high school to the old elementary school during the reunion. Lucy had planned for it. The paper had even mentioned the names of the six faculty and staff members that would be riding one of the old school buses to the site. Lucy had known. She'd known what she was doing. She'd premeditated it.

Taryn shook her head and tried to clear her mind. She needed to focus on her painting. It would be finished within the week and then she'd be gone. On to the next adventure and job. Only, without closure to this one, she might not truly be moving on at all.

For a moment Taryn let herself forget about the worries that plagued her and, instead, absorbed herself in her painting. It was looking good if she did have to say so herself. The school had never looked better. Well, perhaps when it was first built, but it certainly hadn't looked better in a very long time. And it wasn't pink in her painting, either. (Although, truth be known, she was kind of fond of the acid pink walls. They added color to an otherwise dismal place.)

"I tried to like you," she insisted as she dipped her brush in green and worked in some shading on the landscaping at the front entrance. "I wanted to like you."

But she hadn't. From the moment she'd pulled up to the school, Taryn had been uneasy.

How could it be that this place, which had apparently brought joy to hundreds of children over the years, could make her feel so disconcerted?

"It's not a good place," she muttered. "It's not."

When the clatter came this time, Taryn tossed down her paintbrush and began marching towards the building with something not unlike anger.

"I am going to do this, and I will not be scared," she cried.

She slipped through the back entrance with ease; she was becoming an old pro at getting in and out of the school at a rapid pace. This time, however, she didn't pause to wonder about which direction she should go in. She went straight to Classroom Number Five. Mrs. Evans' room.

Now she stood in the doorway and surveyed the shambles. "What do you want?" she screamed. "Who are you? Mrs. Evans, what did you do?"

"Taryn." The voice was soft, but commanding. Taryn startled at the sound and turned quickly in the direction it came from. It came from the principal's office. "Taryn," it came again, this time with more urgency.

The cry that rose in Taryn's throat was unavoidable. "Sarah," she sobbed as she sprinted towards the little office. "Sarah, wait! Don't go anywhere!"

Taryn was not capable of rational thought as she hurried through the door and whirled around the small room, spinning around and around in circles, looking for one of the few people in her life who had truly loved her. Her parents had liked her, that was true, but they'd never shown her love. Distance, coolness, aloofness. That's what she'd received from them. The love was all from her grandmother and aunt. And now they were gone. Gone with Andrew. She was all alone, except for Matt.

"Aunt Sarah!" Taryn wept again. "Please, I need help. Tell me what to do!"

But the room was quiet. If Sarah had been there, she was gone now. Taryn couldn't feel a single ounce of energy that she couldn't see.

Feeling completely defeated and crushed, Taryn dropped to her knees and whimpered, the tears hot and searing on her cheeks. She didn't let out dainty, feminine cries; these were gutted, wretched sounds that echoed up and down the hall.

She cried for herself, cried for Matt and what she knew she could never give him, cried for Andrew, cried for her aunt who had died alone in the woods, cried for the poor kids in Lucy's class who had never had real chances to be adults before passing away...she even shed tears for the dead deer she'd seen on the side of the road on her drive over there. She let it all out.

Then, when she was finished, she stood. Dry-eyed now, and feeling raw yet somewhat stronger, she started for the door.

And watched in horror as it slammed shut in front of her. "Hey, what's going on?" she demanded.

When Taryn reached for the knob, however, it turned bright red and burned her hand. She pulled back, shocked by the blisters that were already starting to form through the broken skin.

"Wha—"

The clatter. At first, she thought it was coming from across the hall, from the storage closet. But then Taryn realized that it wasn't from the closet at all, but from the classroom behind it. She didn't have to look to know that things were once again flying around the room, soaring through the air as though the objects had wings of their own.

Scared and nervous, Taryn slowly backed up to the desk until her bottom hit the edge of it. There was no window in the door, but she didn't have to look to know what was going on; the noise was loud enough.

It sounded as though a tornado was ripping through the building. The din was terrific. Glass broke, shards scattered. Chairs crashed against walls and fractured into pieces. Then there was a popping sound, soft "thuds" that reminded Taryn of guns with their silencer on.

"Good Lord," she whispered. Was someone getting shot?

No, not that kind of sound. But bad.

She stood there and listened until it was over. It didn't last more than a minute or two, but it was long enough. Her ears rang from the racket, and she rubbed at them vigorously, trying to stop the ringing.

"Taryn," the voice behind her spoke again. Taryn straightened tall but did not turn around. She wouldn't risk the hope again.

"Aunt Sarah?" she asked hesitantly.

As though in answer, the Chicago song from the jukebox began ringing out from down the hall. "Look Away" drifted into the office, a peace offering for what had just transpired. The voice was not that of the famous band, but of the teacher. Just a soft, beautiful sound after the uproar she'd just experienced was jarring.

Taryn watched as the redness faded from the door knob. She could leave if she wanted but without warning, she could suddenly feel her aunt's unhappiness closing in around her. They shared that moment of sorrow together as Taryn realized what her aunt had wanted to tell her.

Whatever had happened in that school, the principal had known about it. She couldn't have not known. She'd heard everything that went on. And what had she done? Ignored it? Looked the other way? Was it really that literal?

Her aunt had been a principal, a beloved head of school. She'd protected her students, protected everyone she'd known. And now, in death, she'd used one of her last wild cards up her sleeve to show Taryn that not only was she not alone, but that someone had failed those children in the worst way.

"You didn't fail me, Aunt Sarah," Taryn murmured. "Not ever."

Taryn stayed until the song was over and then she quietly slipped from the office. One more picture of the classroom and she was out.

* * *

SHE FINISHED HER WORK in silence; she didn't even turn her music on. The din in her mind was enough to supersede the quietness. She had enough of a racket going on inside of her, didn't need to add more.

Three hours later Taryn rinsed her brushes with bottled water, carefully wrapped up her canvases, and stored everything in the back of her car. She was ready to get back to her room, back to Matt.

But before she drove away, Taryn paused and really studied the building opposite her. For the first time since her first day, she took a good, long look at what stood before her. The weeds pushing through the cracks in the concrete, the vines wrapping themselves around and within the windows. The damaged roof, the crumbling plaster. The mold. Festering rot.

"Like a person," she whispered aloud. "You couldn't hide, could you?"

The school did not reply, but it was listening.

"All of those years you were a stately building, a solid edifice of learning. You wore your stout cinderblocks and sparkling windows with pride. But then, little by little, you began crumbling. This, this *ugliness* that's here now...it was here all along. *This* is what you were hiding beneath the layers of new paint and Windex and fresh asphalt. Decay and corrosion. Just like a person. Like someone who tries to hide their real selves behind a glossy, polished façade. Until that becomes rancid, too, and you're left with nothing but the putrefaction underneath. You can't hide forever."

Taryn turned then and slipped inside her car.

137

"You can't hide forever," she repeated. "And you won't."

TWENTY-SIX

You sure you feel like going out? You've had a long day."

As though she needed to be reminded. "No, I'm good," she smiled. "Besides, it's your last night. Let's get out of here."

Their plan was to drive to the next county over. They'd heard of a mom 'n pop steakhouse that apparently had fantastic barbecue ribs. Matt was all about the ribs.

"Good, because I was going a little stir crazy in here," Matt admitted. "I got caught up on my emails, took a walk, grabbed some lunch, and sat outside and read for about an hour. Wasn't sure where else to go with the day after that."

"It sounds kind of nice to me," Taryn told him. As she talked, she slipped out of her jeans and sweatshirt and tried on a lightweight floral dress. The loose-fitting cardigan she layered over it would help with the chill. She'd bought both from the thrift store in town. It had gotten a lot of her business since the vandalism. The vandalism that the motel and police had never gotten a lead on.

"Your day does a little more eventful than mine. You want to tell me anything else about it?"

Taryn shook her head. "I don't think so. I'm feeling kind of fragile at the moment. I have a million thoughts rushing through my head. Would kind of like to take my mind off of it."

Matt came up behind her and tugged her hair free of her collar. Using his hand, he smoothed her curls over her shoulders and tucked one long, loose over behind her ear. "Pretty girl," he said.

She stood on her tiptoes and kissed him on the nose. "I felt my aunt today. It was nice. I don't think I'll see her again. But that was fun while it lasted."

"What makes you think you won't see her again?"

"Just a feeling," Taryn replied.

Matt wrapped his arms around her and drew her into him. "Well, I've learned that those are usually pretty accurate."

They stood there in a kind of half-dance, just leaning into one another, and might have remained for awhile except the knock on the door interrupted them.

"I'll get it," Taryn said. "Might be Sandy for that album."

But it wasn't; it was Frieda.

"Hey Taryn," she said. She stood in the doorway and leaned against the knob. Her hair was disheveled and her clothes baggy. It appeared as though she'd lost some weight. The trial had been hard on everyone. She no longer heard the rowdy reporters laughing and socializing as much in the evening. Now they were much more subdued. The reality of the situation was closing in on them. Most were ready to return home to husbands, wives, kids, and their regular baristas.

"Hey, how's it going?"

"It's going," she replied curtly. Taryn and Matt had watched her early on her show. She'd been fired up about something one of her was saying. Her face had never been redder with anger. "You coming back to hang with us in the courtroom?"

"Probably," she said. "I need to finish my real job first. But I'd like to support Lucy."

Frieda cocked an eyebrow and studied her. "Huh. So you don't think she did it?"

"She did it. But I am not judging until I know why."

Frieda chuckled. "So killing seven people is perfectly acceptable as long as you have a good reason?"

Something about her words sent a jolt through Taryn. She'd had the same one earlier that day, at the school. Now, Taryn tried to hold onto the feeling, the little spark. There was something about it that she was meant to remember. It slipped through her mind as soon as it entered, however. Maybe it would come back.

"I knocked on your door because, uh, there might be a little problem."

"Yeah, what's that?"

"That little red number out there yours?"

Concerned, Taryn walked over to where he stood. "Under the streetlamp? Yeah, why?"

Frieda shook his head and grimaced. "Someone did a real number on it."

"What!?"

Taryn was flying out the door before she could finish her thought.

Her car was only about five yards away and parked right under the glaring light. It was in the well-lit part of the parking lot, something her father had told her to ensure when she was alone. And, sure enough, as Frieda had said—someone had done a real number on it.

It was keyed from the rear tire all the way to the front grate. Long, deep marks that, from a distance, could be racing lines. To make matters worse, if that were possible, they'd also dumped a bucket (or something) of white paint right on top. It had spilled down owner the front and sides, peppering her windshield and hood to that it appeared her car had been parked under a tree filled with infuriated birds.

"Oh my God!" Taryn cried. She began stomping her foot, having a tantrum right there in the middle of the parking lot. "No, no, NO!" she wailed with each stamp.

Matt, who had come running out behind her, grabbed her by the arm. "We'll fix it," he soothed her. "Don't worry. I'll stay an extra day. I'll get it done."

"Bastards!" she seethed. "Who did it, Frieda? Do you know?"

Frieda shook her head, looking sheepish. "I literally just got here. Saw this and came straight to your door."

"I've only been home for half an hour," she muttered. "They worked fast. Has this happened to anyone else?"

"Not that I know of," she replied.

"Taryn? Taryn, is everything okay?"

She recognized the voice without looking up. A voice that smooth, that practiced-polite, could only come from Heather.

"Someone damaged my car," Taryn said, pointing at the damage.

Heather walked across the parking lot to where Taryn stood. When she saw the vehicle, she grimaced. Taryn was too busy noticing the woman next to her, though, to pay attention to the blond beauty. Louellen, from the PTA meeting, accompanied Heather that night. Taryn didn't even know they were friends, although she assumed everyone probably knew who Heather and Jamey were.

Louellen did not share the same look of concern and disbelief that her friend wore. In fact, it might have been Taryn's imagination, but she thought she might even look...pleased.

"Is there anything I can do?" Heather asked. "Call someone?"

"We'll get it taken care of," Matt said smoothly. "Thank you, though."

Taryn nodded numbly and thanked the women as they walked away. When they were out of earshot, she turned back to Matt and Frieda.

"Did you all notice anything odd about that that?" she asked.

Matt shook his head. "Did I miss something?"

Frieda slapped him on the back while shaking her head in amazement at Taryn. "I saw it, buddy. You are talking about the splotches of white paint on the ugly one's shoes, right?"

TWENTY-SEVEN

"You sure you're going to be okay?"

"You sure you're going to be okay?"

"I'll be fine," Taryn assured him. "They're coming to get my car this afternoon. Going to give it a whole new paint job."

"I didn't mind paying for it, you know."

"I know." Taryn leaned into Matt and rubbed her head against his arm. "And thank you. But I can afford it now. I'm working in Muddy Creek, after all. Bringing in the big bucks!"

"Well, I am glad I was at least able to get you the rental for a few days."

And she'd let him do that. Because Matt liked feeling useful. She had also let him take her out for breakfast before they took off to the airport. Now, as they walked back to the motel, hand-in-hand, she held onto him and moved slowly. They still had some time, and she wasn't ready to let him go.

"I can stay another day or two if you need me to," he reminded her.

"No, I can't be the one responsible for you missing so much work," she said.

"I can quit my job, Taryn, and go with you." He stopped walking and turned her to face him. In the early morning light, his face looked older. He'd become a man somewhere along the way. She didn't remember that happening and yet, there he was.

"I can't be the one responsible for you giving up your dreams," she said.

"I have new dreams." He had both hands on her shoulders, and now he gripped them tightly, willing her to take him seriously. "I want to do this."

"I can't, Matt," she said with sadness. "I can't do that to you. I can't do that to me. I've known you most of your life. You're one of the few people in the world that're living their dreams. If I was even partly responsible for you not doing that anymore...I couldn't take it. I just couldn't. I couldn't see that happen to you."

"We've got to do something," he pleaded. "Because of this? It isn't working. I need more of you."

"You've had plenty of me," she joked, but he didn't smile.

"I promise, Matt, we'll figure something out. I'll straighten myself up, and we'll do what we need to do. But not right now. Not right this minute. I need to get myself sorted first."

Matt sighed and let her go. He didn't begin walking right away, however. Instead, he turned and looked up and down Main Street. "Ever get jealous of these people?" he asked.

"What people?" There wasn't anyone out on the street that early. Not yet. They'd come in about an hour.

"The ones who can live here, have ordinary lives with children and houses and dogs and family vacations to Pigeon Forge and RVs when they retire. And they make it work because they enjoy it." Matt rarely looked or spoke so seriously. Taryn found it unnerving.

"Sometimes," she admitted. "I am envious of those whose dreams feel smaller than mine. I am envious of those who are easily satisfied." Because she, Taryn Magill, rarely felt satisfied. She constantly felt as though she were reaching for the next big ring on the ladder, following stars she could never reach. And hell, Matt actually DID reach for the stars.

"Don't we deserve some happiness, Taryn?" he asked quietly.

You do, she wanted to respond. But she couldn't. So much to say and she just didn't have the energy to say it.

Instead, she turned and pointed at the house across the street. "There," she said, indicating with her finger. "That's the house where Lukas Monroe lived. Where he was, you know."

Matt grimaced and shook his head. "Poor kid. I just about threw up reading that garbage. You know the father only got five years in prison for what he did? Mother didn't get a thing."

The thought sickened Taryn. She hadn't known that, hadn't done any follow-up. "Do you know what happened to Lucas in the end? Was he okay? I read something about going to live with a cousin or something."

Matt nodded. "Yeah, he was okay for awhile. And then three years later he killed himself. Self-inflicted gunshot wound to the head."

The darkness was everywhere, Taryn realized, if you knew where to find it.

* * *

TARYN HADN'T HAD a smartphone for very long and was still trying to learn how to use it. She had, however, learned how to search for stores with it. It didn't take her long to locate a bookstore at the Huntington Mall.

As Taryn pulled into the huge parking lot, she was frankly surprised that the mall was still standing so many had closed over the past few years, giving way to "town centers" that, to her, looked like a bunch of strip malls connected by green spaces. She'd seen many of the dinosaur carcasses going to waste by the side of the road, everything but tumbleweeds blowing through the empty acres of parking places. Taryn loved to shop, but even she wasn't sorry to see a change in fads where malls were concerned. Something about being inside a building without any windows, unable to tell if it was day or night, while piped-in Muzak tinkered through the speakers depressed her.

The bookstore in the Huntington Mall had what she needed. By the time she checked out she had a stack of Lucy Dawson's bestsellers and three romances. She was on a mission to learn something and entertain herself in the process.

It was too late to go to the school, and she didn't relish the idea of returning to the motel room and sitting around by herself for the rest of the night. Instead, she parked herself inside one of the mall's restaurants and ordered a burger. While she waited, she pulled out the books she'd just bought.

"The Boy in the Tree," "The Girl in the Well," "Avalonia," and "The Light Behind the Door." She'd never heard of the last one but had read the others on at least one occasion.

Lucy's first book was published when she was only twenty years old; Taryn was just fourteen at the time. Technically, she'd been too old to enjoy the books that were marketed at pre-teens. Still, they'd garnered so much media attention that she hadn't been able to ignore them. On one cold, rainy afternoon she'd visited her local library and settled down into a bean bag chair, surrounding herself with copies that were already well-worn. And she'd fallen in love. That was one of the ways her romance with books that weren't necessarily going to get her on the "best read" lists began. Matt was embarrassed by her obsession with Nora Roberts and V.C. Andrews. Taryn did like giving everyone equal opportunity, however–she was just as likely to have a copy of "Great Expectations" on one side of her bed as she was to have "Flowers in the Attic" on the other.

In her defense, while Lucy's books might have been geared towards younger readers, she'd found mature messages within them that were much more prudent to someone of her age.

Reading through the books was a good distraction from thinking about Matt. He hadn't wanted her to go inside the airport with him, had told her it wasn't necessary even when she'd protested, so their rushed goodbye at the curb wasn't exactly fulfilling. She'd see him again soon. As soon as her job ended she'd return home, do laundry and air things out, and then travel to Florida where she'd stay with him for a week or two. That was their routine.

It didn't mean that saying goodbye wasn't difficult.

She would go straight to Florida, but she had a doctor's appointment in Nashville she couldn't miss. Due to her aneurysm and various cardiac issue caused by the connective tissue disorder, Taryn had to have an echocardiogram repeated every six months, and a CT scan each year. She was due for both.

"Avalonia" had always been one of her favorite children's books and now, as she read through it again, she felt herself smiling widely. The tale about the little girl who lived in the mountains and was whisked away to the magical world each night by the winged unicorn hit close to home. As a child who had often felt lonely and out-of-place, Taryn had dreamed of traveling to a place where she was not only accepted, but actually wanted. The magical kingdom of Avalonia, located under the dark waters of Lake Michigan and only accessible by the invisible underwater elevator, was a fantasy she could get behind: miles and miles of book-filled shelves, ethereal music permeating the golden streets, mermaids and fairies soaring through the perfumed air...

Taryn wanted to go now.

In "The Girl in the Well" a nine-year-old child falls into a well on an old farm. For more than a month her friends and family were unable to reach her and provide her with anything she needed. Instead, she became friends with the underground animals that burrowed through the dirt and became her saviors. While the people above her prayed and worried and tried dozens of attempts to free her (all of them outlandish and none of them practical), she took care of herself. She dug out a little house from the packed dirt and drank the nectar from the flowers the little rabbits and moles brought her. She learned to make juice from honeysuckles and to weave together the blades of grass the ants brought her from above to make herself a warm and cozy blanket.

By the time the adults finally rescued her, she was happier than she'd ever been. She hadn't even needed them in the end; she'd tunneled out to the edge of a creek and was able to swim to safety.

"Sad," Taryn murmured to herself.

The last book was not one she was familiar with. She read the title aloud and then opened it, absently picking at the French fries scattered on her plate.

"There was once a little boy, a little boy that lived in a tunnel," she read. "The tunnel was very dark, without any windows. Each day the little boy would wander through the darkness, his hands on the walls, trying to find his way out."

Taryn stopped and looked up. "What the hell is this?" she asked nobody in particular. This was starting like a horror novel, not a children's book.

"He would walk and walk and walk, but he could never see what was in front of him. He'd never seen his face or his hands or his feet. He thought his legs might be purple or even green; only he didn't know what purple or green looked like."

Taryn shuddered, shaking the image from her mind.

"Then, one day, he saw a light at the very end of the tunnel. The light was in the shape of a rectangle. 'It's a door,' he said. 'There's a door at the end, with light. I must go there!'"

Taryn continued to read and grew increasingly uncomfortable as the young boy tried various ways to outsmart the monsters and other things in the dark that kept him from the door. In the end, he made it.

"When he put his hand on the knob and turned it, he was more excited than he'd ever been in his life. Suddenly, his world was filled with light. 'What shall I do first?' he asked himself. 'Should I get ice cream or play in a park or read a book?' But when he saw the mirror in front of him, he knew what he had to do. 'I've never seen myself before,' he cried. 'Now I will finally know how gruesome I am!' When the young boy looked at himself in the mirror, however, he saw that he wasn't green or purple or blue at all. He was not even a monster! He was just a regular little boy. A happy little boy. 'I will never go back into the dark again,' he cried. With that, he closed the door to the dark tunnel and began walking away. With time, he might even forget that tunnel was ever there."

Taryn closed her eyes and rested her head on the illustrated pages. It was not a tunnel, after all, in the book. It was the hallway, the same one from which she, herself, had escaped. The same one she saw in her own dreams.

Lucy was trying to get out of it as well. But she hadn't. She was still in there, still running. The little animals had saved the girl in the well. The winged unicorn had taken the little girl away to Avalonia. The boy had finally found the door in the tunnel. Who had saved *Lucy*?

* * *

SHE HEARD THE CRYING before she saw the source.

Taryn needed caffeine in the worst way. Luckily, Matt had left her a pile of change for the vending machine and now she grabbed a handful of it and went in search of a Coke. They had to restock the machines every day, just to keep up with the demand of the motel's guests. When she heard the sobbing, however, she paused.

A cluster of picnic tables was located behind the motel. They overlooked the stream. Even though it was late, Taryn followed them now. The crying was female, and it was human. This was no ghost.

Taryn was shocked to find herself come face-to-face with Frieda Bowen. No makeup, matted hair, and in her pajamas. And crying like her heart was breaking.

"Hey, are you okay?"

Frieda looked up and for a moment managed to look embarrassed but when she saw it was Taryn she sniffed and wiped at her eyes with the back of her hand. "I'm sorry," she apologized. "You want to sit?"

Taryn nodded and hoisted herself up on the table next to Frieda. "What's going on?"

Friday sniffed again. "I don't know if you watch my show but Louisa Rothburger, that little girl in Florida who was kidnapped? They found her body today. Think she's been dead the whole time."

Taryn had seen Frieda on her show almost every night for a week, bringing on witness after witness in that case. Yelling at them. Demanding answers from them. Almost bringing them to tears. People in the press had called her horrible things. A monster. A barracuda without feelings. Badgering the victims.

And now, here she was, crying by herself behind a motel for the loss of the six-year-old she'd been trying to find answers for.

"These kids," Frieda cried, "some of them don't have advocates. When I started doing this, it was to give them a voice. To help them. But I just don't know how much more I can take."

Taryn nodded. She understood.

"It just...it's taking the life out of me. Taking on other people's sadness."

Taryn could understand that as well.

Frieda brushed a clump of hair out of her face and sighed. "I miss my kids. They're back home with my husband. They don't know what I do, you know? They know Mommy helps other kids, but they don't know the real story. I want to keep that from them. When I'm with them, I am just Mommy. We go to the zoo, get ice cream...but sometimes I look at them and I see what the world is, and I don't want to let go. I am afraid for them."

"I would be as well," Taryn agreed.

"Did you know about Lukas Monroe?" Frieda asked.

"Not until I got here," Taryn replied.

"Neither did I. To think something like that was happening and it didn't even make the news. Nobody cared. Everyone failed him. The school system failed him. The neighbors failed him. His friends' parents failed him. They say he'd been showing signs of abuse for years and nobody said anything. Who was helping him? What about all these kids were hurt and nobody is there for them? Nobody got them justice." Frieda sighed and bowed her head. "I am not doing enough. Sometimes this world just hurts too much."

TWENTY-EIGHT

*T*aryn *rolled around in her sleep*, groaning and crying out into the stuffy room. She was back in the circle of chairs again. The monster danced in the middle, shards of light that wouldn't stand still. The bouquet of flowers was on her desk this time, right in front of her. She could smell them, but she kept them at arm's length, incapable of touching them.

Sickness grew in her belly. She gagged and retched and tried to keep from vomiting, but there were too many emotions running through her mind. Her little body was too small to handle them.

When Taryn woke, her sheets were covered in a filmy vomit.

"Oh, damn," she cried.

Taryn flipped on the light and struggled to get out of bed without making a bigger mess. She was just about to strip the sheets and lay her blanket down on the mattress when her phone rang. It was Matt. Not only was it a ringtone, this time Roby Orbison's "Claudette," but it was 3:15 am. Nobody else would dare call her at that hour. (Not that her phone suffered from incessant calls to begin with.)

"Hey Matt," Taryn started as she gave her fitted sheet a pull. "I just had a nightmare and woke up. Threw up on myself. What's—"

"It wasn't seven!" Matt cried, cutting her off.

"Huh?" Taryn paused, the dirty sheets wadded up in her hands.

"You were saying something about the article earlier, about it being seven people," he said again, more calmly. "But it wasn't meant to be seven. The report said six, six people."

Taryn tossed the sheets down on the floor and scrambled to her laptop. Within seconds she'd pulled up the pictures and was sifting through them. "Well I'll be damned," she said. "How did I miss that?"

"We both missed it," Matt said. "I read it the other way, too."

Now that she was looking at the article, she felt silly. "So Lucy did plan it, but one of them was an accident. They weren't meant to be there," Matt said.

"When I was trapped in that office and heard the stuff coming from down the hallway, that was Sarah trying to tell me something," Taryn said, taking a seat in the rickety desk chair. "Maybe something happened at the school but had nothing to

148

do with the teachers there. It was a parent, abuse that the school knew was going on but did nothing about."

"Like Lukas Monroe and his father," Matt added. "What do you know about Lucy's parents?"

"Nothing," Taryn admitted. "Not a thing."

Both were quiet as they contemplated the situation.

"Which one was missing?" Matt asked. "Which one wasn't meant to be there? If we can figure out who the mistake was..."

"Then we can put this to rest," Taryn finished for him.

"Any ideas?"

Taryn allowed everything that had happened to spin through her mind like a movie reel. She watched each scene carefully, quickly analyzed it. "Maybe," she said at last, as something began to dawn on her. But let me marinate on it. I'm going back to the school again tomorrow. I'm armed with more information. I might find out more now."

"You want me to fly back? I don't like the idea of you rooting around in there by yourself," Matt said worriedly.

"I am going to do a cleansing first," Taryn told him. "Do a protection over the school and me. I've learned a few things from past experiences."

"You have the candles and sage?" he asked. "Where did you find those?"

"In Huntington today," Taryn replied with a shrug.

"Wait, you found ritual supplies at a store in Huntington?"

"Naw, at the Halloween super store," Taryn grinned. "Part of their Halloween sale. It's the best time to be a witch in the south."

*   *   *

"I CLEANSE THIS SPACE of all negative energy," Taryn chanted. "I cleanse..."

The milky smoke trailed behind her, rising from the little bundle of herbs like wisps of cotton. She had started at the library and had slowly made her way from one end of the school to the other, leaving behind a stream of sweet-scented smoke.

At the end of the hall a door slammed shut; the impact caused a piece of the roof above her to crumble and slide to the floor at her feet. Taryn jumped back, nearly tripping over an overturned garbage can, but held her ground.

"Bad energy is gone, only good remains. There is good here," she sang out in a loud, clear voice.

Two years ago she wouldn't have imagined doing such a thing. Things had changed a lot.

"Cleanse this school and make it clear, only good is allowed in here."

A window broke. Shards of glass scattered across the tile; she heard them shower upon the floor like rain. Though she closed her eyes and winced, Taryn ignored the sound. She was not going to let whatever was there scare her out. Not again.

Taryn walked backward, keeping her voice steady and carefully watching the floor as she moved, so as not to trip over any animal bones.

"I cleanse you..."

Parallel with the bathroom doors, she stopped. The fetid scent she'd been smelling since she'd come to Muddy Creek was almost overpowering. The women's door looked at her mockingly, daring her to step inside.

If Taryn was going to do this, she was going to do it right.

Taking a nervous gulp, Taryn made a tentative step towards the door and gave it a slight push. It didn't budge. Taryn closed her eyes and winced. She would be okay; she would be okay...

With a mighty heave, she threw her whole body weight into the door. At first, she thought it wasn't going to move again, but then it swung free, tossing her to the floor. As she and the door swung inwards, the rushing water rushed outwards. Taryn landed smack dab in the middle of a stinking, decaying pool of water that came up above her knees.

"Oh my God," she shouted as she sputtered and coughed, trying to rise to her knees. The room smelled like a tomb, a fusion of sewage and death.

Not wanting to stick around any longer, she splashed through the water and ran back outside, her clothing now clinging to her along with the smell.

She would need to bathe for an hour when she got back to the motel.

Shaking and gagging, Taryn rushed down the length of the hallway, putting as much distance between her and the awful bathroom as she could. She would continue to have nightmares about that for weeks to come.

Now, she entered the gym. "Blessings grace this sacred place it, all joy and peace may it embrace."

The gym, at least, remained quiet. Since it might be her last time, though, Taryn decided to take a chance. "Say cheese," she murmured, lifting Miss Dixie from her chest.

The flash of light from her camera had not even dissipated when the cries rang through the room. The sounds of children laughing and screaming shot out like bullets, full-on war cries of play. "Get her!" they called. "Go, go, go!"

Taryn looked but saw nothing. The scene before was still in shambles, still desolate. The only movement was from a lone field mouse that ran around, searching for a long-lost crumb.

But the children didn't stop. She heard a shriek, then a laugh, and then what sounded like a very real sound of fear. "GO, *go*!" someone squealed again.

Taryn looked around in confusion, trying to force the scene she heard to appear before her eyes. But there was nothing.

"What is it?" Taryn demanded.

And then she looked down.

The cries of laughter and sounds of recreation were not coming from the room in which she stood now, but in the one brought to life on her camera.

The power was still on; the lens cap was still open. And the static images on Miss Dixie's LCD screen had come to life.

Taryn raised her camera back up to her eyes and studied the screen with fascination. On the one side of the camera, the scene was bleak. A room full of garbage and debris. Look a few inches back, however, and the same room was bright, cheerful, and had returned to life. A line of children stood in the middle of the floor; yellow Styrofoam balls held high in their hands. Their contorted faces were gleeful but not with happiness. There was something else, something almost ugly. Taryn shrank from the scene when she saw what they were looking at: Lucy Dawson stood against the gym wall, hands covering her face, while her classmates aimed their weapons at her head and stomach, ready to strike. She was the only one on the other side of the line. It was an uneven sixteen against one.

It wasn't the look of fear on Lucy's face that had Taryn almost crumbling to the ground—it was the disappointment and defeat. The wild-eyed rejection was something only a child could convey.

"Those bullies," Taryn sputtered, angered by something she couldn't understand. "She's just a little thing."

Where were the adults? The teachers? Taryn's pictures flipped through a slideshow Miss Dixie had taken on her own accord, the images moving so quickly they flashed before her like an old flip-book movie. Lucy leaned forward and covered her head with one hand while making a feeble attempt to beat off the offending balls with her other one. The other children offered no mercy. As soon as they threw one ball, another one would bounce off the wall, or Lucy herself, and land right back at their feet. With each throw they grew closer and closer until all of Lucy Dawson's little classmates surrounded her and resorted to beating her from all sides, the balls clutched tightly in their little fists.

"Oh no," Taryn cried. "*Oh!*" Feeling utterly helpless to stop what she was seeing, Taryn turned and began to run from the room.

She was barely to the door when the singing came again. The teacher again, singing about being the person's flame—always being there for them and standing strong. Their loud voice filled the hallway and, like the pied piper, drew Taryn forward until she was standing at the door to the classroom.

"Mrs. Evans, you did this," Taryn sniveled, still haunted by what she'd just witnessed. "But why, why did you do it?"

Lucy had known the teachers were going to be there that night; the newspaper had reported that six of them would be riding the bus over...

The names of the teachers listed one-by-one in the paper, all victims of the explosion...

"Has there ever been a song in your life that you just hated?"

The wooden sign above her began swinging back and forth. Taryn placed her hand on it and brought it to a stop. "Mrs. Evans' Classroom," it read.

"Oh." The realization of what she'd missed hit her like a ton of bricks. "Oh!"

She'd been wrong before, but perhaps never as wrong as she was now. Taryn slumped against the door frame and closed her eyes. The music continued to swell, deafening and passionate.

She'd have to see, of course.

"I think I might regret this," Taryn whispered, bringing Miss Dixie up to her cheek.

Three pictures she took in a row, one right after another. When the last one finished, the music came to a screeching halt.

She thought it might be over then. She'd seen and heard everything the school had wanted. But then, as was custom, the racket followed. Taryn knew enough to stay out of the way, to dodge the flying debris. She was ready with her camera this time, however.

With the commotion continuing, she pulled her back and looked at what she'd just taken. It was no longer trash and broken furniture soaring around the room—it was staplers, tape dispensers, and other office supplies.

The last thing she saw was the row of papier-mâché pumpkins, all made by blowing up balloons. Where they'd been drying on the windowsill, they now lay smashed on the floor, flattened by angry stomps.

Taryn knew she shouldn't keep scrolling back. If she stopped now, then she would be innocent. But if she didn't keep going, she'd be just as guilty as though who knew and did nothing.

The first picture quite literally made her sick to her stomach. Once the vomiting started, she didn't think it would ever stop.

TWENTY-NINE

*L*ucy refused to make eye contact with Taryn when she opened her door. Taryn, for her part, didn't say a word. She clasped Miss Dixie in her hands for support, ignoring the droplets of sweat that ran down her arms and pooled on her hands.

Once inside, Taryn lowered herself to an old rocking chair in the corner of the room. Lucy walked over to the fireplace and busied herself with a figurine of a cocker spaniel, after she turned down her stereo. Neither woman spoke.

It was Lucy who broke the silence at last. "So you know, then."

Taryn nodded. She tried to speak, but a cry was caught in her throat. Her words came out as a croak.

"I'm relieved in one sense," Lucy sighed. "Although it's not exactly a happy conversation starter, is it?"

"Who knew?" Taryn was finally able to manage.

"Everyone."

Taryn looked up from Miss Dixie, eyes wide. "Oh, no. That couldn't be."

Lucy slumped down to the settee, resignation filling her face. "Unfortunately, it is true. I wondered at the time, how many did. In the beginning I told myself that nobody could know, that something would've been done if they had. But..."

"Those walls were paper thin," Taryn said. "The other teachers had to hear most of it."

"Yes," Lucy agreed.

"And the other?"

"Everyone," Lucy said sadly.

"My God, Lucy."

Lucy settled back in her seat and closed her eyes. "You know, for years that messed with me a lot. The fact that everyone knew and did nothing about it made me think I was overreacting, that it wasn't that big of a deal. Can you imagine?"

"No," Taryn said. "I can't."

"I suppose I figured that, you know, if people knew and didn't care then it was nothing. Nobody cared. Bad things happen in the world all the time, things that are much worse than what happened to us. I needed to move on. And I tried! Oh, I did. They did us a great disservice by not reacting. But staying quiet."

"By looking away?"

"Yes."

"Does your attorney know?"

"No," Lucy replied. "I couldn't do that."

Taryn straightened, aghast. "Lucy! You have to tell her! You have to!"

"Why?" Lucy spat with a brittle laugh. "For what purpose? So that everyone can see my dirty laundry?"

"The trial will change," Taryn said in a rush. "They won't be trying you the same way. They'll—"

"You think they'll find me mentally deranged or incompetent? Say I was crazy?"

"Well, yeah," Taryn said. "Not crazy, but that you were under duress. I am sure you have something like PTSD or post anxiety or something. I mean, come on. Who wouldn't?"

"I can't," Lucy said stubbornly. "Where I am from you never talked about these things. Not in public, not in front of people you don't know. Not when it's about...Besides, this isn't about me. It's not my story. It's not my right to tell it."

"But Lucy," Taryn tried again, gently, "people might understand why you did what you did. If they knew. You wouldn't be in as much trouble. And it might help others."

Lucy snorted. "Nobody would care about me, they never did."

"They didn't know about you," Taryn pointed out. "Not the ones who mattered. There is a whole other world out there that could help you; that could maybe help—"

Lucy shook her head no. She was going to be stubborn.

"I know another woman, a reporter. She wants to help. She's a champion for children. She could work with you."

As Taryn sat there, she tried to put herself in the other woman's shoes. To walk around all her life, holding onto a secret like that. Not telling anyone. Never talking about it. Taking abuse for it, when she'd done nothing wrong. And then trying to fix it, probably repeatedly, only to come out as a complete failure.

"How did you know?" Lucy asked at last.

"My camera," Taryn pointed.

"Good camera. You know, it was a camera the first time."

"Huh?"

"A parent," Lucy explained. "They were there in the school and got a picture. Things changed then. That's when it stopped. I thought it was over, I was so relieved."

"But it didn't stop."

"The damage had been done," Lucy said sadly. "Already been done. We couldn't change what had happened."

"Who was that parent?"

"One of the little girls. I don't see her anymore."

"Wendy. I have to ask. What happened to Wendy?"

She knew now that it had been Wendy who had sat next to Lucy in that circle, that awful circle Taryn kept dreaming about. Yet she'd felt comforted by Wendy's presence. That part was still troubling her.

"Wendy was my best friend. I loved her," Lucy murmured. "But she could never handle it. For years I thought she'd forgotten. She wouldn't speak of it, wouldn't talk about it. Nobody would. There even came a time when I'd convinced myself I'd made it all up. We didn't speak of it at the time, nor afterward. Perhaps it had all been in my head. And then she spoke..."

"And that night at the party?"

"The song played. 'The Bluest Eyes in Texas.' You close your eyes for a second, and you're still right back there. You can't escape. That song came on, and Wendy went ballistic. I tried to calm her down but I couldn't. I knew she'd hurt herself. I tried to save her, but I couldn't."

Lucy began crying then, soft sobs that barely made a sound. Taryn was immediately on her feet, wrapping her arms around the other woman's shoulders. "You tried to save all of them," Taryn said, crying along with her. "But who tried to save *you*? Who tried to save Lucy?"

* * *

THE WOMAN ON THE OTHER end of the line had a harsh, impatient voice that grated. She clearly had no time to speak to Taryn, but Taryn didn't let that thwart her efforts.

"Hi, I know you don't know me, but my name is Taryn Magill and I am a friend of Lucy Dawson's," she said brightly.

The curve ahead was a sharp one, and Taryn took it too fast on two wheels. She needed to slow down, needed to pull over. But she was too wound-up to stop. She had to make the call now, couldn't wait.

"Yes." It was not a question. This woman was obviously not going to encourage the conversation.

"Listen, I know you're busy but I need to talk to you. I have information that's going to affect the entire case. I promise."

"You've got thirty seconds," the other woman barked.

Geeze, Taryn thought, *considering your weak witness lineup, seems you'd be happy to talk to someone else.*

Instead, though, she rattled off the condensed version of what she knew. When she finished, the other end of the line was so quiet she thought she'd dropped the call.

Then, "Are you serious? Is this a joke?"

"No joke, ma'am," she replied.

"Do you have any proof?"

"Yes. And we can get more. There were witnesses."

"Holy mother of God, I should have suspected," the attorney exhaled loudly. "Can you meet me in fifteen minutes downtown? The fried chicken place?"

Taryn hung up as soon as she pulled into her motel's parking lot. She only had a few minutes to run inside, grab the photo album Misty had loaned her, and go back out.

Frieda was walking past her door when Taryn reached it. "Frieda!" she called, stopping him in his tracks.

"Hey, what's up? Get your car fixed?"

"More about that later," she seethed, thinking of Heather and Louellen. "In the meantime, how would you like to crack a big story?"

"How big?" she asked, raising his eyebrows.

"The biggest."

"Example?"

"Motive?"

Her smile widened. "You're on! When?"

"First thing in the morning. Meet me for breakfast."

Lucy's permission had been soft. She was still unconvinced; Taryn knew she might ending up hate her. The whole town was probably going to hate her, Taryn, by the time it was said and done and maybe even Lucy. Lucy was right–people were funny about these things. Many would say this was something that should have remained buried, should never have seen the light of day. Too much time had passed. It could only hurt those involved.

But, this time, Taryn was going to do the right thing. It might be a catastrophe. But Lucy deserved it, not to mention the others.

THIRTY

Does she know you're here?"

Taryn shook her head no. "She didn't want to talk about it."

"I can see why." Roxanne Martin, defense attorney, took a long drag of her cigarette and blew smoke in Taryn's face at one of the last places in the country that didn't adhere to any kind of ban (the restaurant, not the county). "You know what this is going to do."

The truth was, she didn't know what it would do. "I'm not sure."

"This isn't just Lucy's life we're talking about here. Look, I like Lucy. I always figured there was something, you know? And hell, in her place, I might have done it a long time ago. But that doesn't excuse the fact that she killed people and now she's dragging half the town down with her."

"Yeah."

"And the embarrassment."

"I'm worried about that part," Taryn admitted. "A lot."

"I'm almost certain that is why this was covered up when it was, for as long as it was. The stigma behind it..."

"It's not a simple bullying case," Taryn agreed. "You know, for a long time Lucy convinced herself that it wasn't that bad. That because others ignored it and let it continue, she was being melodramatic or some shit like that."

"Nothing simple about this one, girlfriend," Roxanne snorted. "Listen, do you know where we are?"

Taryn looked around and nodded.

"No, I just don't mean here, I mean here. This area, this part of the country. Where boys will be boys and men will be men. Where the boys are basketball stars and football heroes and the girls win pageants and become cheerleaders and prance across talent show stages in dance numbers. Do you see what I am saying?"

Taryn frowned miserably. "So you think..."

"I think it's unfair, but these things are not handled the same way. And that will cause problems."

"But if I was a parent," Taryn interjected.

"Damn right," Roxanne agreed, slamming her fist on the table. "If it were my child, blood would spill. But we have to think about these kids, about what it will do to their lives."

"So you won't go forward with it?"

Taryn felt her heart sinking to the pit of her stomach. She hadn't counted on that.

"Naw," Roxanne sighed. "I'll give it a shot. But he might not talk to me, you realize. Just give me what you have."

Taryn reached into her purse, pulled out the two halves of the picture, and slid it towards the other woman. "If you ever want to see my camera, I can show you the rest."

Roxanne took the pieces and studied them. Her eyes clouded over, and she gave an involuntary shake. "Honey, I don't think I'll ever be ready to see *that*."

* * *

SHE DIDN'T KNOW what to do. For over an hour Taryn had walked around town, stopping at the empty storefronts and looking inside, trying to imagine what the town had once looked like, back when it had been active and thriving. She tried to imagine what it could look like, with local artisans set up with demonstrations and musicians strumming on stages of small theaters, bringing the town back to life.

Did she do something wrong? Was this just going to perpetuate the stereotype? Bring more negative attention to an area that had already seen more than its fair share of it?

But it wasn't the *town's* fault.

"Will people see beyond where this took place and look at it for what it really was?" Taryn asked a lamppost. "Or are they going to look at it and laugh, just one more stupid thing from the crazy rednecks..."

She didn't want to be a part of that.

When her feet and heart were hurting equally, she returned to the motel. Everyone had apparently turned in for the night; the parking lot was quiet.

Taryn had only just put the key into her door when it was suddenly jerked open from the other side, the movement sending her flying into the middle of the floor. "Wha–"

In the glow of the stark light bulb, Heather Winters loomed above her, her face stamped with anger and hurt. With her wild eyes, disheveled hair standing out in every direction, and bright lipstick smeared across her cheek she looked far from beautiful–she looked insane.

Taryn scampered to her feet and began backing back towards the door, trying to put distance between her and the woman who raged before her. "Heather, calm down," she began. "I don't know what you–"

"'Calm down?'" Heather screeched.

Well, Taryn thought, that was clearly the wrong way to start.

"Calm down!? Do you know what you're doing to my family and me!"

Taryn shook her head and held her hands out in defense. "Look, I just talked to the attorney, nobody else. If you go to her then you can talk, tell them what you want them to know. And things might be okay."

"I already talked to that woman," Heather snapped. "She called right after you left. Do you *know* what kind of state my husband is in? Do you *know* how hard I've worked over the past twenty years, since we were teenagers even? How much I have invested in this? In my family's life? Do you know what's going to happen?!"

"Do you know what's going to happen," Taryn countered. "How could you let this stay a secret?"

She didn't appear to have any weapons on her, though Taryn knew an angry woman didn't need more than her words and hands when she was mad enough, so she continued.

"Heather," she whispered, "it wasn't Jamey's fault. You've been a good wife. You've done everything you could. But he needs help."

"I've helped him, haven't I?" she cried. "I made him a life entirely different from the one he'd had so that he could start over and forget. All those nights he couldn't sleep, the drinking, the other girls to prove..." Her voice broke then, and it was she who fell to the floor now, crying with her entire body.

"Do you want it to happen to someone else?"

"It can't now," Heather hiccupped. "Lucy took care of that. At least that's one thing she did right."

Taryn sank to her knees beside her and awkwardly patted Heather on her back. "And my car? Why did you hurt my car?"

Heather took a momentary reprieve and looked up at Taryn through heavily mascaraed eyes. "I didn't hurt your car," she sniffed. "Lou and I had just come from supper; that's all. We meet once a week. We're on a committee."

"But–"

"The worst thing I've done is the fire."

"But," Taryn said, confused, "Lucy is the one who started the fire."

"Not that one. Carmie's house, Jamey's mom's place. He hated that old trailer. It reminded him of everything. She was a hoarder, wouldn't get rid of crap. She kept everything from his childhood. It was like a tomb in there. Every time he walked inside he'd come back home, broken for weeks. It was a cleansing, getting rid of all of it." She gave a little sob. "I thought it would let us start over."

Taryn nodding, beginning to understand. "Not that much different than what Lucy did."

"No, not much," Heather sniffed again.

"Heather!"

Jamey stood in the doorframe, his massive shoulders touching both sides. He looked like he'd been running for a very long time. When he saw his wife collapsed on the floor, he lurched and had her engulfed within his arms in seconds. "Oh sweetie," he cooed. "I'm so sorry."

"I'm sorry," she cried, wiping her face on his sleeves. "I was just so angry at her. I thought she could take it back, that nobody would know..."

Taryn looked up at Jamey and bit her lip. "I am so sorry, Jamey. I should have gone to you, first. I was just trying to help Lucy. When I found out..."

"It's okay," he said, "I understand. And, to be honest, it had crossed my mind to say something before. I just didn't know how. It's not exactly something you stand on the street corner and blurt out."

"But why?" Heather asked. "Why put yourself through that? Because of Lucy? Because of what she did?"

"Not just for Lucy," he corrected her. "For all of them."

"Is there anything I can do?" Taryn asked. She'd never seen such miserable looking people.

"Can you be there?" Jamey posed in a small voice. For a second she caught a glimpse of what he must have looked like as a little boy. It only made her only angrier for all of them.

"For you?" she asked, then immediately wondered how he was able to get so many women to do so many different things for him.

"No," he replied, smoothing down the hair on his wife's head. "For her."

Taryn nodded.

THIRTY-ONE

Yor sure you're ready for this?"

Taryn rolled her eyes. "Nobody is going to be ready for this," she assured Frieda. It did not help that even she, the seasoned reporter from the northeast, looked nervous.

"Are they going to talk?"

She allowed Frieda to take her arm and lead her into the courtroom. Heather was waiting for them near the front, a few rows behind Lucy and Roxanne. "The key players," she assured him. "I don't know about Lucy yet."

Taryn quickly made the introductions between Frieda and Heather. Although she eyed her warily, Heather didn't seem to have any more fight left in her. She looked beaten. Like she'd been crying for days. Taryn didn't blame her. She, herself, had been up all night. She wondered if she'd ever sleep again.

The defense had been making their case for three days. From what Frieda had told her, it hadn't been going well. "They've just given up," she'd said. "There's nowhere to go." The case was as good as closed.

And then Roxanne dropped her bombshell. "The defense would like to call Mr. Jamey Winters to the stand."

The audible gasp was heard throughout the courtroom, but nobody reacted more visibly than Lucy herself. When she turned, her face was stark white. She caught Taryn's eye and mouthed, "no, no" but Taryn nodded her head in Heather's direction. Lucy closed her eyes, dropped her head, and turned back around. There was nothing she could do now.

As far as anyone knew, Lucy and Jamey had no connection outside of their childhood elementary school. They were not friends, did not even run in the same social circles. They had not dated in high school, worked with one another, nor were they related. So when he was sworn in and took the stand, you could have heard a pin drop.

After a few perfunctory questions, Roxanne turned her back to the witness, made quick eye contact with Taryn, and then took a deep breath. "Mr. Winters," she began, "did you have any prior indication that Ms. Dawson was going to, in any way, harm Muddy Creek Elementary or the visitors to it?"

"Yes," Jamey answered, "I did."

Someone in the back of the room gasped then immediately stifled the sound. Taryn saw the prosecutor's shoulders straighten, ready to pounce if necessary.

"And what would that entail?"

"On more than one occasion Ms. Dawson told me that she would like to see the school gone, in whatever fashion that could occur, and that she'd like to see many of its former staff members gone with it," he replied.

Taryn leaned forward and held her breath.

"Was this an off-the-cuff remark, Mr. Winters, or something you took seriously?"

"Ms. Dawson assured me that, if she had the means, she would 'wash the sins from the school with fire,'" he said.

A slight yelp, this one from one row behind her.

"Do you know why Ms. Dawson wanted to destroy the school?"

"Objection! Mr. Winters is not a mind reader."

"Overruled," the judge replied, "although I'd be careful where you tread with this. It might not go in your favor. It is your witness, though, Mrs. Martin."

"Thank you. Do you know why Ms. Dawson wanted to destroy the school and any of its staff members?"

Jamey coughed and straightened his tie. His face was starting to turn red. "Yes, for me."

"I'm sorry, can you say that louder?"

Jamey straightened in his seat and raised his voice. "Yes ma'am, she wanted to do it for me."

"Is there a particular reason she wanted anyone dead on your behalf?" Roxanne asked.

"Objection!" The prosecutor once again rose to his feet. "The victims are not on trial here. They are dead, your honor."

"Just bear with me for a moment," Roxanne pleaded.

"Okay, but get to your point, Mrs. Martin."

Taryn watched the defense attorney take a deep breath and turn to face her witness again. "Why did Ms. Dawson want someone dead for you?"

And then, in front of the people he'd known his entire life and those who held him in high regards as a pillar of the community, Jamey spoke for the first time in thirty years.

"Because when I was a child attending Muddy Creek Elementary School, Mr. Everett Scott, our fifth-grade teacher, sexually molested myself and three other young boys in front of my classmates. The sexual abuse continued for a year. And Ms. Dawson was the only one who tried to stop it."

And then all hell broke loose.

THIRTY-TWO

aryn sat on the steps of the old school and, once again, regarded the pictures on her camera. The children throwing the ball at Lucy. The principal's desk. The smashed pumpkins in the classroom.

The tall, good-looking teacher standing before the rest of the class, a prepubescent boy on his lap. The child's shirt off, the teacher's lips on his neck. The rest of the students trying to ignore what was going on in front of them. Some looking down, some hiding their faces, some struggling not to laugh.

Little kids not understanding that sometimes the mind and body's reaction to fright is to laugh, a nervous twitter that didn't mean anything at all. Someone could have explained that to them. Should have explained that they didn't need to carry that guilt with them, or any of it with them. But everyone in their lives that knew had looked away. Everyone.

A principal just a door away, locked in her office, doing nothing to stop what was going on around the corner. And while she might not have *heard* the sexual activity, she most certainly heard the verbal abuse—the shouting, the objects flying around the room, the racket of an angry and fearful man trying to keep and maintain control.

Ironically, in the end it hadn't been the fear that had kept the students from running home and telling their parents what was happening, it was the love. Everett Scott had tried to intimidate with fright. But it had been his ethereal singing voice, almost *womanly*, his Gulliver's Travels style tales, his exuberance even, that had made them want to remain in his good graces. He was charismatic in the way that many abusers are. They'd idolized him. Fought to be in his regards. Clamored over one another for his favors. He'd listened to their problems, bought them presents, encouraged their talents, gotten to know *them*. The attention he showered upon them, the dreams he made them believe they were capable of achieving—they loved him for that. None would risk losing it.

All except for Lucy.

She had seen through it. Lucy was a fixer, a child who wanted to help. Perhaps it had been her eye contact with Jamey while he was at the front of the room. It was the reading sessions when it would happen. Once the assignment was doled out, the chair would be dragged to the front of the room and a child, a special one, would be drawn to the front. Maybe one day she'd looked up and had really seen. Or maybe it was something else. But she hadn't let her adoration stand in the way. And like the child who tried to convince everyone that the emperor was naked, she had spoken out. That had been the start of her own downfall. Everett couldn't have *that*, of course. And he wasn't a *real* monster, he'd probably convinced himself. He would never do anything to hurt her.

But he could convince the others to do it.

Bullying by proxy.

The clash rang out through the window. Taryn imagined history would continue to repeat itself inside the building. Everyone would soon know what had happened, thanks to the picture Misty had tucked away inside her album, but that didn't change the past.

When the sound came again, Taryn rose to her feet. *That was no ghost...*

This time she went through the front door. She was in the classroom in a matter of seconds.

And found herself facing the wrong end of a gun.

THIRTY-THREE

O kay, okay," *Taryn said*, holding her hands up in the air over her head. "Everything's okay."

"How can it be okay," the other woman spat. "You've ruined everything. Everybody knows now. Everybody! Do you know what they're going to say about those boys? They'll laugh, that's what. People don't want to know about little boys. Can't even imagine it! What are their daddies going to say!"

Taryn walked backward until her bottom was up against the chalkboard. She was standing in front of the classroom, Naomi's gun pointed straight at her face.

"Naomi, Jamey wanted to talk about it," she said slowly. "He wanted to help Lucy. Lucy did it for him. She wanted to save him."

She hadn't been able to save the others. Jamey, maybe he had been her last chance.

"Where was she when my brother Ethan died?" Naomi cried. "I got held back that year. We weren't even supposed to be in the same classroom. But there we were. Who saved Ethan? Who!"

"I'm sorry," Taryn cried in return. "I'm sorry!"

"You know out father had just died that summer," Naomi wept erratically. "He died in the mines. An aneurysm. Mr. Scott was good to us. He took us right in, took care of us. We would have had nothing if not for him. He was a good man!"

"Okay, okay," Taryn cajoled.

"And then when it started..." Naomi allowed the gun to shake for a moment, then straightened it. "The kissing, the hugging, the..." She couldn't finish the sentence.

"That's how people like him get victims," Taryn said. "They look for people, for kids, who need help. Who are going through weak times. They prey on those."

"Do you know what it was like to sit there every day? Just sitting there and watching him? He would look at me. Look at me! Like he wanted me to help. And I couldn't do anything. Nothing! And later he would sing. Sing just for us. It was an apology. Any song we wanted sometimes. It couldn't be bad when he sang."

She was rambling now, but if Taryn could keep her talking...at least she wasn't shooting when she was talking.

"Naomi, I am so sorry..."

"And those other teachers. One walked right in one day with her dog when it was happening, she did! Then she just turned around and left. Like it wasn't any of her business..."

Naomi turned and stomped across the room. She stood at the row of windows and looked at the shelf below it.

"Here," she pointed. "It was Halloween. We'd all made these pumpkin things. It took us a week, between covering them and painting them and letting them dry. And then, because of Lucy, he destroyed them. Jamey was up front with him. It was almost always Jamey. Ethan didn't understand. He was as good as Jamey. As smart. As nice. But it was almost always Jamey. He sat there and it was going on and on, and then Lucy interrupted. Just got right up and interrupted."

Taryn had to marvel at the young girl's nerve. She wanted to ask what Lucy had said or done but didn't think it was the time.

"He got so angry. He stood up, marched over here to the window, threw them all down to the ground, and stomped every one of them. All of them." Naomi sniffed. "I cried for a week. It was terrible."

Taryn's heart broke at the fact that the loss of her art project was the only thing that, at the time, her little mind could process as the heartache. She hadn't been able to wrap her head around the other bad things, so she'd thrown everything into her grief over losing her pumpkin.

"Always Lucy's fault."

"It wasn't Lucy's fault," Taryn interjected. "She was a victim, too."

Naomi raised the gun high in the air again and aimed it at the middle of the room and released the safety. "She should've burned the whole thing down," she whispered. "She didn't do it right."

At the same time Taryn dove towards Naomi's feet and tackled her, the gun went off and slid across the floor, but not before clipping Taryn in the side. The pain shot through her searing knife, knocking the wind from her. Doubled over, Taryn tried to pull Naomi back, but Naomi had wrestled out of her grip and scampered away with a shriek. By the time Naomi lifted the gun again and pulled the trigger, Taryn was too late.

THIRTY-FOUR

*H*ey slugger." Taryn opened her eyes and saw Jamey standing in her hospital room, a bouquet of flowers in his hands. "How's it going?"

"They say I am going to live," she replied. "Mostly. How are you?"

"Okay," he said. "Lucy's getting a new trial. I think she might be on her way over here to see you, though. I talked to her this morning. She'll tell you all about it."

Matt, who had been napping in a chair he'd pulled up beside her, stood and stretched his arms. "I'm going to head down and find some of that mud they call coffee," he announced. "Anyone else want anything?"

When he was gone, Jamey took the seat beside her.

"I am so sorry about everything that happened," she began.

Jamey reached over and patted her on the hand, careful of her IV. "It wasn't your fault. It was our fault."

"You were kids. The adults in your life failed you," Taryn said.

"On some things," he agreed, "but we have to take responsibility for what we did to Lucy. And none of us ever did. We all should have gotten help. I should've talked to the police about Lucy. I knew she was going to do something. I'd visited her, you see, just a week before that reunion. When I found out who was coming and what they were doing, I had a meltdown. She was the only one I could talk to. If I hadn't done that..."

"Were you the one with the song lyrics?" Taryn asked. It was one piece of the puzzle she hadn't fit in yet.

"Just the one. 'You've Got a Friend.' That was one of 'our' songs, you know. Told us all that, I found out later," Jamey added wryly. "I cringe whenever it comes on. It makes me want to throw the damn radio through the roof."

"I bet," Taryn snorted. "What a..."

But she found there wasn't a word strong enough to describe her feelings towards the man.

"You know, it was a long time before I realized that he was just a monster. I was screwed up about it for a long time and had skewed ideas about what it meant to be different. We didn't have much diversity here in Haven Hollow back then and I just thought, well, some men were like that."

"Oh," but Taryn said, "but this was about control, about a sickness. Not a person's sexuality or sexual preference or..."

"I know, I know," he agreed. "But as a little kid without anyone to talk to I thought it was because he was a man who liked men. I thought it must mean that I liked men, too. It wasn't until college that I learned it wasn't like that at all. That there was something wrong with him. I guess that's why, with my job now, I try so hard to promote equality and education and diversity. To teach kids about difference and anti-bullying. If I'd known at the time... It's strange, after all this time. When I think of him, I can't help but think of the good stuff. I know he ruined a lot of things, but he also did so many other good things. Like encourage me to go to college one day." Jamey shrugged. "It's confusing."

"Abuse is confusion," Taryn agreed. "Naomi?"

"She didn't make it," Jamey said sadly. "They tried. You tried. If you hadn't gone for that gun, she would've taken you down with her."

"It was my fault. If I hadn't..."

"Not your fault, not Lucy's fault, not my fault. Only one person's at fault here and he's gone," Jamey said.

But Taryn knew Naomi was her responsibility. And she'd carry that with her.

"So many people," Taryn sighed. "Were there others in other years?"

Jamey shrugged. "Probably. He was only there for two years, though. After he left Mrs. Evans took over his classroom. None of us knew where he went. We didn't see hide nor hair or him until that reunion, more than twenty years later. The article in the paper, the mention of him. That was my trigger, why I went to Lucy. I'd had many over the years and Heather helped me deal with them as much as she could. But that time, I don't know. It was worse. Knowing he'd be back here, at the school, it just made it all feel too real."

"So you've talked to Lucy since?"

Jamey bowed his head and sighed. "Off and on, yes. I've spent most of my life trying to apologize for the way we treated her. We were children, of course, and he was encouraging it, but it still wasn't right."

"Jamey," Taryn began as she struggled to sit up in her bed, "I have to ask you something. I kept seeing this circle of desks. Do you remember that? What it means?"

She didn't think Jamey's face could get any rosier, but it did. She thought he might even burst into tears.

"At the end of that school year. I reckon now he was afraid that she was going to talk and he wanted to make damn sure she didn't. So he put all our desks into a circle. He stood in the middle and went around to each person. Made each one of us tell her something we didn't like about her. If there wasn't anything to say, then we were supposed to 'use our imaginations' and make something up."

"Oh. My. God."

Jamey nodded miserably. "I know. They were saying all sorts of petty things. Making fun of the way she walked, the way she ran, how smart she was. Telling her she was ugly. And she just had to sit there and take it. I have never forgiven myself for that. Never."

When Jamey left, there was nothing for Taryn to do but cry.

THIRTY-FIVE

W, *it looks better in your painting* than it ever did in real life," Lucy laughed. Taryn had propped the painting against the headboard, and now she stood back and took a good, long look at it. "I think it came out okay," she smiled.

She was still sore, and it was still difficult to move around at times, but she was healing. Matt had been a tremendous help, of course. He wasn't going to have a job if he didn't start going to work. They only had two more days left there, though. He'd be driving her back to Nashville and flying home from there.

"How are you doing these days?" Taryn asked.

Lucy shrugged. "Okay mostly. I have a new book coming out in the spring. Agent is pretty happy about that. And I've been thinking about taking a vacation."

"Ready for the new trial?"

Lucy smiled grimly. "That's all still up in the air. We don't know what they're going to do yet."

"May I apologize again?"

Lucy perched on the corner of Taryn's bed and lifted her shoulders. "You know, it's okay. I am glad it's all out in the open. Hell, I'm the one who encouraged you to look deeper. Subconsciously I wanted someone else to know. Your reporter friend did a wonderful job on the story. For the first time in a long time, we were able to tell our story. No clichés, no 'gay men are pedophiles' nonsense. No stereotypes. Just the truth. That he was a monster who preyed on young children in a place that nobody cared about at the time."

Taryn nodded.

"When did you figure it all out?"

"Well," Taryn replied, "when I saw that last picture, of course. That sealed the deal. But also, the song. A song everyone else loves. You were talking about two things at the same time."

"Music will take you right back. He would play that song sometimes and I would listen. The length of the song was about as long as it would last. It was the only way I could time it."

Taryn nodded. She'd wondered. And then there were Jamey's eyes. The ones she'd seen in her dream. Lucy had been haunted by more than one thing in that classroom. "I realized that you only thought there were going to be six people on

170

that reunion tour. You hadn't planned on the seventh. That I just kind of knew from instinct."

"Mrs. Evans," Lucy said sadly. "She came at the last minute."

"Not the monster everyone thought?"

"Oh, she was a terribly imposing woman. Everyone was scared to death of her. But she loved those students. She loved me," Lucy swore. "The fact that I had something to do with her death...I will never forgive myself for that. I deserve to be punished. You know, she was the only one who tried to help? She didn't know about the sexual abuse, of course, but she did know about the other. I heard her arguing with him in the teacher's lounge one day. Shouting at him, threatening to go to the police."

"I wish she had," Taryn said.

"Me too. At the time, however, it scared me. I was afraid of Mr. Scott, but I loved him. He made everyone feel so alive, so hopeful. And then he'd turn around and make you feel less than human in a heartbeat. For some of us, though, that little bit of goodness was all we had in our lives. It was in mine. I didn't want to see it go."

Taryn looked sadly at Lucy. It was such a complicated thing, her past.

Lucy smiled again. "You know, on my last day of school at Muddy Creek Mrs. Evans came up to me. 'You are a bright, talented young lady,' she said. 'Do not ever let anything that happened to you here hold you back.' I think she knew then. I believed then that she knew the other things that had happened, too. But that maybe she felt powerless. I have always suspected that she asked for that other classroom so that she could take it over and wipe out the memories."

"Why Jamey, though?" Taryn asked. "Were you all great friends?"

Lucy stood and began pacing around the room. "No, never friends. He was as bad as the others. But at the end of the year, something happened that he couldn't live with. It had all been escalating. I wasn't even going to school half the time. I just hated it. My birthday was that last week, though. I came into school one day right there at the end, and there was a bouquet of flowers on my desk. They were pretty things. I picked them up and started to sniff them, but Jamey knocked them out of my hands. Was a real jerk about it. I cried and cried. It was only later, years later, that he told me the truth—that they'd been full of poison ivy. The other kids had meant it as a cruel joke."

"Oh dear Lord," Taryn cried.

Lucy shook her head. "I believe it was Mr. Scott who gathered it for them."

Taryn rose and walked over to where Lucy stood. She put her hand on the other woman's shoulder and looked down at her, for the first time seeing how small she truly was. "You're not the guard anymore," she told her. "It's not your place. You don't have to stay here and protect them. It's time for you to get out. You no longer have to watch over the school or the kids. Please."

Lucy took her hand and squeezed it. "You know, I have fought and fought now for most of my life, trying to find my way out of that classroom. And most of the time I succeed. Only..." She looked away, and Taryn watched as her face seemed to fixate on something in the faraway distance. "Only sometimes I wake up at night, and I am right back there. I think, in the end, none of us escaped that classroom. We all eventually find our way back some time or another. And one day it will just be impossible to leave."

That rectangular-shaped light at the end of the dark tunnel did not always turn out to be a door, Taryn realized. And sometimes the monsters were real.

* * *

"ARE YOU GOING TO BE OKAY?"

Taryn knew Matt wasn't referring to the long, and probably uncomfortable, ride that stretched out ahead of them.

"I don't know," she answered honestly. "Probably."

"I can't take another one like this," he tried joking.

"Nor can I."

"Do you think they'll be okay?"

But Taryn didn't know that either. She wanted to say yes, but only time would tell. Jamey was doing what the others in his young life had failed to do—he was protecting children. And Lucy was writing for them. The others, the ones they'd lost along the way, would never get another chance.

"I am hopeful that Lucy will get the mental health counseling she needs," Taryn said at last. "The rest of them, too. Misty, Jamey, Heather..."

"One thing I don't understand," Matt said, "is that if the angry ghost was the Scott fella then who was the other one? The one crying? The one in the hall? What was all that?"

Taryn rested her head in her hand and stared out the window. "It was Lucy," she said at last. "Lucy was right. None of them ever truly made it out of that school. A part of her will always be there."

"Would you have killed him?"

Taryn shrugged. "No, I wouldn't have. I believe in the justice system too much. But then, look what happened to Lukas Monroe. His father got five years, and Lukas ended up dying as well. There are no winners here."

"And the other teachers? Did they deserve it?"

"No. But they deserved something. They allowed something terrible to happen."

Matt pulled out onto the main highway and laid on the gas, wanting to put as much distance between them and the town as quickly as he could.

"You know," Taryn laughed, "Lucy told me something about her teacher that's a little ironic."

"Oh yeah? What's that?"

Taryn could hear Lucy telling it even now.

"My grandmother had died right around Christmas. A few weeks later, after winter break, I went back to school. I was feeling sad and upset. But, that night before, I could have sworn I heard her singing in the living room by the Christmas tree we still had up. I wanted to tell someone but I didn't want them to think I was crazy. Mr. Scott was decorating a bulletin board and I volunteered to help him. I don't know why, but I ended up telling him what had happened. I expected him to tell me I was nuts or laugh but, when I was finished, he turned to me and said, 'Why Lucy, I think that is just beautiful. And I firmly believe that ghosts are here to watch over us, protect us, and love us.' I know he did a lot of terrible things but when I am feeling at my best, I think about that, about how he made me feel. It was a gift."

Bloody Moor, Book 8 Excerpt

One

"*Are you sure you want to travel to Wales alone?*"

Taryn tried not to let Matt's legitimate concern annoy her. He had, after all, known her for more than twenty years and had seen firsthand some of the scrapes she was capable of getting into. However, she was also an adult; she could take care of herself.

"I'll be all right," she replied brightly. "It will be fun!"

"You don't need me to come up there and help you pack or anything?"

Right, she thought sarcastically. *I want you to fly all the way from Florida to Nashville to help me throw some sweaters into a suitcase.*

Instead of being a smartass, however, she rolled her eyes (he couldn't see that, after all) and plastered good humor into her voice. "Nah, I'll be okay. Almost packed. Got everything together."

"Passport?"

"Came in the mail yesterday," she answered. "Expedited."

"Travel toiletries?"

"Bought some of those cheap bottles from Wal-Mart and filled them up with my regular stuff."

"Warm clothes?"

"Cardigans, leggings, and long-sleeved tops," she told him. "It's all about layers."

"Extra batteries for Miss Dixie?"

Taryn paused above her suitcase, a roll of underwear in hand, and glanced over at her camera. The beat up and gently loved Nikon watched her from her bedroom bureau. "Two in my checked bag, one in my carry on."

"So where are you flying into and how will you get to this town of Lampeter?"

Knowing that Matt would not be satisfied until she pacified him with the answers he sought, she tossed the underwear into the suitcase then slid down to the floor. "I fly into London. From there it's a train to Cardiff, a switch to Carmarthen, a local bus to Lampeter, and a pack mule the rest of the way."

"They still have those?"

"I'm kidding," she laughed. "Well, about the pack mule. I imagine I'll walk from the bus stop to the house."

"Worried?"

"Nah," she shrugged. "The only thing I'm concerned about is dragging my luggage through all of that. I'm trying to pack light, but even my 'light' is a lot for regular people. To be honest, I am kind of hoping they lose my bags."

"What for?" Matt sounded genuinely baffled. To his organized mind, a deviation from a plan could cause chaos to ensue. Matt did not do chaos.

"Because," she explained, "if the airline loses it then they're responsible for getting it to me. They'll drive it right to my door. Or, you know, where I am staying. Hopefully not this door. That would be a problem."

"Well," Matt said with a bit of hesitancy, "I guess it's okay to be inconvenienced if the inconvenience is in your favor."

"That's the spirit!"

Matt was silent for a moment and all Taryn could hear was the ticking of her living room clock. It was shaped like Elvis, and his legs danced back and forth with every tick of the minute hand. She'd paid $5 for it at a flea market.

Finally, he spoke of what was on both of their minds.

"Speaking of spirits..."

Taryn sighed and crossed her legs. They were already aching and she'd barely been on them for more than an hour. She needed to get in and see the doctor before she left, but that wasn't going to be possible; she flew out in two days.

"The house is haunted, but I'm not there for that," she replied at last. "I'm just there because the new owners are renovating it and opening it as a high-end hotel and wedding destination. They're just using me for my artistic talents. Not my, you know, my..."

"*Other* talents?" Matt offered.

"Of which I have many, as you well know," Taryn replied primly.

Matt laughed, but it was strained. "I read up about the house. It's meant to be one of the most haunted places in Wales—in the U.K. even! Are you sure you want to..."

"I do," Taryn replied firmly. "I read those stories as well. I am feeling much stronger these days, much more confident in what I am doing. And besides, nothing truly terrible has happened to me on any of my jobs. I've always come out fine."

"People have attempted to murder you on at least four occasions," Matt pointed out.

"'Attempted' is the keyword. Nobody's succeeded yet."

"If you're feeling poorly, though," he spoke gently, "then you might not be as strong as you once were. That could work against you."

Taryn supported her back against the foot of the bed and closed her eyes. It was true; she *was* getting worse. Things got a little harder for her each day. There were now even days in which it was difficult for her to even walk down to the mailbox at the end of the apartment building. Someday, possibly soon, she might even find herself relying on a wheelchair. But until that day came...

"I'm fine," she said. "I know what I am up against and, Matt, there might not be a lot of time left. Not being morbid, but if I can do what I love, why not do it? I might not have the chance to go to Wales again, to stay in a mansion and work. I mean, for crying out loud, the Holy Grail was supposed to have been stored there for awhile!"

"I can always take you there myself," Matt interjected. His stubbornness bore through her. "I don't care if you can walk or not. I'll carry you around on my back if you want to go."

"And I thank you for that, as awkward as that image may be, but there are some things I just need to do on my own," Taryn said. "While I am able."

"Okay," Matt sighed. He knew when he was defeated.

They let the silence drift between them, each lost in their respective thoughts. Elvis continued to shake his hips in the other room. Taryn was afraid she'd hurt his feelings. Matt's pride wasn't something easily bruised but, where she was concerned, he had a soft spot. He wanted to take care of her, had been trying since she was a little girl, even though she was the one who used to beat the bullies off *him*. And he felt helpless—not just because of her illness but because her job and life had little to do with him and lately the division was growing stronger and stronger.

She might not need him at all. That's what he was thinking; she knew it.

"Sooo..." he finally said at last. "The Holy Grail, you say? I didn't read that part of the mansion's history. Want to fill me in on it?"

Taryn opened her eyes and smiled. "Sure! Okay, so supposedly back in the seventeenth century there was this..."

It was nearly midnight before she hung up the phone.

* * *

The corridor was thick with night as Taryn soundlessly made her way down the tunnel of blackness. Her feet padded so softly on the cold wooden floors that she might have been a ghost herself. Above her, the ceilings soared, amplified in height by her sleep.

Taryn stretched out her arm and let her fingertips trail along the oak-paneled walls. Cobwebs clung to her nails, balls of sticky string that felt alive.

She turned and began her descent down a wide staircase, the marble floor now cold and uninviting. Piano music played somewhere, the ethereal notes hollow and bleak. Her skin chilled beneath the silk covering pulled across her shoulders. Yet, even in the darkness, she was calm. The blackness closed in around her, soft and warm. She was gliding down the stairs now, moving through the air as though on a cloud; her feet and legs were not moving.

Death, death was all around it. She could smell it, taste it even. It clung to the floor and walls, filled the air. She swallowed and tested the bittersweet taste. There was sorrow, but hope. It did not frighten her.

Up ahead the music grew louder. The tonal song rose and fell in volume. She longer she walked, the farther away it seemed to get. The corridor, dark with its wooden panels and even darker portraits, rose above her on both sides and appeared to go on forever. There were no twists or turns—this house was not a labyrinth but one massive passageway.

Someone was going to die.

She knew it, could feel it, but while the thought should have brought sadness and perhaps a sense of fear, it did not. She was accustomed to death. She welcomed death.

As the last notes of the somber ballad filled the air, Taryn sighed; the sound shook the house's foundation.

She was death.

TWO

*T*aryn *took one last look around* her apartment and then, feeling oddly sentimental since she normally couldn't wait to get away from the place, took a picture of it.

Taryn hated her apartment most days. She'd tried to pretty it up by hanging dazzling paintings on the walls (some hers, some not), draping colorful throws on her sofa and chairs, and setting out her collections of sea shells and candlesticks that she gathered from her travels. Still, it did little to hide the overall dinginess, cramped space, and smell of old cheese that drifted in from the elevator.

Thanks to a job that had gone awry and netted her an insurance payout (or pay*off*, depending on how you looked at it), she could have afforded better. The idea of moving, however, sounded draining. Besides, she was rarely there anymore; Taryn only spent a stretch of two to three weeks at home in any given timeframe.

"Why *Wales?*" her favorite server at her favorite Nashville pancake house had asked over dinner the night before.

"I don't know," Taryn had shrugged. "The job offer kind of came out of nowhere and it just felt right."

What she *didn't* tell her server over pecan pancakes and warm maple syrup, was about the astrologer. She didn't want to appear unstable, after all.

Taryn had visited the astrologer a month before. She'd gone to him intermittently over the years, mostly because she kept hoping that he'd eventually get something right. Although he'd never been entirely *off*, his answers had mostly been vague. Taryn wasn't sure she put a lot of faith in horoscopes, you could read most any sign's fortune for the day and apply it to yourself, but there was quite a bit of work that went into her astrologer's report, so it felt more scientific.

Even before her camera started showing her the past, she'd sought proof of the supernatural. Anything to give her hope that there was something out there bigger than herself.

On her last visit, she'd gotten her wish.

"You want to see a map of the world?" he'd asked. "See where you might have the best luck?"

"Sure," she'd replied. "Might help when the next job rolls around."

He'd first brought up a map of the United States. She wasn't surprised to see that a fate line ran right through southern Georgia. The time she'd spent on Jekyll Island,

and later St. Simon's, had certainly been memorable. She'd created some lovely paintings there, too.

Nor was she surprised to see that destiny and love lines ran through southern New Hampshire. Her aunt Sarah had lived there, after all, and Taryn had inherited Sarah's ramshackle farmhouse. She was currently in the process of having it restored and often played around with the idea of making it her permanent home.

She was a little surprised, however, to see that Florida wasn't on her map at all. What did that mean for Matt?

"How about we check out Europe?" he'd asked with a grin.

Whether she totally believed in his work or not, Michael Thurman was an immensely likable and intelligent guy. He was absolutely excited by what he did and could talk for hours about his enthusiasm for Chiron.

"Sure. Let's see Europe."

Taryn had never been to Europe–she'd never had the money on her own. Her parents, now deceased, had traveled there often. They'd left her with her grandmother during those trips, not that Taryn had minded. She preferred being with her grandmother over traveling with them.

"Anything in Ireland?" she'd asked, peering across his desk as she tried to get a better view of his computer screen.

"No, not that I see," he'd replied, much to her disappointment. "But here, look at *this*."

She'd patiently waited as he'd printed off a copy of the map and had then leaned over the desk with him as he'd pointed out little squiggly lines of green, black, red, and blue. "See these," he gestured with his index finger.

She'd nodded.

"These are your fate, destiny, work, and love lines," Michael had explained. "You have a strong destiny line going through the Czech Republic and a love line running through Italy."

Taryn smiled. She'd always had a thing for Italian guys. Matt was part Italian himself.

"But right here," he pointed, "*this* is where you need to be."

Taryn could see a place on the map where all the lines intersected, causing a big blob of color. "What is it?"

Michael had laughed then, momentarily relaxing his normally piercing eyes. "*It's* Wales. Almost right there in the smack dab middle of it."

"So what does it mean?" Taryn had asked. "That I should go to Wales?"

"Maybe." Michael had shrugged. "All four of your lines intersect there, which could mean something positive for you."

"Does it say anything about a past life?" She was always hoping to get some glimmer of a past life from him.

"Could be. That could be where your destiny comes into play. My guess is that, if you went there, excellent things would come of it. I certainly wouldn't discount the idea of traveling there."

Taryn had thought about that on the drive home and for the rest of the week. Wales. Her ancestors on her mother's side were from there, but the lines went back very far. She didn't even know their names. Wales was certainly not a destination she'd entertained herself with. Ireland? Sure. England? Possible. Italy? Definitely. But Wales? She wasn't even sure she knew what was *in* Wales. The word brought up nothing but Princess Diana.

One week later, however, she'd received the email.

Dear Ms. Magill,

On behalf of the Ceredigion House, I'd like to introduce myself. My name is Joe Butler and, along with my siblings, we recently inherited the home from our deceased parents. The house was originally started in the 17th century but has been completely modernized. For the past fifteen years, it has been used as budget accommodations. My siblings and I, however, are now interested in having it completely rehabilitated and turning it into an upscale hotel and wedding destination, with my wife and me acting as managers. It is unique in structure and land mass, although I admit it needs quite a bit of rehabbing. I'm sorry to say that it has been on a decline over the past ten years and will take much work to bring her back up to standards. We recently became aware of your fantastic work and were hoping that we might entice you to join us and work with our architect to help bring it back to life.

If you'd please contact me with details regarding your schedule and fees, I'd be most delighted.

Joe Butler

Naturally, Taryn had immediately opened a new tab and Googled the house. She shouldn't have been surprised to see its Welsh location and, yet, she was. In fact, she'd sat there for the longest time, just staring at the Google map. Right in the middle of Wales. The dash of pleasure that coursed through her veins had her shaking.

Perhaps, by the sheer number of times she'd visited the astrologer, she'd evened the odds. He had finally gotten something right!

Of course, Joe Butler hadn't been kidding about the state of the house.

"In need of some rehabbing, my foot," she'd laughed aloud.

The house, which was not so much a *house* as a mansion, looked on the edge of deterioration. The older pictures of it from the 1980s showed a beautiful manor home, complete with stone walls sprouting ivy up the sides and an immaculate circular driveway lined with lush foliage. Current pictures showed crumbling columns, broken windows, and droopy scaffolding that looked as though it were placed to give the appearance of renovations to distrustful guests.

TripAdvisor reviews claimed that it was "too old, smelled bad, and lacked hot water."

Well, she'd stayed in worse.

Taryn's reputation as a talented artist with a knack for looking at something in disrepair and seeing its former glory had taken her to stunning buildings across the United States. Her clients often hired her to work with architects in restoration projects, although she'd also been hired by private members of the community. Some had wanted renderings of the family farmhouse before it was torn down, for instance. Or a painting of the old homestead—a house that was only partially standing, thanks to a fire and even more destructive natural elements.

She'd always prided herself on her vast imagination; being able to look at something that was falling apart and seeing what it used to be, what it could be *again*, was fun. And she loved to paint.

Two years ago, however, things had changed. She no longer had to rely solely on her imagination. Her beloved camera, Miss Dixie, had started showing her the past. Not on every job, and not always images she desired to see, but it was starting to happen more and more frequently.

She could take a picture of an empty room and come back with a space full of period furniture.

Taryn was now able to see the very past she used to long to visit.

Of course, the ghosts had come then, too.

Taryn was still trying to deal with *that* particular aspect of her newfound talent. The ghosts were unsettling—restless, sometimes tragic figures that needed her help in the most confounding ways. She'd found herself in more than one scrape although, to be fair, it was the living she normally needed to fear the most.

Ceredigion House was waiting.

"Maybe for a long time," Taryn whispered as she shut her door and locked it.

As Taryn entered her stinky elevator, rolling her bags behind her with the feel of Miss Dixie bouncing on her chest, she felt hopeful.

A BROOM WITH A VIEW EXCERPT

Chapter One

L IZA JANE HIGGINBOTHAM was a witch.

Mind you, not the kind of witch that conversed with black cats or could make herself look like a supermodel with a wave of her hand (although that particular skill would've been useful on a number of occasions) but a witch, nonetheless.

When she was twelve she'd watched a movie about a girl who came into her witchy powers on her sixteenth birthday. "Teen Witch," it was called.

She wasn't *that* kind of witch either.

Liza Jane had been born a witch, known it most of her life, and considered it as normal as her hair color.

(Okay, maybe not *quite* as normal as her hair color. Thanks to Clairol and some plastic gloves, she'd been dying her hair for so long she had no idea what her natural color was.)

Nope, she thought as she gave the last box on the U-Haul a good, solid kick with her tennis shoe and sent it flying down the icy ramp, *she was just a regular witch with few useful and exciting skills.*

Sure, she could get rid of negative energy around a place, was a pretty good healer, and could see into the future with a little bit of help from some of her tools— but she couldn't make herself invisible or turn people into frogs.

Had she been a *TV* kind of witch, she'd have just wrinkled her nose a few times and in an orderly fashion sent those boxes flying into the house, where they then would've graciously unpacked themselves. Then she would've spent the rest of the afternoon lounging on a perfectly made bed (*not* made by her, of course), watching Rom-Coms, and feeding herself strawberries.

And later she would've turned Jennifer Miller into a cockroach. Just for the fun of it.

But she could *not* send all the boxes into the house like that, she couldn't afford to get cable, and there were no strawberries available in Kudzu Valley in December.

Shivering even inside her thermal coat, Liza Jane rubbed her chapped hands together and hopped down from the back of the truck. She blew out a puff of air, her breath making a large round cloud before floating away, and watched as the box slid off the ramp and landed with a thud at the bottom. One side was completely caved in. She hoped there wasn't anything breakable in it. She hadn't taken the time to mark any of them. It was going to be complete chaos for awhile.

Divorce was making her more unorganized than usual.

And she was still a little miffed that she'd missed Thanksgiving back north. But she'd had to get out of there as quickly as possible. She'd had to, even if it meant eating chicken nuggets and fries instead of turkey.

"What the *hell* was I thinking?" she muttered to herself as she turned and looked at her new house.

Well, technically, her *old* house. She had lived there, once upon a time. She'd been six then and now she was in her thirties so it had been...

Well, she didn't need to think about how many years ago that was. She was already depressed enough as it was.

Her grandparents' white farm house rose before her in the dreary winter sky, proud and neglected. White paint had chipped off and now sprinkled the dead, brown grass like dirty snow, leaving behind naked patches of worn wood. An upstairs window was boarded up, the glass missing. A black garbage bag covered another. A window unit in the second floor master bedroom had leaked and dripped over the years, leaving a stream of discolored water running down the side of the house. She was almost certain the front porch was leaning, too.

Liza Jane cocked her head to one side and studied it. *Yep,* she thought, *it was definitely crooked.*

"At least it has electricity and running water," she stated cheerfully.

Nothing answered her back. She was surrounded by more than fifty acres of mountainside and pastureland. Her grandparents' farm. Her *family* farm. Her heritage.

Damn, it was dismal.

She knew it would look better in the summertime, when the trees were bursting and full of leaves and color, the fields were lush with wildflowers and thick grass, and the sky a brilliant blue.

But for now everything was dead. Dead and gray. Even the tree branches were gray. How was that *possible?*

Her divorce was almost final. She just needed to sign the papers. Her high school sweetheart had left her for the woman at Starbucks who made him his latte every morning. (Well, actually he was marrying the trombone player in the pop opera group he managed. He'd just initially left her for the Starbucks chick. There had, apparently, been many women. Many, *many* women.)

Back in Boston she'd lost her fairly interesting and well-paying job as the administrative assistant to the director at the nonprofit organization she'd been with for two years. She'd been unceremoniously fired when everyone on her floor, including some donors, overheard her yelling obscenities over the phone to her husband's lawyer.

She'd let the happy new couple have her house in Wakefield. She'd loved that house, had enjoyed everything about it. But once she'd discovered that Latte-Girl had gotten busy on her kitchen table and Trombone Chick had blown more than her mouthpiece on Liza Jane's $2,000 leather sofa, the bloom kind of fell off the rose.

"You're being very immature about this," her husband, Mode, had told her when she'd handed him her house key.

In her mind, Liza had stuck her tongue out at him and snarked, *I thought you thought people overused the word "very."* Instead, she'd kept her face impassive.

"You own this house outright," he'd continued, growing increasingly agitated by her lack of fight. "You don't have a *job.* You won't be able to support yourself. Your money will run out soon. You've *never* been good at money management, Liza. It makes no sense for you to leave the house. Jennifer and I will be fine someplace else. We won't have any problems settling in." He'd paused at that moment and leaned in closer to her. Then, with their faces only inches apart, he'd put his hand on her arm. "It's *you* I'm worried about."

His self-righteousness had been the last straw. She'd told him where he could stick her house key.

Now, since she'd signed over the house to him and he'd given her half its appraised worth, she was moving back into the only other thing she owned besides her ratty car—her grandparents' dilapidated farm house in Kudzu Valley, Kentucky.

Liza Jane was depressed.

"Promise me you won't kill yourself," her mother, Mabel, had shrilled over the phone on Liza's drive down. "Nobody would even know forever, you being out there by yourself like that!"

"Please consider medication or a therapist," Mode had cajoled her with fake worry and sincerity.

"Don't do anything stupid down there," her younger sister, Bryar Rose, had warned her. "Like join Scientology or get bangs."

"Well, maybe just a *little* something," she muttered, flipping her hair back from her face, her teeth chattering in the gusty wind.

For a moment, the air around her stilled. The time-honored words she chanted ascended from her like a soft breeze, comforting her with their familiarity and cadence. They gently lifted the ends of her hair and swept across her face like motherly hands, their warmth nearly bringing tears to her eyes. Her heart raced and for just a second she felt a surge of adrenalin, like she could take on the world if she wanted.

And then it stopped.

Grinning with satisfaction, Liza opened her eyes and studied the farm house again. The porch was perfectly straight, not a board out of place.

"Yeah, well, I deserved it," she snapped to the crows that flew overhead.

Then, feeling a little drained and hung over from what she'd just done, Liza Jane proudly marched up her new steps and into her new life.

∞ ∞ ∞

When Liza Jane had last been in Kudzu Valley it had boasted a Taco Bell, Burger King, and McDonalds. There was talk back then of putting in a Walmart on the new by-pass that circled around the mountain and circumvented the small downtown area that consisted of two cross streets and one red light.

That Walmart never materialized; the by-pass was a lonesome stretch of road that passed through what used to be farm land and a drive-in. Five families had lost land to it all in the name of progress. It did, however, get travelers to the next county over three minutes faster. This was important since Morel County was dry, making it impossible to (legally) buy any kind of alcohol.

Liza's grandfather, Paine, had died ten years earlier. Her grandmother, Nana Bud, had passed away two years ago. The old farm house had been empty ever since, although it had been winterized and a neighbor had watched over it and taken care of any repairs it needed.

Liza had gone down and taken a look at things back in the summer, before her big move, so she kind of knew what she was getting herself into. Still, there weren't many conveniences. For one thing, it was completely devoid of food, unless you wanted to count the bag of birdseed that someone (her grandfather probably) had left out on the back porch in the 1980s and the small piece of moldy cheese that had led a mouse to his last fatal adventure.

Liza Jane needed supplies.

Other than the tiny food marts attached to some of the gas stations, there was only one grocery store in the entire county. It was a discount chain that sold fatty beef, bait, generic canned food, and bulk bags of cheap cereal.

She could roll with that. At least it was cheap. And right now she needed cheap. She was not only moving to Kudzu Valley, she was opening her own business. The money her grandmother had left her two years ago and the divorce settlement would not last forever.

She'd declined alimony.

As Liza slowly pushed her cart down the unfamiliar aisles and loaded up with boxes of Rice Crisps and Frosty Tiny Wheats, Liza became acutely aware of someone's eyes drilling holes into her.

Her senses stayed at a heightened state of awareness these days; when she'd let them slide in the past her husband had gone on a one-man tour of the local single ladies and she wasn't going to make *that* mistake again. However, she did make an effort to turn her senses down when she was out in public so that she didn't pick up on every Dick, Jane, and Bubba's feelings and thoughts but even a Normal would've felt the sharp eyes stabbing into their back.

"Liza Jane Merriweather!" The loud, reedy shrill came from less than ten feet behind her and had Liza startled, despite her mindfulness.

When she turned, Liza was face to face with a tiny, elderly woman carrying a yellow shopping basket overflowing with at least two dozen packages of frozen spinach. Unlike many of the other shoppers, who looked like they'd stumbled out of bed without getting dressed or brushing their hair or teeth, the little woman before her wore a blue-tailored suit and was in full makeup.

Her lavender eyeshadow framed small, beady eyes behind thick bifocals and her clunky heels sounded like shotgun blasts as she marched over to where Liza Jane patiently waited. Her hair, permed and sprayed within an inch of its life, was a brilliant purple.

Liza closed her eyes for a moment and reached forward, focusing on the woman's mind. She frantically attempted to extract a name or memory, since it was obvious she was meant to know the person whose arms were now outstretched and gearing up for a hug.

The only word she could come up with was "Pebbles."

"Just look at *you!*" the woman crooned, squeezing Liza Jane in a bony, yet tight, embrace. The combination of Marlboro Lights, Aqua Net, and Elizabeth Taylor's White Diamonds was almost overpowering. "You're so grown up now!"

Liza plastered what she hoped was a respectful smile across her face and gently untangled herself. She was afraid to squeeze back too hard; in spite of the woman's grip her shoulders and arms felt brittle. God forbid she break somebody on her first day out in town.

"Yes," she replied courteously. "I've grown up a little."

"Liza Jane Merriweather," the woman murmured again, shaking her head in apparent disbelief. Her hair didn't move an inch. Liza had to restrain herself from reaching out and touching it. "I just *can't* believe it."

"Well, actually it's Higginbotham now," Liza helpfully corrected her. "I got married."

"Oh?" At the mention of a husband the woman's eyes sparkled. "Is he here with you?" She began looking around, as though Liza might have hidden him under a gallon of milk in her shopping cart.

"Er..." Liza felt her face turning red. "He's um, back in Boston. We're still, uh, getting some things together. For the move down here."

There was no need to go into the messy details of her impending divorce right there in the grocery store aisle. People were already stopping, pretending to be keenly interested in the nutritional values on the backs of discount cereal boxes while they listened to the two women chat.

"Oh, well, that's okay. I bet you don't remember my name. Do you remember my name," she demanded.

Liza, taken off guard, found herself flustered as she regarded the impatient woman. She reached out again, but came back with nothing. If she'd known her in the past, it was as a child and she'd made little to no impression on Liza.

"Well, I er, I *think* so..." Liza murmured, embarrassed. *Give me a break, lady, it's been almost thirty years*, she thought to herself at the same time.

"It's *Penny*! Penny Libbels!" she cried, slapping Liza Jane on the arm with unexpected strength. "I was your granny's best friend, may she rest in peace."

"Oh, *Pebbles*," Liza Jane nodded now. "Okay, that makes more sense."

"You never *could* say my name right." Penny stared at her wide-eyed and Liza wondered if she was waiting for her to try to say it *now*.

"Um, well, I was young I guess," Liza faltered.

Liza had never been particularly good at small talk. Or grocery stores.

"I hear that you're opening one of those New Agey herbal shops here," Penny pressed, squinting her purple eyes under the harsh fluorescent lights. "You aren't gonna be selling those *drugs* are you? That *meth*?"

At least three more people stopped what they were doing and turned to look back at them, not even trying to hide their curiosity. Liza randomly grabbed at a can of pineapples behind her and clutched it tightly, its metal hard and reassuring under her fingertips. She was about to dig a hole into her hands from the wringing and had already popped an acrylic.

"Well, um, no," she sputtered. "Nothing illegal. It's a holistic clinic, a day spa really, with herbal remedies and massages and–"

"Not one of those places with *hookers*," Penny lowered her voice to a stage whisper, her eyes darting around as she pursed her lips.

"Oh no! Just teas and lotions and regular old massages. Nothing bad," Liza promised.

Oh dear Lord, make me disappear, she prayed silently.

Liza thought she might pass out. One woman passing by actually grabbed her young son by the arm and pushed him ahead of her, as though Liza was already a lady of the night, hawking her body and illegal drugs in the fruit and cereal aisle.

"Hmmm," Penny pursed her lips again so tightly they were almost white. "Well, you *might* do okay here. We're not Hollywood, though. I don't know how many people need those New Agey things. We got a," her voice dropped back down to a stage whisper, "*chiropractor* last year."

Liza nodded her head, pretending to understand the implication.

"He's just *now* starting to catch on," Penny continued. "The ladies here are good Christian women and they don't like being touched in certain places by men who aren't their husbands. But I suppose since you're a woman, it will be just fine."

Penny did not look hopeful.

It was now all Liza Jane could do to keep a straight face. The can of pineapples began to shake in her unsteady hands as she forced her body to control itself. She mentally gathered her thoughts together and forced her breathing to slow down and ease up. Then she ran a quick, but effective, little charm through her mind that sent a wave of coolness through her body, relaxing her muscles and nerves. It wasn't much, but it would hold until she reached the check-out counter.

"Well, I certainly hope people will give me a chance," Liza replied diplomatically once she'd collected herself together.

"Well, at least you don't *have* to work since your husband has a good job. Rosebud was always bragging about his work with the music group. I'm sure your little business will get along just fine and dandy. It's nice for a lady to have a hobby these days," Penny crooned, patting Liza Jane on the arm. "I'd better skedaddle now. I'm making a pot roast for dinner after church tomorrow. Have you found a church yet?"

"I, er..."

"Never mind. You're coming to mine! Elk Creek Primitive. We don't allow none of that singing or music nonsense that the Baptists and Methodists seem to carry on about but you'll *love* our services. They run all morning and our preacher truly gets the spirit deep inside him. I will see you at ten!"

Before Liza could answer, Penny was scurrying off through the considerable number of onlookers, her purple hair a helmet raging her into battle towards the produce.

Since it was a dry county and beer was unavailable, Liza turned and headed back to the candy aisle.

She was going to need a lot more chocolate than she'd initially planned for.

∞ ∞ ∞

In spite of the old house's "quirks" (she was going to call them "quirks" because, at the moment, that sounded less intimidating than "problems") she loved it. It was spacious and full of charm and character.

More importantly, it smelled and *felt* like her grandparents, and she missed them something fierce. She hadn't visited them nearly as much as she'd wanted to as a child, and hardly at all as an adult. Still, they had regularly gone north and visited Liza, her mother, and her sister on the major holidays and during Paine's vacations.

Liza had looked forward to their visits more than she'd looked forward to the holidays themselves.

Liza didn't think there was a finer woman in the world than her Nana Bud had been, and most everyone who'd known Rosebud in her lifetime would have probably agreed.

Liza's heart had broken when Rosebud passed away.

Her death was especially difficult for Liza since she'd been in Spain with her husband at the time and, due to the standard form of miscommunication exhibited by her mother and Bryar Rose, she hadn't found out about it until her grandmother was already dead and in the ground.

Liza, filled with grief she didn't know she was capable of feeling (she didn't remember her father *or* his death) she'd lashed out at everyone from her husband to the poor plumber who'd just come to the house to unclog the guest toilet. In fact, her relationship with her sister Bryar was still strained and had only started to improve when talk of her divorce from Mode began.

Nothing brought sisters, or women in general, together more than a shared enemy, and Bryar always *had* enjoyed being in the middle of drama.

Liza regretted not attending the funeral; she was even more ashamed that she hadn't seen her grandmother in more than a year when she died. She'd always assumed there would be more time.

She guessed everyone thought that.

Liza Jane thought the guilt of not being there for someone who loved you and having nobody to blame but yourself had to be one of the most dreadful feelings in the world. It was for her, anyway. Rather than being at her grandmother's side, she'd been following her husband around like a puppy on the beaches of Marbella during breaks while he gawked at the topless women and their rosy nipples.

She'd been there when her grandfather Paine had passed away peacefully at the Hospice Center. She'd even been holding his hand when it happened. But that was different.

She'd loved her grandfather but hadn't known him well. He'd always been a quiet, gentle soul who didn't offer much of himself to anyone but his wife. And he'd lived a good, long life. When he'd passed on, Liza had been sad but it had felt *right*. He'd suffered for so long, his death was as much as a relief as it was a release.

As soon as they're returned from England, the last leg of the tour, Liza had locked herself in the guest room. It was the only place in the house Mode said he felt comfortable with her keeping her "supplies" as he called them. (He'd always claimed he was fine with her being a witch and had even considered it a fun little novelty at first, but now Liza was convinced that he'd been partly afraid of her. And rightly so. He *should* have been afraid. Very afraid.)

She'd stayed in that room for two days, holding her own vigil for Nana Bud. On her altar, she'd lit candles and placed Rosebud's picture and some of the cards she'd sent Liza over the years. She'd chanted, she'd meditated, and she'd offered thanks for having someone like her in her life. She'd called to the elements and sought peace within herself.

Mostly, she grieved.

Mode had left her alone. When she'd emerged at the end of the second day, hungry and exhausted, he'd glanced up from a Science Fiction book he was reading and asked her what she wanted for supper, like she'd just returned home from the movies.

"Jerkwad," Liza muttered now as she remembered the moment in total clarity.

Not all witches were made alike. While they could do similar things and for similar reasons, they were all individuals and had their own unique traits. Unfortunately, sometimes for Liza, one of her strongest traits was that she could remember things that happened ten years ago in total, accurate detail as though they'd occurred just moments earlier. She wished that gift had kicked in while her father was still alive but, like some of the other things she'd learned about herself, witchery and the skills it entailed seemed to be an ongoing process.

But as for Mode..."*Jerkwad*" was one of the nicest things she'd called him. When *his* grandmother had died, she'd been there for him. She'd even arranged the funeral, since both of Mode's parents were dead.

And she'd taken care of all the guests who had filed in and out of the house after the internment. He, on the other hand, never brought up *her* grandmother again. Didn't even offer to send flowers to the cemetery.

Asshat.

Now, as she paced alone through the rooms of the old farm house and touched its walls, feeling the same places her grandparents had also touched, she could feel a part of them near her. It was both peaceful and comforting, even when thoughts of Mode threatened to tear her up inside. (Asshat or Jerkwad aside, they *had* been married for a long time and she *was* grieving a part of him—the part she wanted him to be anyway.)

The overstuffed chairs covered in rainbow-colored afghans held imprints from their bottoms. The stale scent of cigarette smoke (even after being diagnosed with lung cancer her Papaw Paine hadn't given up his Marlboros) that still lingered in the air even after eight years, lace doilies on every flat surface, hundreds of ceramic teapots and ladybug statues, and homemade rag rugs scattered throughout the house were constant reminders of the two people who'd meant the world to her.

Liza vaguely remembered living there in the house with her mother and sister after her father died but those memories felt more like dreams. Still, while they might not have been strong, something about the house *felt* like home anyway. When she'd returned to Kudzu Valley to take stock of the situation after her separation from Mode, she'd known instantly that the idea she was flirting with in her mind was the right one.

As soon as she'd turned off the main road and entered the downtown proper, a calmness had settled over her. The mountains were lush with leaves then, their colors almost unnatural. She'd rolled down her windows and deeply inhaled the town right there on Main Street.

The air itself tasted of freedom.

And when the old farm house had come into view, despite the headache she was getting from the various washouts in the gravel, she'd *felt* her name being called, not heard.

Liza had no experience when it came to living in the country, or even living in a small town—at least no recent experience.

"You lived at home for college for Chrissakes!" her mother had scolded her. "You've never even been responsible for a house by yourself!"

Which was true, unless you wanted to consider the fact that Mode only did what he thought he *had* to.

"You've never lived more than a ten-minute walk to a store," her sister had pointed out, which was *also* true, although to Bryar "the Boondocks" meant someplace that couldn't get Chinese delivered to you thirty minutes or less.

At least in her adult life, Liza had *never* lived in isolation, never lived without neighbors within a stone's throw distance, never lived without an active nightlife and restaurant scene just minutes away (now, if she wanted to go to a nightclub, she'd have to drive for more than an hour and a half), and had never been responsible for only herself.

Hell, she'd only even lived by herself just recently. After moving out she'd ended up renting a dinky little apartment in Beverly that cost a fortune but had a closet the size of a shoebox and a view of a couple who were either newlyweds or just really, really amorous.

Still, standing there in the yard, *her* yard now, and feeling the ground beneath her feet—the same ground generations of her relatives had stood on as well, she knew she was home.

She knew it as a witch; she knew it as a woman.

"You can *have* it," Bryar Rose had sworn as soon as Liza asked her permission to move into it. "What the hell am I going to do with it?"

Her mother had echoed the sentiment.

She didn't remember the shotgun house on Ann Street where she'd lived with her real father or the trips to the local park she'd apparently taken with him when he was alive (though she'd seen the pictures). Her only memories of Kudzu Valley had come from her brief and infrequent visits growing up. In her college sociology class, however, she'd read about how people from Appalachia could get the mountains in their blood and never really shake them. No matter where they went, the mountains stayed with them, softly beckoning them to return home.

Liza figured she was one of those people. All those years of living in the city, she'd teared up every time she'd watched "Matewan" or "Coal Miner's Daughter" or even "Next of Kin" and "Justified." Movies set in eastern Kentucky or nearby had pulled at her, even the bad ones, and she'd watched the credits feeling a yearning, like she was missing something she'd never even had.

∞ ∞ ∞

T he farm house had four bedrooms and two had actual bedroom furniture. Another was what looked like her grandmother had used for a junk room. It was a mess but, more importantly, if she was going to get that board off the window and replace the glass she'd have to straighten it up. As it was, there was no direct path to get to the other side of the room.

There wasn't a *path* at all.

The room was full of boxes of patterns dating back to the 1970s, scraps of random material, Christmas tree lights, bags of unopened junk mail, and boxes of 3-ply toilet paper. Seriously, there was more toilet paper than two people could ever use. And her grandfather had been gone for a long time.

"Aw Nana Bud," Liza chuckled. "You really got the use out of your Sam's Club membership, didn't you?"

Well, at least she wouldn't have to stock up on that necessity any time soon. Nana Bud had always believed in being prepared; you could never have too much toilet paper or chicken broth.

She bought both every time she left the house, even if it was to just make a run to the post office.

With Luke Bryan blaring on the portable CD player she'd found in the room she was using as her own bedroom, Liza sashayed around, singing along and bobbing her head in time with the music while she sorted and organized.

She'd listened to country music stations on the whole ride down. It might have sounded stupid to others, but one of the things that excited her about living in Kudzu Valley was the thought of being a part of those things the songs talked about: a sense of community, bonfires with neighbors, and adventurous drives down backroads that turned to dirt...

After what she'd been through with Mode and his menagerie of extracurricular activities, she couldn't wait to dive into the bucolic life those singers crooned about and live a more peaceful existence.

Goodbye to pop opera bands, naked boobs on the beach, and 2:00 am Chinese. Hello to four wheeling (whatever that *really* was), horseback riding (she could learn), and gardening (she *did* have a green thumb).

When Luke got into his song about the woman dancing in his truck, Liza, who was in the middle of bending over to pick up an old tennis racket, paused mid-air.

Did she need a truck?

Oh, she thought with glee. *Maybe I **do** need a truck.*

The idea thrilled her to the bone–the thought of cruising through town sitting high above the road, being able to haul...stuff.

But she changed her mind as quickly as the idea came to her. She *had* a car and Christabel had been good to her. More than that, when she made the payment on her next week, she'd own her free and clear.

And it only took six years.

"Okay, okay," she grumbled aloud, just in case Christabel had been able to hear her thoughts and desires from her position in the driveway. There were times when Liza was certain her car had a sixth sense, but she hadn't been able to prove it yet. "No truck for me. I have a good car."

Sighing with regret, Liza leaned back over to reach for the tennis racket again and then popped back up.

"Hey," she cried, her eyes bright with excitement. "Do I need a *gun*?!"

A heavy box of books fell off the top of a shelf just then and came within a hair of crashing down on her toes. Liza had reacted quickly enough that she was able to stop it mid-air and gently move it a few feet to the left before letting it continue its drop.

"Yeah, yeah, yeah," she muttered again. "I hear you. Grandpa. Or Nana. Or whichever one of my dead relatives you might be. I won't get a gun. I don't even know how to use one."

Before returning to work Liza did stop and listen to the room for a few minutes, however. If there *had* been another energy there moments ago, it was gone now.

If either one of her grandparents had been watching over her, and in the very room with her, they were no longer there.

Liza was sorry about that.

Chapter Two

*P*ROSTITUTE RUMORS aside, Liza Jane really felt like her life was going to fall into place in Kudzu Valley.

Her new business, The Healing Hands, was on the corner of Main Street and Broadway. At one time Kudzu Valley had been a thriving railroad town, a town built to house the workers of the tracks that ran right through the middle of downtown. The houses and businesses were all laid out in a perfect grid, a perfectly planned community.

At one time the town boasted not one but *two* cinemas, a handful of restaurants, two department stores, and several dozen locally-owned businesses.

There had even been a drive-in and Liza could almost remember going to it as a child, sitting on the hood of the car with nachos and popcorn between her and a man who was now blurry in her mind.

However, things had changed. More of the storefronts were empty than used now, their dusty windows overlooking a street that saw little traffic. Liza expected to see a tumbleweed blow by at any moment.

A crazy part of her considered running out in the middle of the road and laying down under the one and only red light, just to see how long it took for a car to come by.

But that would've been immature. Right?

Now everyone just drove to the next county over; the next county that served alcohol and had a Walmart.

Still, whether the town was dead or not it still needed *her* kind of business; she was sure of it. There wasn't a single place in town where anyone could get a massage and more and more people were looking for natural treatments for their ailments. There were forty-thousand people in Morel County and some of them were bound to get sick and in need of somebody to pound on their backs and legs for half an hour.

Liza Jane Higginbotham was just the person to do the pounding. She had a lot of issues to work out.

It took her several tries to get the key to turn in the lock. When kicking, cursing, and throwing a mini tantrum with her red hair flying from her knitted cap and whipping her in the face didn't work, she turned to something else.

Liza calmed down, gave up the lock and key, said a quiet little charm to herself, and then let go of the knob and watched as the door creaked open in reluctant welcome.

"Yeah, well, you and I need to work on that," she murmured as she stepped inside.

Of course, she wouldn't *always* be able to charm it open. She'd have to figure out what made it stick and get that fixed and go about things the right way as often as she could. In the meantime, however, she was keen to explore her new building now and she didn't want to wait.

There were three rooms downstairs: a large space upfront, a bathroom, and a smaller room in the back.

The smaller room was around 10 x 20, an awkward size, and had unfortunate peeling linoleum on the floor (and smelled faintly of pickles for no discernible reason whatsoever) but she could work with it. With new floors, new paint on the walls, a privacy screen where people could change clothes, and some aromatherapy it would be a fine treatment room.

Someone had tried painting the bathroom a shocking shade of blood red, without priming it first. The original blue bled through in parts, making it look like someone really *had* splashed blood against the walls. She wasn't totally against the *Texas Chainsaw Massacre* look but figured it might not be soothing to some of her more sensitive clients.

There was also an upstairs' apartment which was available for her use as well. It consisted of a living area with a dining space in the back, a bedroom, a galley kitchen, and a bathroom that had a toilet and shower, but no sink. (The sink wasn't missing; there just wasn't enough room for one.)

Liza had no reason to live in the apartment but she *could* use it for storage. She hoped that her actual products, as well as her services, would bring her some income. She had oils, herbs, tinctures, supplies for making one's *own* tincture, and even gemstones for sale. She'd also ordered a ton of lotions, bubble baths, creams, and organic juices and supplements. She was eager to start making her own body scrubs and shampoos, too, and stock them as well.

She used to get a kick out of making them and using what she could, giving the rest out to friends for Christmas but Mode had ridiculed her for doing it whenever he saw the opportunity.

"Why do you want to keep buying brown sugar and olive oil?" he'd ask with that condescending smirk of his. "I'm making good money now. Just go to the mall and pick out what you want. It will save you a lot of time and you're not really saving us money by doing this. I don't know why you want to do it."

What she *wanted* was to make her own damn bubble bath. She didn't care that the DIY approach wasn't saving them money, she just enjoyed it. And she secretly thought they were safer and better for her skin.

Besides, it wasn't like she had much of anything else to do anymore anyway.

She hadn't worked in years. When she'd gone back to school and received her massage therapist license she'd had a ball doing the certification and being in a classroom setting again. Liza had always liked school. Then she'd taken the job at the day spa and that had been fun, too, even though it was only part time. At least she was getting out of the house.

And her clients *liked* her.

Since she'd married Mode, most of the people she knew were *his* people. There were the bandmates, *their* girlfriends, their publicity people, their accountants, the groupies (oh God, the groupies-who would've thought a pop opera group brought groupies), and so on and so on.

She hadn't had her own people in a very, very long time. But then he'd talked her out of working at the day spa, convincing her that she'd be much happier traveling and going on the road with him. "Just think of how much fun we'll have going to South America, Scotland–Japan even! You can do whatever you want while I'm on the road!"

Starry-eyed and full of wanderlust those things *had* sounded great to her at the time. So, even though she'd paid good money to get her license, and she liked the people she worked with, she'd quit her job and let the license expire to become a stay-at-home wife who traveled with her husband.

Of course, in reality the traveling rarely happened. Sure, they'd gone on a few trips at first, and they'd had a wonderful time during those trips. Mode was a different person away from home. He was charming, knowledgeable, and relaxed. The tours were exciting. Those trips had reminded her of why she'd fallen in love with him in the first place.

But later when it came time for him to travel to San Francisco for a week he'd told her that the other members of the group were starting to complain since they couldn't bring *their* spouses with them.

"Sorry honey, but you might want to sit this one out," he'd said with concern.

"But we pay for my way, and my meals. Couldn't their spouses and girlfriends do the same? It's not like the group is paying for me to go."

He'd nodded in agreement and swore a little to show his "irritation." Then he'd said, "Let 'em simmer down a bit. Then you can come on the next one.

Of course, the next one would come around and he'd said the same thing.

"I think I'm going to get my massage license back," she'd declared one June morning, five years ago. "I've painted every single wall in the house, learned to crochet and made more afghans than I ever thought possible, and have dug around in the garden so much I'm afraid if I go any farther I might hit Hell. I need a *life*."

"I like having you at home, though," he'd all but pleaded. "You don't know how much it means to be able to come home to a place that's clean and ready for me. To know someone is inside and has food waiting. The traveling is getting old. You being there for me at home is what makes it bearable."

Liza had gathered her nerves at that point and said what had been on her mind for months. "Well maybe if I got pregnant...I mean, I think we *can* now. And I am really, really ready."

He'd looked away then, his face blank. When he'd turned back to her he'd been all smiles again. "Well, it might be hard if you're on the road. We're leaving for Bermuda next weekend and you can go with us. I was going to surprise you!"

So, for the next five tours she was "allowed" to travel with them. That had continued on for a year and a half. Then it stopped again. She'd brought up pregnancy three times after that but he'd always changed the subject. She'd finally just stopped.

In hindsight she realized that only *one* of the members had complained of her presence—the one he was currently engaged to. A trombone player. She'd been too blind to see it, or else too scared to look into it properly.

"Serves me right," she spat.

Her voice, stronger than she'd realized, echoed in the cavernous room. It was a little thrilling. "I spent all my free time helping others see their future. I was too dim-witted to look at my *own* present."

At least she had some money. Along with the house and property, when Nana Bud died she'd left both Liza and Bryar a tidy sum from her life insurance policy and stocks she'd purchased back in the 1970s. In total, Liza Jane's part came to more than $125,000. (Which made her wonder what her grandmother had left Mabel. She'd never asked her mother.)

At one time, it would've been a fortune. Now she was going to have to make it stretch a good while to cover her expenses for at least two years, until her own business hopefully (definitely, think *positive*) took off.

So far she'd used it to rent the apartment in Beverly, move to Kentucky, get the house up and running, pay the rent for her building four months in advance, purchase all the supplies she needed to get her business up and running (massage table, products, waiting room furniture, decorations, etc.), her recertification, and to get the utilities on for everything.

And then there had been a few new outfits. Just because.

She shuddered at the amount she'd already spent.

"I *will* make this happen," she promised herself, tossing her head back so that her hair shook in the shadowy light. "This *is* going to work for me."

The overhead lights flickered off and on, a strobe-light effect from the energy that flew from the snap of her fingers.

She felt good, she felt positive.

She was going to do this, do this well, and not use any magic at all.

Oh, who was she kidding? She'd use as much as she could. A girl *had* to eat, after all.

∞ ∞ ∞

Liza knew whose voice she'd hear on the other end of the line before she was halfway across the room. Always a glutton for punishment, she continued towards the phone all the same. It was either now or later, after all.

Mode's voice carried that pleasant, cheery tone that had irritated her so much at the end and made her swoon in the beginning.

"Hi Mode," she said carefully, and then cringed. She'd promised herself to avoid that if she could.

Nana Bud had believed that names had a tremendous amount of power attached to them, some of the greatest power that existed.

"Don't use someone's name when you're mad or flying off the handle," she'd warned her when Liza was nine and first starting to recognize the fact that she could do things that others couldn't. "If you use their name in anger, you're trapping both of you in a web you'll likely never get out of. And the same–don't say it in love unless you're real sure you mean it. That's the thing that will bind you best of all."

Still, as she spoke Mode's name aloud she was reminded of the number of times her mother had made fun of it.

"*Mode,*" she'd shuddered. "That's ridiculous. It sounds too much like '*commode.*' He should at least go by a nickname. He shouldn't tempt the fates like that."

"I'm assuming you're settling in down there in little old Kudzu," he said.

Condescending prick, she said soundlessly and then watched as the book she'd left on the coffee table the night before shot up in the air and slammed back down, sending the TV remote clattering to the floor.

She was really going to have to get a grip on her emotions. Now was as good a time as any to start trying.

And maybe she should give him the benefit of the doubt. After all, her goal was to live a peaceful life that was free of stress and unwanted excitement. She could start by being civil. Besides, she couldn't be sure if he was *truly* being condescending or if it was his legitimate attempt at being cute/friendly and just sounded smarmy because she was currently pissed off at him for cheating on her and ending their marriage.

Oh, screw peaceful and relaxing, her inner mind snapped. There'd be plenty of time for that later. She'd stick with the condescension because that's just the kind of mood Mode put her in anymore.

So far in the conversation, he'd rambled on about himself for at least six minutes, giving her information about his upcoming tour and problems with the guest bathroom's pipes in her old, *their* old house.

"Lizey?" he asked, his chipper tone falling an octave. "I asked if you were settling in down there."

"Fine and dandy," she replied tightly. "I'm assuming *you're* settling into little old Jennifer."

"Jennifer's fine," he replied, not losing the smile from his voice but speaking slowly, as though speaking to an insolent child. "Are you sure you're holding up? It's an awfully big house for just one person and you're not used to being by yourself and having to do things alone."

Except for all those weeks you went off and left me alone while you were on tour, she mentally snapped back at him. "I'm fine," she replied instead. "I like being by myself. At least I know I am in good company."

"But still...you know you can always come back up here when you're ready. Your mom or sister will be sure to take you in and help you."

Every hair on Liza's head rose to angry attention. *You don't even know who I am*, she wanted to scream at the top of her lungs. *You never let me be myself so you don't know what I am capable of! Don't you remember? Don't you remember that first year and what...?*

Her silence appeared to make him nervous. "Is there anything I can do for you on my end? Any way I can help you with, you know, official business?"

What he *really* wanted to know was if he could do anything to help her clear the rest of her part of their storage unit out faster. If he could do anything to stop the loose ends of mail she figured were still being delivered to his house. If there was anything he could do to speed up the divorce process...

He was asking if he could do anything to help cut their ties to each other quicker.

"Not a darn thing," she said. "I'm moving just as fast as I can."

"Oh! I know you are! I didn't mean to imply that you were dragging your heels or anything," he said smoothly.

Yeah, the way you didn't drag your heels when you invited your mistress to move in with you before I'd even packed my suitcase, she thought wryly.

"Now we'll be out of town for all of next month," he said. "I'm going on tour with the group and we have sixteen dates on the west coast. So if there's anything you need from up here– "

"You telling me so that I can come up then and you two won't have to run into me?" she finished for him. "Because I can tell you now that I won't be coming up there until after Christmas, probably. I have to start working on my business this week. I have men coming in next week to start construction and I can't leave them alone without any supervision."

Liza, who'd sat through most of the conversation feeling a bit depressed, straightened her back now, proud at how official she'd sounded. *Ha! Take that. I have work, too!*

"No! That's not what I meant at all. I just meant that Larry and Sheila next door have the spare key," he replied, his voice beginning to sound a little strained.

Liza was now confused. Her mind began to spin as she traveled backwards in time to the incident involving the house key and the ensuing argument. "Well, I still have my key. Remember? I tried to return it to you and you wouldn't accept it. You brought it to my apartment and said that I needed to keep it until everything was final, until the house was completely in your name."

"Yes, well, we um..." Mode let his voice trail off his until his end of the line fell uncomfortably silent. It was in the silence that the implication of what he was saying struck Liza square in the middle of the forehead.

Damn her third eye.

"You had the locks changed," she accused him, unable to keep the high pitch of anger from creeping into her voice. "Well I'll be damned."

Mode coughed nervously and through the line she could see the tips of his ears, rosy from the anxiety he was feeling. Soon he'd be unbuttoning the top of his shirt. *Good.* "It's just that there's been a lot of thefts in the neighborhood recently and–"

Enjoying his discomfort more than any decent person should, Liza allowed him to ramble while she closed her eyes and let herself drift hundreds of miles away and back in time.

On the movie screen behind her eyelids she could see them a few days ago, the catalyst for the current conversation.

There was Mode, with his stubby beard, tweed jacket he'd picked up at Goodwill, and red suspenders that she'd always thought looked ridiculous but kept quiet about because she didn't want to hurt his feelings.

And then there was Jennifer, pacing around the living room like a caged cat in her black tights and deep orange tunic sweeping her knees. Her voice was controlled but her skinny little shoulders were hunched forward and her eyes were bright with blue-tinted rage. "I don't want that *woman* to have a key to my house Mode."

"She's not 'that woman' Jen. Liza's a great girl. She'd never do anything to hurt you or us!" Mode, who abhorred conflict, looked crushed. His eyes were lowered to the travertine tile Eliza had installed two years earlier and his mouth dropped at the corners–the way it got when he thought the world was stacked against him.

"She's vindictive and mean-spirited and I don't trust her as far as I can throw her," Jennifer spat. "Change the locks!"

Liza chuckled at the scene playing out before her eyes on her own private movie screen.

She was the vindictive one who couldn't be trusted? She hadn't been the one to make it her goal to sleep with a married man on a twelve-city tour and document the affair in Instagram posts.

Liza still couldn't believe they'd carried on that affair as long as they had without her knowing. When he'd told her about the Starbucks girl and that he was moving out, she'd thought he'd gone insane. Insanity she could fix. But when she learned he was actually leaving her for someone he worked with, that was different. That was serious. That's when she knew she'd lost him.

Mode was still babbling some nonsense when she interrupted him. "Sorry, I've got something on the stove. I'd better go."

"What? You're cooking! That's great. I am so glad that you're—"

She'd never know which part of her cooking made him "glad" because she hung up before he finished.

Eh well, she shrugged as she stared at the blue light on her phone's screen.

Perhaps she *was* a little vindictive. After all, she hadn't made an entirely innocent exit from their house. With Bryar at her side, begging Liza to let her curse something or put out a good hex, she'd loosened some things in all the toilets so that they'd overflow and run for the entire two weeks that the happy couple was on vacation, removed the new thermostat which effectively left them without air or heat until they could call someone in to replace it, and then removed all the towel racks and light bulbs and taken them with her.

Just for the fun of it.

∞ ∞ ∞

The last of her boxes were unpacked.

Liza's meager personal belongings were either neatly stowed away in closets or arranged on bookshelves and credenzas throughout her grandparents' house.

Her house.

She wasn't sure it would ever completely be *hers*, but she knew she belonged there.

Liza didn't bring much with her. The few items she'd deemed important enough to transport from Boston were sentimental and random. In fact, from the looks of some of the things she packed, Liza was now worried she might have unknowingly suffered from some kind of mental breakdown before she left. Her belongings had clearly not been chosen by someone who was in full control of their decision-making and cognitive skills.

For instance, she hadn't brought a single cup or plate or towel with her yet somehow managed to carefully pack the collection of foreign Coca-Cola bottles she'd gathered during their international travels. They were now artfully displayed on a library table in the living room.

She'd forgotten to pack any underwear (and, since all her drawers were empty when she left the house, had no idea where they were, which was a little disturbing) but *had* packed a box of nothing but melted candle wax that she'd collected from all the candle holders in the house. Yes, she liked to melt down the old and make new candles but why had she deemed *that* wax necessary?

And then there was the plastic bag full of more than three-hundred corks.

Still, she'd managed to bring every single item of clothing she'd ever owned, including the sweatshirt she'd cut the neck out of back in 1989 when she was just a kid. Well, other than her underwear. *That*, she'd managed to leave...somewhere.

"Liza Jane," she declared, her voice booming through the empty rooms. "You're a little pathetic."

The dryer buzzed in response, a reminder that she needed to change loads. The sheets and blankets on the bed were clean, but musty from non-use over the past few years. She'd spent the previous night coughing and sneezing. She wasn't ready to throw them out yet so she hoped a good dousing with Tide and that fabric softener with the annoying white teddy bear who was always laughing would help.

Momentarily forgetting her self-deprecating speech to herself, Liza scurried to the dryer to take action. With each thing she'd done that morning, she'd mentally hit Mode over the head with it.

He didn't think she could hack it. *He* didn't think she'd stay down there. *He* didn't think she could be alone.

Liza Jane was a stress cleaner. She enjoyed dusting, washing dishes, mopping, and organizing. It just wasn't cutting it today, though. The more she thought about Mode's phone call, the madder she got.

Thinking about Mode frolicking around her house with Jennifer did not help. Changing her locks. Ha! Like a lock could keep *her* out.

Mode would've known that, too.

Oh, he *knew* she was a witch. He was embarrassed by it, but he knew. "Just don't do anything out in public, okay?" He hadn't even had the decency to look ashamed or embarrassed when he'd asked.

"Like what, Darren?" she'd snapped. "Ride my broom? Turn the waiter into a frog?"

She'd looked at his face then and saw that it wasn't awkwardness of her abilities that had him humiliated, it was old-fashioned fear. He was afraid of her. She'd softened a little then and changed the subject after promising him she wouldn't make a public spectacle of herself.

Hours later something must have clicked inside and he'd felt guilty. As a peace offering, he'd brought her a broom, one of those old-fashioned ones that looked handmade and like it belonged by a storybook witch's front door.

In fact, it *was* now standing by her front door. She was sentimental, after all. And it was a nice broom.

Still, his ideas never wavered. Two years later he asked her to move her altar out of their bedroom and into another room of the house. He claimed it was for the sake of "space" but she'd read him like a book. It was easy to do it by then. She only had to lightly press her thumbs together. She'd pressed them on his temples once, and then on his third eye, and they'd been connected ever since and would be forever.

Until *she* ended it.

"Well, shit," she sighed, looking around her living room again.

Her face cooled just a fraction and she closed her eyes to gather herself together again. She was angry at herself, angry for allowing him into this space, for making her angry *here*. Somewhere that had nothing to do with him. This space was meant to be hers and she'd all but invited him inside and asked him to throw darts at her.

It wasn't fair. Why couldn't her life be fair for a change? She'd given up years of it for his career. She'd helped put him through that last year of school, the year his parents died and their account (and subsequently his college funding) had been frozen.

She'd dropped out herself to work two jobs so that he could start his business and had then traveled all over the world with him so that he could work with the pop opera group and feel "fulfilled." She had put off having children because he wasn't ready, let her massage license expire so that he could have someone at home, kept the house clean, hired the maintenance workers, kept his records and balanced the checkbook, hid her magic and—

Liza, in the midst of her depressing and angry march down Memory Lane had not counted on the fact that the house could read her thoughts. She wouldn't make *that* mistake again.

Before she'd finished her last thought, two things happened at once:

The front door swung open from the pressure of a hearty knock...

And two of the foreign Coca-Cola bottles sailed off the shelf on the other side of the room, hovered dramatically in the air before proceeding to spin around uncontrollably, and then crashed to the ground, showering the living room with a thousand glittery shards of glass.

Liza, hand covering her mouth in embarrassment, was left staring at her visitor in shock.

"Um, hi?"

The curly-haired brunette holding a corning ware dish covered in aluminum foil gave her a baffled grin. "I'm your neighbor from the next farm over. Um, welcome to Kudzu Valley?"

ABOUT REBECCA

Rebecca Patrick-Howard is the author of more than a dozen paranormal books, including several true haunting accounts. She lives in eastern Kentucky with her husband and two children.

Visit her website at www.rebeccaphoward.net and sign up for her newsletter to receive free books, special offers, and news.

LET'S CONNECT!

Pinterest: https://www.pinterest.com/rebeccapatrickh/
Website: www.rebeccaphoward.net
Email: rphwrites@gmail.com
Facebook: https://www.facebook.com/rebeccaphowardwrites
Twitter: https://twitter.com/RPHWrites
Instagram: https://instagram.com/rphwrites/

Want access to FREE books (audio, print, and digital), prizes, and new releases before anyone else? Then sign up for Rebecca's VIP mailing list. She promises she won't spam you! *And she'll never sell your information or use it for anything other than sending you her newsletter.) You may easily opt out at any time.*

http://eepurl.com/Srwkn

REBECCA'S BOOKS

Taryn's Camera Series

Windwood Farm (Book 1)
The locals call it the "devil's house" and Taryn's about to find out why!
Griffith Tavern (Book 2)
The old tavern has a dark secret and Taryn's camera's going to learn it soon.
Dark Hollow Road (Book 3)
Beautiful Cheyenne Willoughby has disappeared. Someone knows the truth.
Shaker Town (Book 4)
Taryn's camera is finally revealing a past to her that she's always longed to see–the mysterious Shakers as they were 100 years ago. But is she seeing a past she hadn't bargained for?
Jekyll Island (Book 5)
Jekyll Island is known for its ghosts, as well as its fascinating history, but now the two are about to take Taryn on a wild ride she'll never forget!
Black Raven Inn (Book 6)
The 1960's music scene...vibrant, electrifying, and sometimes even deadly...
Muddy Creek (Book 7)
Lucy did a bad, bad thing when she burned down the old school. Now it's up to Taryn to find out why.
Bloody Moor (Book 8)
The call it "the cursed" and the townspeople still fear the witch that reigned there a century ago. But this haunted Welsh mansion has more than meets the eye!
Sarah's House (Book 9)
Taryn's Pictures: Photos from Taryn's Camera
Taryn's Haunting

Kentucky Witches

A Broom with a View

She's your average witch next door, he's a Christmas tree farmer with sisters named after horses. Kudzu Valley will never be the same when Liza Jane comes to town!

Broommates
When Bryar Rose makes a fool of herself on national television, it's time for her to return to Kudzu Valley. But now that she's accused of murdering half the town, will anyone truly accept her?

A Broom of One's Own
What does a witch do when she can't get rid of the restless spirit that haunts the old cinema? Call for backup! (A Taryn's Camera/Kentucky Witches crossover)

Nothin' Says Lovin' Like Something from the Coven (coming soon)

General Fiction

Furnace Mountain: Or The Day President Roosevelt Came to Town
When Sam Walters invited the president to visit his Depression-era town, he never dreamed of what would happen next!

The Locusts (Coming Soon)

Things She Sees in the Dark
Mallory's cousin was kidnapped when she was eight years old and Mallory saw the whole thing happen. She's suffered amnesia ever since. Now, 25 years later, her memories are starting to return. Can she solve the case that no detective has been able to crack? And will she live through it, if she does?

Superstition Mountain

Superstition Mountain
Wren has just taken a job in Superstition Mountain, Kentucky where the locals are friendly, the scenery gorgeous, and all the urban legends and folk stories come to life!

Pretty Polly (coming soon)

True Hauntings

Haunted Estill County
More Tales from Haunted Estill County
Haunted Estill County: The Children's Edition
Haunted Madison County
A Summer of Fear
The Maple House
Four Months of Terror
Two Weeks: A True Haunting
Three True Tales of Terror
The Visitors

Other Books

Coping with Grief: The Anti-Guide to Infant Loss
Three Minus Zero
Finding Henry: A Journey Into Eastern Europe
Estill County in Photos
Haunted: Ghost Children Stories from Beyond
Haunted: Houses

Reviews for the *Taryn's Camera Series*

Windwood Farm

"This is an absolutely wonderful book and I didn't want to put it down. It was exciting and sad but it was uplifting too." (Kim @ **The Open Book Society**openbooksociety.com/)

"I won't spoil anything but this book has great characterization, loads of atmosphere and is never dull. The first book in the Taryn's Camera series so roll on number two!" (**A Drunken Druid's Reviews** the-drunken-druid.blogspot.com/)

"The author does a great job painting just what life in a small town in Kentucky is like. She also writes a great mystery." (Lisa Binion @ **The News in Books** thenewsinbooks.com/)

"while I do not believe in ghosts and such, this book was written in a way that I was able to enjoy it and go along for the ride and "believe" the story."- online reviewer

"a great chiller that was perfect summertime reading!"- online reviewer

Griffith Tavern

"I actually love Rebecca's descriptive style of writing which kept feeding my imagination and continuously created images and pictures in my mind"- online reviewer

"If you like old houses, historic preservation, AND creepy ghost stories, it's right up your (darkened, cobwebby) alley"-online reviewer

"This was a book that was an absolute pleasure to read. A book that I couldn't wait to get back to"- online reviewer

Dark Hollow Road

"Her characters are rich, her story lines are enticing and as a reader these combine to make for a lovely journey through a small southern town"- online reviewer

"I've enjoyed all of the Taryn's Camera books. They have so many things I love – old houses, ghosts, a likable main character I can relate to, and realistic descriptions of small town Southern life. But this one goes a step further, addressing real life issues with a depth of emotion that can only come from someone who knows this region and its issues firsthand. Highly recommended."- online reviewer

Shaker Town

"a paranormal whodunit with lots of surprises"- online reviewer

"As always wonderful thorough research was done. Great presentation. I did not want to stop reading until I finished"- online reviewer

"Wonderful story, history, background and my favorite characters! You won't be disappointed with this newest adventure of Taryn and her camera!"- online reviewer

COPYRIGHT

Made in United States
North Haven, CT
03 September 2022

23605754R00124